THE
GREENLEAF
MURDERS

THE GREENLEAF MURDERS

A Historic Homes Mystery

R.J. KORETO

LEVEL
BEST BOOKS

First published by Level Best Books 2022

Copyright © 2022 by R. J. Koreto

Author Photo Credit: Dutch Doscher

First edition

ISBN: 978-1-68512-208-9

Cover art by Level Best Designs

This book was professionally typeset on Reedsy.
Find out more at reedsy.com

Once again, to Liz, who made our house into a home.

Praise for The Greenleaf Murders

"A delightful who-done-it in which the house is as engaging as the wonderful heroine. Readers will want to get lost in these rooms and these pages."—*Cate Holahan, USA Today* bestselling author of *Her Three Lives*

"If you love houses and puzzles - which I do - you will be captivated by *The Greenleaf Murders*, the first in Richard Koreto's new series. Equally sure-footed in the gilded age of the mansion's heyday and the contemporary world of its decline, Koreto has woven a pretzel of a plot, introduced a charming new heroine, and whetted appetites for more grave deeds and grandeur."—Catriona McPherson, multi-award-winning author of the Dandy Gilver series

"I believe I was secretly born to be an architect, which is probably why I so enjoyed this mystery of a stately NYC mansion and its role in murders both past and present."—Lisa Black, *NYT* bestselling author of *Every Kind of Wicked*

"*The Greenleaf Murders* mixes a modern suspense mystery with the love of old-world mansions and iconic High Society. Buried secrets threaten a family clinging to their former glory as two murders surface, a century apart. Koreto weaves a story that creates the perfect tension between the beauty of the golden era and the fear of a killer in plain sight."—L.A. Chandlar, national bestselling author of the Art Deco Mystery Series

"One would think that a murder mystery featuring old homes, architecture, and rich blue bloods would be a dull read, but that's not the case with R.J.

Koreto's finely-written "The Greenleaf Murders." Filled with twists and turns and sharply-drawn characters, this well-done novel is very much recommended." —*Brendan DuBois, award-winning and New York Times bestselling author*

"Set firmly in the 21st-century but glancing back toward The Gilded Age, *The Greenleaf Murders* explores twinned stories of manners, morals, and mystery across more than a century—with a grand family mansion as the cornerstone for each. Like his engaging new heroine—architect Wren Fontaine—R.J. Koreto proves himself a master craftsman throughout, with a keen eye for all the right details."—*Art Taylor,* Edgar® Award winner, author of *The Boy Detective & The Summer of '74*

"Koreto weaves past and present into an engrossing tale of old and new New York. Fans of Fiona Davis will delight in this blending of history with present-day issues, proving that the more things change, the more they stay the same. An engaging heroine uses her knowledge of history to unravel a century-old family secret and solve a very recent murder as she restores a landmark home in Manhattan."—*Victoria Thompson, USA Today* bestselling author of *Murder on Pleasant Avenue*

Chapter One

L ast night, Wren had dreamt she went to Manderley again.

When she was fifteen, her mother had given her a copy of *Rebecca*, saying it was one of her favorites. A voracious reader, Wren finished it in a few days, but her reaction was not what her mother had hoped for.

"Rebecca was horrible, but Maxim was no prize either. And the second Mrs. De Winter—kind of wimpy."

"You didn't like anyone in that book?" asked her exasperated mother.

"I liked Mrs. Danvers. I know she was insane, but she really appreciated the house. If people had been nicer to her, maybe she wouldn't have burned it down. The best part of the book was Manderley. I'd have liked to live there, in *splendid isolation,* and Mrs. Danvers would take care of things. She was the only one in the book who knew how to *do* something."

Her mother just stared. What teenaged girl talked about living by herself in an ivy-covered British mansion? She kissed her daughter on her forehead. "Wren, you really are an old soul."

But although Manderley was her first love, Wren proved fickle, and also fell in love with Holyrood House, Blenheim Palace, and Versailles.

A succession of guidance counselors worried about Wren, although she gradually learned to make friends, and even go on dates. However, nothing could replace her love for houses, and it was a foregone conclusion by college that she would become an architect like her father and spend as much time as possible working with *houses* and not *people.* And not just any houses, but the kind no one had lived in for a long time.

As Wren approached 30, her father made her a junior partner and told her if he could close the deal with Stephen Greenleaf, he'd let her take full responsibility for Greenleaf House. Once the proposal they had worked on so hard had been completed, Wren couldn't think about anything beyond spending her days in that Gilded Age gem, one of the largest private residences ever built in New York City. Over the years, like the second Mrs. De Winter, she dreamed of Manderley, never more than when she was hoping for the Greenleaf job.

She came home late one evening after visiting a job site and found her father in the study of the home they still shared. Living at home had become a temporary convenience while she was at graduate school, which turned into a habit, as they liked each other's company. Not that either would admit it.

She watched him sketch. Although the firm had an office in midtown Manhattan, her father preferred to work in the study of their Brooklyn townhouse. For normal work, she knew it was safe to interrupt him, but not while he did the sketches—his avocation, his passion, just him and his pencils, creating columns and cornices, chair railings, and gargoyles. The only light poured from the desk lamp, illuminating the fine paper and her father's high-domed forehead. She wanted to know if he had heard anything—but had to wait patiently.

Eventually, the scratching stopped, and he put his pencil down.

"If you haven't eaten yet, Ada left her spaghetti and meat sauce in the refrigerator. She's a fine housekeeper, but that particular dish is a little common."

"Only you would describe a dish of pasta as 'common.'"

"You know what I mean. And if you don't understand the context, you shouldn't be an architect."

"Fine. But I think it's delicious."

"Yes," he said, with a touch of impatience. "I didn't say it wasn't delicious. I said it was common." He swiveled in his chair and smiled. "But you're really here to ask if I've heard from Greenleaf? I told him today that we couldn't put aside our other projects indefinitely. And that Bobby Fiore was the only contractor we could trust, and we couldn't ask him to postpone other jobs, so with a few arguments about the price, he agreed."

Wren laughed, did a little dance, and punched the air. Then she ran and hugged her father, which he tolerated. "I knew you'd convince him. You are the most wonderful father."

"Wren. Take a seat." He said it in his even, measured tone, the one he used for serious discussions. Wren wiped the smile from her face, pulled up a chair, and tucked a rebellious lock of hair behind her ear. In the half-dark room, he took her hands in his.

"I have no doubt that you have the technical skills for this job. My concern is the personal skills. These are the Greenleafs. They were a force in this city when it was still New Amsterdam. We see their house merely as an architectural jewel. The family sees it as a symbol of how tightly they are tied to the history of this city. They are different from other people."

"People are people," she said.

"First of all, no. People are different. And even if you were right, people are not your strong suit."

"I've worked well with our clients," she said defensively.

"You referred to one of our clients as 'a pompous bourgeois vulgarian.'"

Wren rolled her eyes. "Let's not go there again. I didn't say it to his face, just to you."

"Do you think you hid your feelings?"

"You've said worse," she countered. Then realized she had lost the argument when his eyes went up to the framed certificate on the wall—the Pritzker Prize, often called the Nobel Prize of architecture. *I've earned my right to arrogance. You have a long way to go.*

"Just remember that these people pay our bills. I know we often work to protect them from their own worse instincts, but let's try to be a little more politic. Your mother used to say you lived in your own special world. But you have to join the rest of humanity every now and then. And that brings me back to Greenleaf House. This is the very important symbol of what was once one of the most important families in this city. Keep that in mind when dealing with Stephen Greenleaf."

"We've already had several meetings, don't forget. He didn't seem that unusual to me—runs his own asset management firm. I've dealt with Wall Street types before. It won't be a problem."

"Wren." Again, heavy on her name—all her life, this had been the sign of a serious conversation. "The Greenleafs made their money before there was a Wall Street. People like this are unusually touchy about their families and histories. Now that you're actually starting, his behavior may change. There could be some emotional repercussions. To make this a success, you will have to watch out for those feelings and manage them."

"And you're about to say—again—that I understand houses but not people."

"Let's just say it's more of an effort for you. You can work with people. You just don't like to. But I made you a partner. So you can't just do the fun parts of your job. You have to do it all."

"Yes, father," she said. He was serious, so there could be no more pushback from her. No verbal fencing. He wanted her to live up to his expectations.

"It isn't your father who's asking you, Wren. It's the senior partner of this firm, Ms. Fontaine."

She nodded. "I understand, *Ezra.*"

And then he lightened his face with a smile. "But before we move on to the particulars, there is one more piece of advice, this time from your *father.* It may be hard to remember in any residence we work on, but especially in one with more than 70 rooms, it is not just a house. It's someone's home. It was Mr. Greenleaf's childhood home, in fact, and his aunt has lived there her entire life. You're not very sentimental Wren—and that's fine. Neither am I. But please remember that—it's not just a building. It's a home."

He let go of her hand. Her father was done on that topic, at least for now. "To the job at hand. Like most rich men, now that Stephen has made up his mind, he wants to start immediately. I told him you'd be there at 9:00 tomorrow. Bobby will come later that morning—he was almost as excited as you are. Good luck," he said. "And by the way—this will take up a lot of time. I trust you won't let your 'group' activities interfere." His tone always managed to add the quotation marks around "group."

"Be fair. We raise a lot for charity. But I have my priorities in order. Anyway, before I begin tomorrow, do you have any further hints into what he plans to do with that house?"

"You were there with me, Wren. He said he wants a residence and that 'future plans are uncertain.' Some of the smaller rooms merged—people expect larger bedrooms now. More bathrooms. But still a residence."

"But what is he going to do with it? Not live in it himself. No one lives like that anymore, even wealthy people. He just has his elderly aunt in a little apartment. What is going to happen to that house?"

"The house isn't our client. Stephen Greenleaf is. And for reasons of his own, he doesn't want to share the house's fate."

"He didn't say anything? Come on, *Ezra*. You, me, and Stephen—all of us Columbia University graduates. You're an adjunct professor. He's a former member of the Board of Trustees, and the Greenleafs have been donors to the school since before they built that house. You teach in Greenleaf Hall. You're telling me that after a couple of drinks in the faculty club, he didn't drop some hints on what he plans to do once we're done with it?"

He smiled blandly and spread out his hands.

"Wren, please don't press him. If you get off on a good first step, he may share his plans with you. Now, I'm going to wish you good luck. You no doubt have things to organize tonight." She was being dismissed. Her father turned away to resume his sketching without another word, and Wren quietly left.

She had kept the Greenleaf file in her bedroom, wistfully thumbing through the photos and the specs, and spent the next few hours reviewing it and furiously making notes on her tablet. Even as a teen, when the boys and girls she had known were poring over pictures of musicians and sports stars, she was comparing the relative merits of Doric, Ionic, and Corinthian columns and admiring the beauty of a fan vault. She had sulked when her parents had said they were not going to install mullioned windows in her bedroom. *Even as a child, I wanted my room perfect, for a splendid isolation.*

Wren had fantasized about making Greenleaf House perfect again, just like it was when gentlemen in top hats and ladies in long skirts walked the halls, and the house was scented with cigars, port, and lavender water.

At 9:30, she suddenly realized she was starving. Nothing new there—simply forgetting to eat. Ahh...but there was Ada's spaghetti and meat sauce in the fridge! A few minutes in the microwave, and Wren was savoring the filling starch and meat. Restored and renewed, she dove back into the Greenleaf file and didn't even hear her father pass by on the way to his own bedroom.

"Really?" he said. "It's come to this?"

Wren's face flamed. Seeing herself as others saw her was not her strong suit, but even she realized what a sight she must've made, sitting in bed and dressed in her plaid pajamas, surrounded by the Greenleaf papers, with a plate balanced on her knee, and the tomato and meat spread around her mouth as if she were six.

Don't show weakness, she told herself. "I don't really think it's right for the senior partner to comment on the junior partner's dining habits, *Mr. Fontaine*," she said.

"It isn't the senior partner of this firm who's disappointed. It's your father, *Wren*." He gave her his half smile and headed off to bed. She sighed and began cleaning up.

* * *

It was spring—no need for a coat, but not yet so warm that she risked arriving sweaty to Greenleaf House on her first day. Because she was an architect, she knew people assumed she'd wear something black and cutting edge, but she had no interest in looking like an avant-garde artist. She kept it simple by having a closet full of pants suits, professional and practical, and a generous leather bag. It had been a present from her father when she had received her license to practice. It was large, useful, and appallingly expensive.

"How can you convince our clients you will make their residences both functional and elegant if you don't look functional and elegant yourself?" her father had said.

Still feeling a little guilty over last night's spaghetti binge, she had only buttered toast and coffee for breakfast. She wondered if the senior partner might've given her a soulful, fatherly farewell to the junior partner as he sent her off to her first big job. But she didn't expect it, and in fact, he didn't. As he had said, they were not sentimental.

She arrived as planned a little after 9:00. "Make them wait for you," her father had advised. No doubt Stephen Greenleaf would already be there, eager to get her started. She was curious about the elderly aunt who still lived there, with a companion. In previous tours of the house, there had always been a reason not to meet them. "She's sleeping now...at a doctor's appointment." He had seemed hesitant about it, and Wren wondered what the full story was. Well, he'd have to introduce them eventually.

She hoped they weren't going to be difficult, but remembered what her father had said about being accommodating.

She rang the bell, and while waiting, looked again at the façade, the red and grey patterns, the elegant arches, the columns and balconies, and the magnificent bay windows. Her childhood dreams came back. Greenleaf House was one of the few grand Gilded Age homes in private hands, and perhaps the last still owned by its original family. Imagine being all alone in one of the grand rooms with its perfect proportions—marble and brass and hardwood.

Stephen broke into her dreams by opening the door. He wore a well-tailored suit—clearly he was planning to go downtown after the introductions. "Wren—so glad you could start on such short notice. Do come in. We have coffee going in the kitchen, and I understand the contractor, Mr. Fiore, will be coming later?"

"Yes. He's eager to begin. And I can assure you again—Bobby Fiore has worked on many of our jobs. He's well-versed in unique houses like this."

"*Unique.* Well said," said Greenleaf. All right, she was off to a good start.

The kitchen didn't seem to have changed much since the house was built, but not even the finest houses ever bothered making their kitchens fancy—they were exclusively for servants. This one had been given a grudging upgrade decades ago—a bulky gas range and a fridge that belonged in the Smithsonian.

"I know," said Greenleaf, following Wren's eyes. "As we discussed earlier, there's nothing really historic in this room. Everything gets ripped out, and we add Sub-Zero, Viking—the works, and plenty of electric power. I did offer an upgrade years ago, but Mrs. Ryan—my mother's housekeeper-companion—stiffly told me she was used to this. It wasn't worth a fight. And that brings me to my next subject." He sighed and ran his hands through his hair. He didn't want to discuss this.

"I was my parents' only child, and I grew up in this house. I know what you're thinking—what a privilege to live in a place like this—"

"I've been thinking of nothing else," Wren jumped in. "I would've given anything to grow up in this residence." She worried she had said too much. The interruption surprised him, but then he smiled.

"I'm sure," he said. "Maybe once, it would've been a privilege, when there was money for maids and kitchen staff, but by the time I came along, there wasn't even enough for maintenance. You've seen the drafty windows, the leaky roof, and peeling paint." He shook his head. "Anyway, although the house was left to me after my parents died some years ago, we lived here with my father's sister, Agnes, and she has a right under my parents' will to live here for the rest of her life." He sighed again. "She's around ninety, and doesn't get around much. The thing is—she hates the idea of any changes. You will have to work around her—so to speak."

"I understand. We've done special work before, around a family."

"You know houses. Well, my Aunt Agnes is as much a part of this house as the walls and plumbing. Even when she was born, the world our family had inhabited was already gone. It's as if she remembered the life of her parents and even grandparents."

"You may find it hard to believe," Wren said. "But I do understand what that is like to feel part of another time." He looked at her closely, trying to see if she was just humoring him. *Or does he think I'm as crazy as his aunt.*

"Perhaps. You work on old homes, so I can see that. But for you, it's probably just a matter of attitude. For Aunt Agnes, it's a way of life."

"It's a certain...dementia?" she asked.

"If only," said Greenleaf, with a grimace. "Anyway, I wanted to give you this background, so you understand where my Aunt Agnes is coming from, and why she'll be resentful. If you're ready, I'll take you upstairs."

Again, Wren couldn't stop admiring the magnificent ironwork on the railings, and the quality of the marble stairs. The hallway seemed to soar to the heavens, an impression of infinite height, infinite space. Yes, the place needed work, but the fundamentals were good. What the house lacked, it seemed, was someone to love it. She didn't think Stephen did. She knew that the first time she met him. This house was just a problem he had to deal with. Wren saw no signs of people here, no hint of clutter, more like a poorly funded museum, she thought. It was clear that no one truly lived here anymore, and hadn't for a long time.

"It's an unusual name—Wren," said Stephen. "A family name?"

"I was named for the great English architect, Sir Christopher Wren. A bit of humor of my father's." The party line since she was 10.

"Ah, your father. We finalized the very substantial fee for your firm's services. I wonder how much more it would cost for the firm's senior partner to show up." His look was half challenge, half amusement. It was a test—but she had prepared.

"I assure you that, like my father, I am a fully qualified architect, with the addition of a degree in art history." Her father had warned her against false modesty on the job—no one paid the firm's enormous fees for a diffident professional. But as it so often happened with her, it came across as harsher than she had intended. Less self-assured than snippy. "I am well-acquainted with houses that are not just homes but works of art in themselves."

Greenleaf nodded—again, the answer seemed to please him, which reassured her. *See, father, I can do this.*

He led her to the suite, the little apartment where his aunt lived with her companion. He knocked, and a moment later, the door was opened by a sixtyish woman, tall and lean, black hair pulled back severely and a slightly disapproving look, even for the master of the house.

My God, it's Mrs. Danvers.

"Mrs. Ryan. You are well?"

"Yes, thank you. And you, sir?"

"Fine, fine," said Greenleaf. The conversation was completely automatic. This part of the house, Wren noted, was the only part still lived in. No museum-like perfection here: books and magazines and pill bottles, and she saw that the little sitting room was well-lit with modern fixtures. But the furniture looked to be original to the house. Aunt Agnes was giving no more concessions to modernity than was absolutely necessary. She saw a small writing desk Wren could tell was a valuable antique, with fine stationery, a selection of fountain pens, and books of stamps. Interesting to see someone who still wrote letters. An old-fashioned radio stood in the corner—but it looked fairly new, probably a retro design to give clear audio with a 1950s look. No television.

In a large leather wing chair sat a small woman—she was very old, but not her eyes, which took in everything. Stephen bent over his aunt, and she raised her cheek to him for a dutiful kiss.

"Aunt Agnes, good to see you again. I came to introduce you to Wren Fontaine, the architect who will be overseeing the renovations of the house."

Aunt Agnes slowly turned to focus intently on her. Curiosity? Yes—and suspicion.

"Our family has lived in this house for over a century. I was born in this house. And no slip of a girl is going to throw me out." Wren didn't know whether to laugh or cry—Miss Greenleaf was talking like a Victorian character.

"For heaven's sake, Aunt, no one is throwing you out. You know full well that this is your home for the rest of your life."

"Then why are you bringing in *her*? To turn this into a hotel?"

"Of course not."

"You—architect lady. Tell me what you're going to do here."

Wren glanced at Stephen, who quickly nodded.

"Your nephew has engaged me to renovate and repair this house. Much of it is falling apart. I'll be enlarging some of the smaller rooms and adding some new bathrooms. But my orders are to keep this as a residence."

The old lady's eyes went back and forth between Wren and Stephen.

"So, you've finally come to your senses and decided to move back here—"

"Aunt Agnes—"

"Everyone says you've been very successful. You'll sit at the head of the

10

table again, like your father, grandfather, and great-grandfather."

Stephen sighed dramatically. "Aunt Agnes—never mind. I'm not going through this again."

But Miss Greenleaf was ignoring him, Wren saw. The house would be repaired and the Greenleafs would take their place at the head of New York society. Wren recalled her father's warning. These were *Greenleafs*; Stephen's aunt turned back to Wren.

"My grandfather built this house for his wife. He was a great man. All their children were born here. All their grandchildren were born here. They were leaders in this city, pillars of the community. In this house, every important person in New York, every leading family, visited. Theodore Roosevelt dined here...."

Greenleaf rolled his eyes. He had probably been hearing that speech for the last half-century. Then he caught Wren's eye—and winked.

"Come now, Auntie. We Greenleafs weren't all so perfect. Maybe we need to tell Wren about your Great Uncle Ambrose." At the mention of that name, Aunt Agnes swiveled back to her nephew, and her hands gripped the arms of the chair. "How dare you bring him up in front of strangers. How *dare* you!"

Wren took an unconscious step back from the woman's vehemence.

The old lady started coughing, and Mrs. Ryan swiftly stepped in with a glass of water. She sipped slowly, and calmed down. *Oh yes, these are not like other people.*

"I'm going to help Wren get started now, Auntie. We'll be back again later." He kissed her again, but she didn't seem to notice, and Wren was deeply grateful she could leave with Stephen. He closed the door behind them.

"You see what we're up against? I bet you had wondered why my family and I live in an apartment building on Central Park West instead of here. I bet you're not wondering anymore." He didn't wait for a reply she couldn't formulate anyway.

"Come. We call this the ancestor hallway." Gilt-framed oil portraits lined the walls. "These are my great-grandparents, the original owners, Benjamin Greenleaf, and Susan Greenleaf, nee Vanderwerf." Black suit and a late-

Victorian dress, in deep green. Benjamin didn't look like a commanding captain of industry. He had a dreamy look about him, as if he were an artist. If this house was his vision, that was understandable. Susan was beautiful—Wren had heard that she had a reputation as a lovely and lively hostess. Still, there was more than that. Of course, you couldn't read personalities just in an oil painting, but Wren thought she saw some mischief in those eyes. They must've been some pair, the dreamy husband and the extrovert wife.

"My grandparents, Caleb and Eleanor." A tuxedo and a simple but elegantly patterned dress, and bobbed hair: The next generation, adjusting to the 1920s, as the Gilded Age became a memory. "And my parents, James and Julia." A blue suit, and a red dress that was reminiscent of Mamie Eisenhower. This final portrait was not as well done as the other two. Was there less money left for the finest portraitist? "So, what do you think?"

What did he expect her to say? "You favor your mother," she finally said. Stephen nodded.

"Yes—you have an artist's eye. But one more to see."

He led her into an empty bedroom at the end of the hall. It was furnished, but tarps covered the bed and dresser, and like the other empty rooms she had seen, it smelled stale. No one had lived there for a long time. The walls were bare except for another portrait, a bearded man in nineteenth-century clothes. Was it her imagination, or was he smirking?

"And this is the younger brother to my great-grandfather Benjamin, Uncle Ambrose, whose very name infuriates Aunt Agnes." He didn't look like his brother. He had a beard, for one thing, and looked a lot more resolute, with a strong chin and a darker complexion. Wren could imagine him as an industrialist—no, something more flamboyant. Perhaps a sea captain.

"You know, my great-grandfather knew what his brother Ambrose did. My grandfather knew what his uncle had done. And my father was told as well, when he came of age—and I'm sure Aunt Agnes knows too." He shook his head. Wren felt a response was required.

"What did he do?" It came out as a whisper.

"That's the funny thing. My father never got around to telling me. All I ever heard was that whatever it was, it happened in this room."

Chapter Two

The temperature seemed to drop ten degrees as Wren tried to connect this forgotten, shabby room with one of the most magnificent residences in New York.

Greenleaf laughed. "I'm sorry. The penalties of coming from a prominent family obsessed with its past. I do admit it's fun to have a gothic touch in your history. I always imagined they caught Uncle Ambrose in some dingy Bowery dive with an opium pipe. "

What now? Should she laugh or offer sympathy? Or be offended? But she was saved by the bell, as they heard the doorbell ring. "Ah, that must be Mr. Fiore," said Greenleaf. They stepped out of the room, and Greenleaf firmly closed the door behind him. Wren felt doubly glad, not only to be away from Aunt Agnes and Uncle Ambrose, but to see Bobby, whose well-grounded personality was the antidote to family ghosts.

When Greenleaf opened the door, Wren caught him stepping back to look at the façade with a workman's appreciation.

"Ah, Mr. Greenleaf. Good to see you again, sir." He gave him a strong handshake with a calloused hand. "I'm very excited about working with Wren on your house."

"Come on in. We have some coffee in the kitchen. I'll give you the keys, and you can take it from there."

Bobby looked appreciatively around the kitchen. Kitchens were a favorite room to work on—all the possibilities to make them real showplaces for the wealthy people he tended to work for.

Greenleaf pulled a keyring out of his bag with more than a dozen keys, some of them older than he was. "I scooped up every key associated with this house." Everything from modern Medeco keys to old bit-and-barrel—so-called skeleton keys. "Bedrooms. Storage rooms. Whatever. Only my parents' housekeeper really knew what went where, and she's been dead 20 years." He dropped them on the battered kitchen table. "Bobby—you can put your van in the garage. This house hasn't seen a car since we sold my father's ancient Mercedes years ago." He stood. "Keep me posted on your progress, and let me know if you run into any problems, especially with...well, you know." He pointed upstairs. "I told Mrs. Ryan that she soon won't be able to use the kitchen. But there's a small fridge and microwave upstairs, and they can order out. I have to get back to the office now. Looking forward to seeing your work." He quickly shook hands with both of them and left.

"All right, then," said Bobby. "That was quick."

"He doesn't like being here. He doesn't love this house. He doesn't even like it," Wren told him. "You haven't met the residents yet." She gave him a quick rundown on Aunt Agnes, Mrs. Ryan, and the ghost of Uncle Ambrose. He nodded.

"So more than the usual run-of-the-mill crazy," he said. Then he gave her a look—Bobby knew Wren well. "But Aunt Agnes loves this house, doesn't she? I know whose side you're on." She blushed a little and shrugged. "We'll save Aunt Agnes' rooms for last. Most of the big stuff is the electricity and plumbing, before we get to crown moldings and painting anyway." He pulled some papers out of his bag. "If you want a real mystery, never mind Uncle Ambrose. Did you take a look at the electrical requirements he wants? Especially here in the kitchen? It's industrial-level power. If that's what he wants, fine. But why?"

Wren frowned—it was odd. "Why indeed? Did you ask?"

"Yes. He said he was advised by a friend who had similar work done. It must've been a very knowledgeable friend. His requests were very accurate. Over the top, but the technical details are precise. Is he planning to live here, after we're done?"

"He told us he can't reveal the final plans at this time—but that wiring is just another mystery. I think he's planning to sell it. But who would want something this large as a residence in this day and age? Is this about who he's going to sell it to? Is this house part of a secret investment scheme? Anyway, Aunt Agnes is living here, and I think she would fall apart at the idea of this being sold even after she's dead."

"It sounds operatic," said Bobby.

"You would know," Wren said. "Were you out last night?"

A smile lit him up. "The Barber of Seville. I can never get enough of Italian operas."

"You're biased."

He laughed. "Wagner is fine, but nothing beats the Italians. I have my portable sound system in the van for when we get started."

"Does your crew like opera?" Wren asked.

"My business. My truck. My music," he said. He drained his coffee. Wren picked up the keys—for a while, she could pretend she was mistress of Greenleaf House.

"Let's get to work."

They spent a couple of happy hours going over the needs of each room and how they'd preserve the artistic features with the upgrades. Some of the smaller rooms would be knocked together to form larger rooms, but Wren hoped to keep the basic proportions. In the 19th century, bedrooms were just that—a place for your bed. But unlike nineteenth-century robber barons, the merchant princes of the twenty-first-century wanted king-sized beds and more in their bedrooms. Still, Wren was determined to keep the beauty, the ideals of the nineteenth-century builders who created this residence, all the design details, all their care in workmanship.

Eventually, they couldn't put it off anymore; they had to review Aunt Agnes's suite, without Stephen running interference.

She knocked, and again, the expressionless Mrs. Ryan opened it. Aunt Agnes was still in the wingback chair, reading a book whose cover clearly identified it as a "sweeping saga."

Wren took a breath. "Mrs. Ryan, Miss Greenleaf, please excuse us. We need to review these rooms, especially the bathroom. It shouldn't take long. This is Bobby Fiore, our general contractor, who will be supervising the workmen, electricians, and plumbers."

Bobby gave a quick salute, but neither woman said anything. Nothing extensive was planned for this area, except for the bathroom, so after making a few notes, they entered the bathroom and stepped back 80 years.

"Wow," said Bobby. "I've seen some old bathrooms in my time, but not like this." A small clawfoot bathtub, with a shower extension, along with the most basic sink, toilet with a high tank, and medicine cabinet whose mirror seemed permanently fogged.

"My grandmother always marveled at modern bathrooms. Now I know why," Wren said.

"It suits us fine," said Aunt Agnes. She apparently was not confined to her chair, and, walking slowly, had slipped in behind them, closely followed by Mrs. Ryan. "I was a little girl when this was all installed, right before the war. This was always my room. I don't want it touched."

Why hadn't Stephen himself explained this to his aunt, Wren wondered. But maybe he had, and she was just being stubborn. Time to show she could deal with difficult clients.

"These fixtures were the most advanced in their day. But they're inefficient now. And falling apart," Wren said. People were awkward, but houses were easy for her to discuss. She saw the layers of sealant where desperate plumbers had attempted to keep the pipes working without replacing anything. "There are leaks—the ceiling below is heavily stained. We need to replace the pipes. We'll need new tiling, new fixtures, everything." Aunt Agnes didn't yield. "We have catalogs of new fixtures," Wren offered. "There are many choices for that same classic look, and you and your nephew can choose what you want." Wren didn't want to seem like the enemy here.

She braced herself for an explosion, but Aunt Agnes just looked sad.

Wren took a breath. She knew she had been right—she and Aunt Agnes shared a love for this house. "Miss Greenleaf. I want you to know I have been in dozens of beautiful houses. Maybe hundreds. Few are as wonderful as this one. I adore it already. I envy you getting to wake up here every morning. I could not hurt it. It would be like hurting a person. When I am done, I want this to look like it did the day your grandparents moved in. It is important that you know that. If you do not recognize your house when I am done, then I have failed. And I don't ever fail."

Aunt Agnes just stared, and she realized she was being sized up. She recalled Greenleaf's comments—"Dementia? If only." No, she was clear-minded. That was the problem—at least from Greenleaf's perspective.

"My nephew is a fool in many ways. Like his father. And he doesn't love this house. But I think he may have chosen wisely in hiring you. My grandfather, and I knew him well, loved this house he built. He said no one, not even his own children, appreciated it as much as I did—it's what made us close. I think you appreciate it as much as he did." She paused.

"Will you be working in the library?"

"Eventually, yes. We'll be working on every room."

"It's been closed since I was a girl. Stephen says it isn't safe anymore, but I should like to see it again." Unsafe? Maybe Stephen just didn't want his aunt wandering around the place.

"When it's been fixed up, I'll take you there myself."

"Thank you."

Bobby caught Wren's eye and smiled. They walked back downstairs.

"You say you don't like people. But you did all right with the old lady," he said.

"Yes, I did. But it wasn't about her. It was about the house. I was just lucky she and I share the same passion."

"At any rate, you calmed her. I think she already likes you better than her family. Anyway, I think that's it for today," said Bobby. "I'll arrange for a dumpster. We'll start ripping things out downstairs. This'll be quite a show, but we'll get through it together. Nut cases and all." He gave her a salute, and headed out the front door. Wren went back to the kitchen to make some notes about the house and the items she wanted to research. She vaguely heard the front door but ignored it until Mrs. Ryan showed up in the kitchen with a man behind her.

"Someone to see you, miss," she said. Her look said, *this is not your house, so why are guests calling for you here?*

Wren went into semi-panic. She didn't recognize the man, but if he was visiting her, it was probably someone she *should* know. This was going to be awkward. Any hope that Mrs. Ryan would introduce them was dashed when she turned on her heel as sharply as a marine on guard duty and left.

He appeared in his mid-thirties, dressed neatly in a suit and tie. He looked around with undisguised curiosity before looking at Wren.

"You're Wren Fontaine? Of Fontaine Partners, Architects?"

"Yes…" she said.

He pulled out a wallet and showed her a badge. "Sergeant Enrique Ortiz, NYPD. Your office said you were here. May I have a moment of your time?" He sat opposite her at the kitchen table. "Can I ask if you know a woman named Karen Lavendell?"

"I don't think so. It doesn't sound familiar. What—"

"She was chief acquisitions officer, and a partner, in a company called PH Hospitality. Is that familiar?" He smiled. "I see by your face it is."

Wren was a little embarrassed at being so obvious. "Yes. I do know about the company, although I've never done business with them. But what is—"

"According to Ms. Lavendell's calendar, she was going to call on you. She had notes about you and your firm."

Irritation began to replace confusion, as she looked at Ortiz's bland, slightly smug face. "What is this about? Have you arrested her for something?"

"What makes you think she's been arrested?"

"You're a police detective," said Wren.

Ortiz nodded slowly. "Yes, that's a fair conclusion. I've never met an architect before, but I imagine that clear, logical thought is essential for your profession. But no, Karen Lavendell is not under arrest. She's dead. She was murdered. And 'call Wren Fontaine' was the last task she entered.

Chapter Three

Wren started to say something several times, stopping each time, while Ortiz looked patiently at her.

"I'm sorry," she finally said. "But although I know of the company, I've never even heard of Karen Lavendell." She still didn't see where this was going—she assumed this was a mugging, a carjacking. Wasn't that how people were killed?

He answered her unspoken question. "You see, she came here from Boston and was staying in a hotel downtown, and was found in the rear service entrance, shot to death. But she wasn't robbed. Her wallet was still with her, with cash and credit cards, cell phone, jewelry. So, I'm looking for a motive. I haven't had a chance to research it much. Can you tell me anything?"

Wren took a breath and organized her thoughts. "They develop old homes, mostly in New England, into inns and small hotels. The 'PH' stands for 'Private Hotel.'"

"Why do you think Ms. Lavendell was hoping to meet with you?"

"I have no idea. I could only speculate."

Ortiz grinned and spread out his arms. "This is not a courtroom. Speculate away."

"All right. Perhaps she wanted to talk to me about a project."

"And you're an expert in historic renovation?"

Was he teasing her? "It's the focus of my practice," she said. *How prim I sound.*

"Would you have gone to work with them? Again, we're just speculating. This is all new to me, so I want your opinion. I'll keep it confidential."

20

She took a breath. "No. I probably wouldn't work with them. They don't have a great reputation in the industry."

"They're crooks—their buildings fall down?"

Wren smiled and shook her head. "That's not what I meant. This business is very heavily regulated. You can't do anything really terrible, that is, dangerous." She felt comfortable now, talking about something she knew. "But you can still do second-rate work. As a professor of mine said, you can have a Hyundai, or you can have a Mercedes. They both meet certain engineering standards but think of the difference. PH Hospitality work was Hyundai work."

"Ahh." He looked around. "This is some house. This gets Mercedes work?"

"This gets Rolls-Royce work," said Wren.

Ortiz laughed. "I like that. I like that a lot. You know, I looked up your firm before I got here. You and your father—you're big shots." Wren wondered how her father would react to being referred to as a *big shot*. "I imagine Karen Lavendell would know that too. I wonder why she'd waste her time trying to get your prestigious firm to work on her second-rate projects?"

Wren had no answer to that. Fortunately, Ortiz didn't seem to expect one. He stood and pulled a card out of his jacket pocket.

"My card, in case you remember something later. By the way, is this home being converted into a hotel?"

"You'd have to ask Stephen Greenleaf. As the owner of this house, he's my client."

"Of course. Like priests and lawyers, architects have confidentiality agreements built in." She assumed he was joking. "So, how do I leave this place? "

"I'll see you out," said Wren. They walked through the magnificent foyer, and Ortiz continued to look around. Wren realized that detectives might be like architects, curious about their surroundings.

"So this was someone's house? That is, just one family lived here?"

"It was a different world," said Wren. He nodded.

She closed the door behind him. Wren walked back to the kitchen, Ortiz's questions still bouncing around her head. She didn't know Lavendell, but she bet Lavendell knew their firm and the unlikelihood that Fontaine Partners would work with them. So why did Lavendell want to meet with her?

* * *

Wren finished making her notes, then spent the afternoon following up with suppliers—those who could give twenty-first-century quality with a nineteenth-century look. It was always going to be a compromise, she noted ruefully. You couldn't find anyone to do some of that old work anymore, like finding someone who could still drive a hansom cab. But she could come close. She found some possibilities and knew Bobby also had contacts, third-generation suppliers who might have just the thing in the back of a warehouse, long forgotten.

Ortiz had asked her if Greenleaf House was going to be a hotel. She thought about wiring. Greenleaf had wanted more power than was really necessary for a home. But if he was planning for a commercial kitchen…

When she was done, she took the subway back to Brooklyn, considering what to tell her father. He was in the study going over some paperwork.

"Off to a good start?" he asked.

"Yes. On the right foot with Stephen, but even better, struck a good tone with his aunt, who lives there, and may be obsessed with the place. I think she sees me as a kindred spirit. But one rather odd thing happened." She told him about the police visit.

"That is odd. We've never had any business with PH Hospitality—and never will. I don't know this Karen Lavendell, either. Why would she think we'd work with her?"

"I thought about that. Maybe she hoped to find out more about the house from us."

"Equally foolish of her. But maybe she was foolish. Anyway, I'm sure this will turn out to be nothing."

"And there was something else I wanted to run by you, though. I was talking with Bobby about the power requirements for the kitchen. It's enough to run a small restaurant."

"Odd, but not impossible," said Ezra. "I assume Bobby can easily handle that. Is this a problem for you?"

"A house must follow a purpose—you taught me that. I want to know the purpose."

"Ah, but you know the house's *purpose*, dear daughter. You are more concerned with the house's *fate*. And that is out of our purview."

* * *

Wren was even more excited the next morning—off to a good start and confident she had everyone's good will.

Bobby had already arrived with his crew, and they were starting by ripping out the old kitchen. He and Wren had optimistically done the paperwork already so they could start work immediately. Bobby gave her a quick salute, as opera poured out of the portable player.

"Tosca?" she ventured.

"Very good! You're learning. The ladies are upstairs. Mrs. Ryan peeked in to make sure we weren't stealing the silver."

She had a sheaf of plans, and began reviewing with Bobby the structural requirements along with the artistic ones. There were engineering concerns affecting supporting walls, pipes, and wires, along with artistic ones—the plaster designs on ceilings, the door hinges, and the wooden floors. Later she'd walk through the house alone, taking stock of every room. That was the best part of the job. Could a house be a best friend?

But for now, there were modern-day tasks. "By the way, I just wanted to give you a head's up—we had a police detective here yesterday. I told my father, but I should tell you too, in case he comes back." She told Bobby the story.

"Dear Lord, I wonder what that's all about. I know about the firm—same rumors you probably heard, shoddy work. It'll probably turn out to be something personal, nothing to do with the business, but I'll let you know if they call me."

"Well, they certainly called Stephen. He left a message earlier saying he'd be coming by."

They were finishing up their plans for the day when they heard someone coming through the door upstairs.

"Wren!" It was Stephen Greenleaf. He came downstairs quickly. "About the late Karen Lavendell. I went 10 rounds with some police detective about her. I found out that she was reaching out to you, which was quite a surprise. What the hell is going on here?"

After considerable thought, Wren decided this was a rhetorical question. She watched Greenleaf's eyes go back and forth between her and Bobby.

"Wren—did you meet with her?"

"No. I didn't even know who she was. The police asked me about her, but I had no idea why she would want to speak with me. Was she a friend of yours?"

"A friend? Dear God, no." He shook his head and glanced at the workmen, prying the walls apart. "Can you two join me upstairs?"

Without waiting for an answer, he headed back upstairs. Bobby and Wren looked at each other, shrugged, and followed him to the Rose Parlor, a small room off the foyer, and sat on faded furniture from the 1920s.

Greenleaf made an attempt to pull himself together and absently fixed his tie. "I'm sorry—it's been a bit of a shock. Lavendell and PH Hospitality have been after this house to turn it into one of their hotels. I'm working on…along somewhat different lines. Anyway, I need you to be extra careful not to tell anything to anyone from PH Hospitality—or, God help us, to my aunt."

"I was wondering if she just wanted to talk with me about a project," said Wren.

"You and your father are way out of her league. No, I bet she wanted to pump you."

"Well, she wouldn't have gotten anything from me or Bobby. I assure you, we know how to be discreet."

"Of course. Sorry if I…anyway, the police, a Sergeant Ortiz, tracked me down at my office. So he was here, as well?"

"Yes. I wasn't able to tell him anything I haven't told you," she said.

"Does my aunt know he was here?"

"I'm afraid so. Mrs. Ryan answered the door."

"Dammit. Aunt Agnes will be all over me on this. What a mess. Listen, Wren, Bobby—I don't control what you do outside of this job, but keep in mind that I don't have a good relationship with those people. That's all I'm saying. Now, I have to account for my time with that cop, as if I were a suspect."

"Why would you be a suspect?" Wren asked.

"Karen Lavendell and I have met before. And as I'm sure Sergeant Ortiz found out, it wasn't pleasant."

* * *

Wren finished the day, and gave her father the update.

"So our client may be a murder suspect?"

"I'm wondering if Karen Lavendell was just trying to find out if I could give her an inside edge on what Stephen Greenleaf is doing. Not so much as being indiscreet, but influencing Stephen to work with them. Do you think that PH Hospitality wants to take over Greenleaf House and is pressuring Greenleaf to sell out to them?" she asked.

"Very possibly. Wren—let me know right away if they get in touch with you again. They're controversial, and now they're somehow involved here. Let me know if anything else happens. Right now, I have a client call in two minutes."

Wren retreated to the kitchen, where she had coffee. What a way to start. But she wasn't going to be surprised again. She fired up her laptop. She needed to find out more about PH Hospitality. Also, what would happen if Miss Greenleaf asked why there were police in the house? Just tell her to talk to Stephen—not her problem. As Bobby might say, "Not our circus. Not our monkey."

* * *

25

The next day started well. Wren had made a bargain with herself that she wouldn't seek out Aunt Agnes but wouldn't shirk from her while going about her work. She gathered she hardly ever left her suite anymore. But there was a chairlift installed on the servant staircase on the back, and Mrs. Ryan accompanied Aunt Agnes on daily walks as the weather allowed. Wren saw her that morning, reviewing that extraordinary foyer, the lady of the manor from a day when such things mattered. As a girl, had she listened to endless stories from older relatives about how things were in the old days, until she thought they had happened to her? Wren hadn't even grown up there, and yet could still picture herself having tea and cucumber sandwiches in the morning room.

Wren imagined what their walks were like, Mrs. Ryan escorting Miss Greenleaf all the way to the avenue, where she would bitterly comment on how the shops of her youth had been replaced by a Thai restaurant and a store selling obscenely expensive sneakers.

Shortly after they returned, Wren found herself outside making notes on what they'd need to do to keep the façade in repair. A wrought-iron fence separated the house from the sidewalk, and, stepping back to get a better view, she saw a man leaning on the fence and staring at the house—certainly forgivable.

Or maybe at her—which was not.

"You're working here?" he asked. He looked a little older than her, nicely dressed in a jacket and open-necked shirt, and with a cheerful smile. Her first inclination was to respond sarcastically, but she resisted the temptation, and instead just smiled and nodded.

"I've always loved it. One of the most beautiful homes in the city. I'd heard it was going to be renovated and restored." Karen Lavendell, and now this stranger. Had Stephen taken an ad? "You must be the architect." He looked at the sign on the fence, noting Fontaine Partners as architects and Fiore Construction as general contractors.

"How do you know I'm not the general contractor?"

He just grinned and shook his head. "Not dressed like that. You must be the Fontaine."

"I'm *a* Fontaine. Wren Fontaine." He laughed. *He thinks a lot of himself.*

"After Christopher Wren? I like that." At least she didn't have to explain it.

"My name is Conor, Conor—"

And then Mrs. Ryan came out the front door, glaring at Conor.

"I saw you from the window. What are you doing here?" She looked at Wren. "Miss Fontaine is working—why are you interrupting her?"

Wren wondered if she was somehow in trouble for letting this stranger interrupt her. Was Mrs. Ryan spying on her from upstairs? Would this appear on her report card: "Wren is a good worker, but somewhat distractible."

But what happened next surprised her even more. Conor didn't wilt, but laughed again and pushed open the gate. Mrs. Ryan continued to frown and came down the steps. Wren thought that Conor was being brave to the point of recklessness. A few more steps and they were face-to-face, and then Conor leaned over and gave her a kiss.

"Aren't you happy to see me, mom?"

Chapter Four

"We just didn't expect you this early," said Mrs. Ryan.

"My schedule opened up. And I was just starting what I suspected would be a pleasant conversation with architect Fontaine here. I'm sorry, Wren, I was just about to give my full name, Conor Ryan. Mrs. Ryan is my mother, as you see. Mom—has Aunt Agnes been giving Wren a hard time?"

"I don't know what you mean," she said.

"Yes, you do. Come with me, Wren. I'll put in a good word for you with the old lady."

"I wish you wouldn't call her the 'old lady,'" said Mrs. Ryan. But Conor just shook his head.

So the companion's son had a connection here. Wren wasn't sure she liked him—he seemed a little too full of himself. But if he had a connection with the house, he could be helpful, even if he just put in a good word with the "old lady."

The three of them walked upstairs while Mrs. Ryan briefly updated her son on how various siblings and other members of the Ryan clan were doing, and from her tone, they generally did not meet her standards.

But Wren noticed how Aunt Agnes lit up at seeing Conor. She was reading in her chair, as before, but this time she greeted her visitors with a wide smile and open arms.

"Conor! Give your aunt a kiss!" He was apparently an honorary nephew. He leaned down and obliged her. Then he reached into his jacket pocket and pulled out a small gold box. "Oh, it's marzipan. How thoughtful. You never forget."

"She's not supposed to have it," said Mrs. Ryan. Everyone ignored her, and Aunt Agnes happily bit into a bright red candy strawberry.

"Your work is going well?"

"Yes, coming along nicely."

"Why aren't you married yet?"

"Haven't found the right girl."

Aunt Agnes looked over Conor's shoulder to Mrs. Ryan. "This city is wall-to-wall Irish. You wouldn't think it would be that hard to find a nice Catholic girl for your son."

"I'll work on it," said Mrs. Ryan drily.

Miss Greenleaf knew of a time when few Catholics would've entered Greenleaf House, unless they wore maids' uniforms.

"Aunt Agnes, I am sorry things are such a mess here. But I'm sure it'll be a whole lot better when it's done. Now, I met your architect outside, and I have a good feeling about her. She loves this house as much as you do. I can tell by the way she was looking at it, so let's work with her."

Aunt Agnes took a look at Wren, who felt like she was meeting a new friend's mother for the first time.

"You've always been good with people, Conor, so I'll be as flexible as I can. I will do you this favor, Miss Fontaine, at Conor's request, because I know he appreciates the history of this house. His ancestors didn't own this house, but he has a respect for it. " She gave him another fond look and took another piece of marzipan. Mrs. Ryan jumped in and seized the box, saying they should save some for later, and Conor took the chance to give Wren a smile, who felt she owed him a smile back.

"A pleasure meeting you," Wren said. "But I have to get back to work now."

The next few hours went smoothly, and Wren was planning to take her sandwich and eat by the park when she saw Conor come down the stairs.

"Thanks for the good word," Wren said.

"My pleasure. Now, it looks like lunchtime. Would you like to join me?"

He had done a nice favor for her, but it wasn't lunch-worthy. She brandished her lunch bag. "Just eating in the park."

"If I buy a hot dog, can I sit with you?"

"All right," said Wren, after a moment's thought. It was casual enough.

They found a bench to themselves—it was a workday and still a little cool.

"You're probably wondering about me and Aunt Agnes," he said. "The truth is, the Greenleafs were very good to me. My mother was a Murphy before her marriage, and the Murphys have been working for the Greenleafs one way or another since this house was built. My mother is descended from Kevin Murphy, who was the original coachman here. She had been a maid here before her marriage and did occasional work even after. As a small boy, she'd bring me along and park me in front of a TV, but I'd wander off to explore. Even then, the place was beginning to fall apart. When my father died when I was nine, I had two much older sisters, who were already on their own—the army and college—so my mother and I moved in so she could be a sort of cook/housekeeper, gradually becoming Aunt Agnes' nurse/companion. Anyway, old Mr. Greenleaf—Stephen's father—put away some money for me for college, and Stephen added to that later on when he started making it big on Wall Street, and Aunt Agnes was generous with her own inherited funds."

"A bit of noblesse oblige?" Wren said.

"Absolutely. But kind nonetheless. They saw I was bright, helped me apply to college, get scholarships. Aunt Agnes especially took interest in me. I know." He became sarcastic. "I know what you're thinking: This sounds almost feudal, the distinguished old Greenleafs giving money to the Irish help. Such condescension! It's the way they saw it, I know, especially Aunt Agnes, but it was welcome nonetheless. You probably noticed from the state of the house that the money was running out—Stephen was the first one to start making real money again. But they still wanted to play philanthropists." He looked uncertain. "I see how this could look humiliating. I hope you don't think less of me for taking their money."

"Why should I? Why should anyone? And after all, you do bring her marzipan." He just looked at Wren for a moment, and she was afraid she had gone too far, but then he laughed.

"Oh, all right. You can be sarcastic too. I deserved that. And I am grateful, no matter how they gave it."

"What did you get your degree in?"

"Undergraduate degree in information services, followed by a master's in library science."

"So you're a librarian?"

"Sort of. I work for a research company. Corporate clients mostly. It gives me flexible hours, so it's good for now."

She was about to say she had to get back to work, but then she remembered this was someone who no doubt knew a lot more about the house than she did.

"One question you might be able to help me with—Miss Greenleaf seemed very interested in the library. She specifically asked about it. Stephen was able to give us only a limited number of papers relating to the house, and I wondered if you knew if she might have squirreled away some old documents."

Conor raised an eyebrow at that. "You think she has some information about the house that Stephen doesn't?"

Wren shrugged. "She doesn't seem to like her nephew very much—but I doubt I'm telling you anything you don't know. She may have some papers he doesn't know about. You seem to have a better relationship with her. It would be helpful if I had them."

"You're not talking like an architect," he said.

"Do architects talk in a special way?" she asked. "But I have a background in art history as well. So I know that documents, plans, old blueprints can end up in funny places."

He had struck her as glib, but now he just stopped and thought that over. She wondered if she had triggered something.

"That's…interesting," said Conor. "I mean the idea of putting it all together."

"Houses don't exist by themselves," said Wren. "I think of how they were decorated and furnished—how they were used."

"And the people who inhabited them?" He raised an eyebrow. *Oh, he was right!* "But you're wondering about my mother and Miss Greenleaf. Rather an odd couple, you're probably thinking. Actually, not odd, very much in tune with each other."

"It's none of my business," she said, hearing the priggishness as the words came out. She wished she could handle interactions like that more smoothly, as she knew her father would.

"It's all right. It is strange—something you don't see anymore, just read about in old novels. But about any records. From time to time, Aunt Agnes has mentioned family papers, but we've always thought she was just confused. As you can imagine, the Greenleafs are a somewhat patriarchal group. I don't see anyone sharing anything with her. But if I hear anything from her, I'll pass it along."

"I'd appreciate that," she said, and they started walking.

"One more thing you might be able to help me with," Wren said. Her curiosity overcame her usual shyness, and she found it easy to talk with someone as open as Conor Ryan. "Stephen showed me a room that belonged to Uncle Ambrose, and I—"

Conor started laughing. "That didn't take long, did it? How did that come up?"

"Miss Greenleaf was being difficult, and Stephen teased her about him. She was enraged—I thought she'd have a heart attack. I asked Stephen for the story, but he said he didn't know."

Conor nodded, and they continued walking. "There are rumors, but nothing more than that. For what it's worth, I think Stephen was honest with you. He really doesn't know—and it's interesting to speculate on why no one told him. Also, for what it's worth, I think my mother knows, but she won't tell me. Perhaps—" Then he stopped and shook his head. "But speaking of murder, can we jump ahead a century? I hear there was a murder related to this house yesterday."

"Did Stephen Greenleaf mention it to you? It didn't get much mention in the news."

"No, Stephen didn't tell me anything about it. But research is my business. The dead woman, Karen Lavendell, worked for a firm that buys old houses and turns them into hotels. I wonder if she wanted to turn Greenleaf House into a hotel. That interests me." Yes, Wren thought. Using Fontaine Partners to pull strings with the Greenleafs.

"I thought you were just interested in this house's past," said Wren. "But it seems you're interested in its future too."

"We're the same that way," he said. "It's because we're interested in the house's past that we're concerned about its future. It's been a bit of a hobby of mine, the history of Greenleaf House. There are still some things I want to find out. If PH Hospitality were to buy it, God knows what secrets would just be dragged out into dumpsters. I wouldn't like that at all."

"It would seem that Lavendell's death delays those plans. Maybe even stops them."

Conor gave her a sharp look. "Are you saying—" he said and stopped again.

She caught his meaning and felt her heart lurch. "I'm sorry—I wasn't accusing you—"

He laughed. "Of course not. My job makes me paranoid. Look, I'll put my cards on the table. You and I both have an interest in this house's future. I know that Stephen is your client, not me, but I think we can help each other, for the good of the house."

He handed her a business card. A very plain design, "Sapiens Corporate Research, Conor Ryan, Research Manager." Just a phone number—no email, website, or even address.

"Can we continue this conversation later today at my office? Is 4:00 convenient?"

She thought it over. Again, this was all uncharted waters for her.

"All right, but I can't make any promises," she said.

"That's fine." He seemed relieved.

"You will have to tell me where. I've never seen a business card without an address."

"My employer is a little nervous about privacy. It discourages people from showing up unexpectedly." He pulled out a pen and wrote out a West Side address on the back, in the garment district, which Wren thought an odd place for a research firm.

They had reached the house.

"I'm going back to work," he said. "I'll see you later." He headed for the subway. Wren took out his card and looked at it again. Even the simplest designs could hide secrets—she knew that from houses. And it held true for people, and the cards they carried. He said his job made him paranoid. Why would a simple librarian job make anyone paranoid?

But more to the point was his knowledge of PH Hospitality. The news items hadn't connected PH Hospitality to Greenleaf House, and Conor said he hadn't spoken with Stephen about it.

So how had he concluded that PH Hospitality was interested in the home?

Chapter Five

Wren found Bobby supervising the kitchen work. "Glad you're back," he said. "It's going well, but we have a chance to get started on the roof. The man we want for that job has some time now, so let's grab him while we can."

"Yes. Almost no one knows how to work on copper anymore."

"You're right on that. There is nothing that lasts longer—or costs more. A copper roof will survive for more than a lifetime," he said. But the Greenleaf House roof was finally showing signs of its age. It had been around for several lifetimes, and if it didn't need a full replacement, it likely needed some heavy maintenance. "If you remember, we saw what we could from the windows, but now we need to get up there proper, through the attic. The way isn't clear, and I don't want to cut anything we don't have to."

"Of course. I'm curious myself to see how we can get up there."

One of the heavy, old keys opened a door to a long-unused hall on the top floor, forgotten storage rooms, and abandoned servants' quarters.

"There must be a way up there without taking the ceilings apart," he said.

Wren paced along the hallway—she could feel it. Houses, especially great houses, had fixed proportions—and this one was off. She could read them. *Wouldn't it be great if I could read people, read Conor, as easily?*

"It's too short," Wren said. "This corridor is too short. Do you have the measurements handy?"

"No, we don't have the plans for this—it probably wasn't considered important enough to save. But I know the length of the corridor right below this. Let me get my equipment, and we can compare." Bobby had a laser distance meter, quick and accurate. While he got it, Wren peeked into the empty rooms. Her childhood dream of living in such a house in "splendid isolation" gave way to the realization that even the most dedicated introvert would need a team of servants—not just Mrs. Danvers. Oddly, Stephen had asked for these small rooms to be brought up to code and turned into little bedrooms. Why more bedrooms in such a big house?

Bobby came back, and a few minutes later, he confirmed several feet were missing from the end of the hallway.

"Your instincts are already as good as your father's," he said, which pleased Wren more than she wanted to admit. "Now, let's see what I can find." The light was dim up there, so he had brought a heavy-duty work light and shone it at the wall at the end of the hallway. They looked closely, and he slowly felt the wall.

"Ha!" he finally said. "Feel that. There's a seam there, plastered and painted but not completely covered. There was a door here once. There's something behind here. Soon Bobby was cutting through the wall—the ancient panel quickly fell off, revealing a steep set of stairs. It led up to a small attic, which granted easy access to the roof without necessitating damage to the ceiling. They carried up the work lights, with the aid of long extension cords, and flashlights. Wren was just five foot four, but even so, she could barely stand in the little attic, and Bobby had to stoop.

"Yes, perfect," he said. "This will do nicely." Wren was busy looking around the small room. Nothing but dust, but it was dry—the roof still held, even as the old pipes had rotted elsewhere. The only item was an old sea chest. A remnant from an old clipper ship? It was in good shape, the wood solid, the metal not rusted. It could be valuable. As Bobby examined the ceiling, Wren carefully opened the hasp and swung it open. She lifted the flashlight....

"Jesus Christ!" Wren fell back as a wave of nausea washed over her, and she fought dizziness.

"Are you hurt?" asked Bobby, running as fast as he could, bent over. The sea chest didn't contain any treasures. It contained a skeleton.

"Jesus Christ indeed," said Bobby. He stepped closer. "Looks real, all right." They both just stared at the skeleton in silence for a few moments. "I suppose we ought to call someone," he said.

Wren forced herself to think. There were procedures for this. "Actually, we have to call the police."

"Do police investigate murders that old? I'm guessing this has been in there a while."

"It doesn't matter. There are rules if you find a body while digging a new home foundation, for example, and I'm sure this isn't different. We'll have to call the authorities." She wondered which particular department in New York handled that—then remembered she had Sgt. Ortiz's card. As good a place as any to start. And she'd need to call Stephen.

For a moment—just a moment—she thought of dumping this all on her father and getting back to work. He could have the people—and she'd have the house. But again—she was now a partner.

"Let's go downstairs, and I'll start making calls," Wren said. Back in the hallway, she called Stephen first.

"It's Wren. Something came up. Nothing directly to do with the house. But Bobby and I uncovered a forgotten attic when looking for access to the roof. We found an old chest with—well, with a skeleton."

That's when it hit her. The Greenleafs literally had a skeleton in their closet. She coughed to cover up a sudden laugh.

"A what?"

"A skeleton. I'm guessing it's been there for some time." She tried to sound in control—she was in charge and didn't want to sound panicked.

"What the hell, Wren? Is this someone's idea of a joke?" She didn't answer.

"I'm calling the police," she said.

"What—why?"

"It's the law. I can't just leave the bones there. Anyway, I'll call Sergeant Ortiz, who interviewed both of us."

"Oh, all right. I suppose there's no helping it. I've got some meetings, but I'll be there when I can." He ended the call.

"He's not too upset?" asked Bobby. "I'm guessing he would've been happy if we had just put out the box on recycling day."

"Probably. Especially after the Lavendell murder." Wren pulled Ortiz's card out of her wallet and called him.

"Ortiz."

"Sergeant? This is Wren Fontaine. We spoke at Greenleaf House."

"Yes. Did you remember something else?"

"No. It's something new, and I didn't know who else to call. In a long-sealed attic, we found a skeleton." It was quiet for a while.

"Excuse me. Are we talking about a full human skeleton, or just a few bones?"

"I didn't count the number of bones. But it seems to be a full skeleton. A skull, ribcage, arms, and legs."

A long quiet. "All right. See that no one disturbs it. In fact, could you or one of your workmen stand guard? I want to make sure no one connected with the house gets curious. I'll be there shortly. Have you told anyone else?"

"I was with our contractor, Bobby Fiore. And I called Stephen Greenleaf, who said he's coming."

"All right. But no one else in that room until we get there." He hung up.

Wren took a deep breath. "I have to tell my father, but that can wait until tonight. Good grief."

Bobby nodded. "But on the bright side, I saw it's going to be easy to get to the roof from there."

"That's good," Wren said, but she was hardly listening. She suddenly thought of Uncle Ambrose smirking downstairs and wondering if she had just found out why.

* * *

Bobby said he would watch over the entrance, and that he'd examine the ceiling in preparation for going onto the roof while waiting for Sgt. Ortiz.

She headed back down to do some examination of the dining room—and ran into Mrs. Ryan on the stairs. Wren groaned inwardly. She knew she had to tell her something, with police on the way. She wished she had insisted Stephen come immediately so he could've broken the news.

"Miss Greenleaf heard noises and asked if everything was all right," she said.

"Everything is fine. We had to break into the old attic stairs to get to the roof. We are sorry for the noise." Wren felt Mrs. Ryan's eyes burn into her, and once again, Wren felt like a naughty student. Mrs. Ryan had probably gone to a parochial school and learned her talent for glares from the sisters.

"Thank you. I'll tell Miss Greenleaf."

"Just one more thing. Mr. Fiore and I found something in the attic that, ah, for official reasons, needs an official examination. Some police will be arriving, and Mr. Greenleaf has already been notified. But it's nothing to worry about." Wren gave her what she hoped was a reassuring smile but doubted she had succeeded. Again, Mrs. Ryan looked like she was going to ask questions, but stopped herself.

"I see. I will tell Miss Greenleaf that as well. That attic has been sealed for years. I am sure she will want to speak with Mr. Greenleaf when he arrives." She turned and left.

There was no point in just waiting and brooding, so she busied herself in the dining room. When the doorbell rang, she walked quickly to the front door, wanting to beat Mrs. Ryan there so she wouldn't have to face her again. Sgt. Ortiz stepped in, accompanied by a small team, including an older man whom Wren immediately recognized. He gave her a quick wink, and that was all. Those in the group generally didn't acknowledge each other among strangers—it wasn't something you wanted to explain.

"A skeleton, Ms. Fontaine?" asked Ortiz.

"That's what I said."

He sighed. "Thank you. We have to look into this and take photos." He gestured to the older man. "The remains will be examined by Dr. Erik Leopold, from the medical examiner's office, who has a sideline in historical forensics." Oh yes, Wren knew that well.

"It'll probably be the oldest crime scene we've ever seen. Out of our jurisdiction," Dr. Leopold said, rubbing his hands. "Nevertheless, this is going to be fun."

Ortiz didn't look amused. "I may be wasting your time," he said. "But with one recent murder connected with this house, I want to be sure—and you already are involved in the Lavendell case. Ms. Fontaine—please show the way."

Bobby was waiting for them at the bottom of the attic stairs, and Wren introduced him.

"I set up several work lights up there, so it's easy to see. And only Wren and I have been upstairs."

Ortiz looked at the freshly opened doorway.

"How long has this been sealed?" he asked.

"From the workmanship and materials, I'm guessing more than a century," Wren said. Ortiz nodded.

Bobby led everyone upstairs.

The lights didn't do much to rid the room of its haunted look, throwing into relief the old, stained beams and nails, the cobwebs and dust. The sea chest and its occupant looked like a stage set, the skeleton at the twisted angle where they had left it.

A photographer quickly pulled out a camera and took a series of photos. When he was done, he nodded, and then Dr. Leopold and one of the crime scene investigators knelt by the body, looking almost gleeful. Well, Wren concluded, she loved old houses. Why shouldn't they love old crime scenes?

"The decomposition would've dissolved any clothes," said Dr. Leopold. "But we seem to have a pair of shoes in here." He pulled them out.

"Those are women's shoes, but not fine. Those are likely a maid's shoes," Wren said. Leopold gave her a knowing look. Somehow, simple clothes like these gave Wren a greater connection to the past than the fanciful ballgowns found in museums. She saw something very real in this unknown woman, who made beds, dusted furniture, and met her friends at Coney Island on days off, where they flirted with young men.

She saw Ortiz raise an eyebrow at the exchange she had with Leopold, at her caring about the clothes while he cared about the body.

"Can you tell how she died?" asked Ortiz.

"You don't ask for much, do you?" said Leopold. "We first need to figure out if it is, in fact, a she."

"You said those were women's shoes. Was cross-dressing common a century ago?" asked Ortiz.

"And you're assuming it's a century ago. One thing at a time—but yes, it is a woman. The shape of the hips. And I think she was in her twenties. Now, for how long she's been here.... Let's have a look at the teeth...Sally, just hold the flashlight." He looked closely at the teeth. Ortiz stepped closer, and so did Bobby and Wren—both curious, but not wanting to call too much attention to themselves and get sent away.

"Okay, we're in luck. She had dental work, not a given once upon a time. Now, we could bring in a forensic dentist, but from what I know, this is turn-of-the-century work."

"No one does work like that anymore?"

"Oh dear lord, what a ghastly thought that someone is out there practicing dentistry like this today! No, she's definitely been here a long time. No longer your responsibility, Sergeant."

"Glad to hear it," he said. "But I'm still wondering how she died. I'm imagining she was murdered. Otherwise, why stick her in the attic?"

"That'll be tough, but we'll see what we can do...her neck wasn't broken. No damage to the skull...." His eyes traveled over her ribcage. "All right—we may have something here. Damage to a rib, and it wasn't long before she died, because the bone hadn't even begun to heal—this looks like a bullet wound. I bet the bullet is still here somewhere." They peered into the chest with their flashlights. "Aha! You're going to love this, Enrique. We have the bullet, and it's in good shape." The crime scene officer picked it up with tweezers and dropped it into a plastic bag.

"So what are we going to match it with? Was it the gun that killed President McKinley?" asked Ortiz.

"Nice suggestion—could be. But actually..." She produced a magnifying glass and examined the bullet in the quiet room. Then she said something to Leopold, and he said something back, but they were both too quiet to hear.

"Do you want to share with the rest of the class?" said Ortiz.

The officer turned around. "On the other hand, I don't think you're going to like this at all," she said, but she was grinning, and Leopold was shaking his head. "Remember how I told you the bullet that killed Lavendell was

41

unusual? An old alloy we haven't seen in decades? This bullet looks the same. It belongs in a museum. Now I'm going to have to get this back to the lab to do a full ballistic comparison, but I'd be willing to bet a week's salary that this comes from the same gun that killed Karen Lavendell."

Ortiz just stared. "So, you're saying that the same gun was used to kill two people more than a century apart?"

"That's exactly what I'm saying," said Leopold.

Chapter Six

"Two people—with the same century-old gun," said Ortiz, more to himself than to anyone in the room.

"Could be one," said Leopold, with a chuckle. "Just look for a 140-year-old hitman." The other cops laughed, but Ortiz didn't seem to hear.

He eventually roused himself. "We're taking the body and the shoes pending a ballistics report."

Everyone left the attic, Ortiz departing last, shaking his head. "I'll have a full report on the body, such as it is," Leopold told Ortiz. He gave Wren another wink and left.

"OK if I go back up to examine the roof?" asked Bobby.

"Just wait until we've removed the body," said Ortiz. "I can hardly call that a crime scene, not after all this time."

"Thanks. I'll just go check on my crew," he said and headed downstairs.

Ortiz disappeared into himself again, and Wren thought it might be time to get back to work herself, when she heard the door and then quick footfalls on the staircase. A breathless Stephen Greenleaf looked back and forth between them.

"What the hell is going on here?"

"A long-dead body in your attic," said Ortiz.

"Who is it?"

"I was hoping you could tell me. It's a young woman who has been there for a long, long time. Any stories of family members disappearing?"

"Those were definitely a servant's shoes," said Wren.

"You're sure?" said Ortiz.

"Old clothes, old houses. They go together," she said.

"All right. Anyone, Mr. Greenleaf? Any stories of people disappearing? Family legends? I gather your family has been here since this house was built."

"No, not at all. I have no idea who that was or how it came to be in my attic. That room was sealed long before I was born."

"Why?" asked Ortiz. "Why not just lock the door?"

He shrugged. "Maybe they wanted to keep the servants out of there."

"Or because they threw one in there. Do you still have servants here?"

"Just Mrs. Ryan, my aunt's companion. The two of them are the only residents here, as I told you already. My aunt is 90 years old, and I don't want her upset. Neither of them could possibly know anything about this."

Ortiz stuck his hands in his pocket and looked around. "This is some house, sir. I have never been in anything like it. It's like being in a museum."

"It's not a museum. It's our family home," said Greenleaf.

"But not really, sir, is it? You don't live here anymore. Just your elderly aunt and her companion, in one little corner. 'If these walls could talk.' That's the phrase, isn't it? What this house has seen—it's enough to give me chills."

"Theodore Roosevelt and his wife dined here," said Greenleaf heavily.

"He was a war hero, knew his way around a gun. I wonder if he shot that young woman?"

Even Wren realized at that point that Ortiz was baiting him. Greenleaf started to answer, but then stopped.

"I do need to speak briefly with your aunt and Mrs. Ryan. It will just be a few minutes."

"Why is it necessary to solve such an old murder?"

"We have reason to believe the same gun that killed this woman killed Karen Lavendell. Which reminds me—are there any guns in this house? Have there ever been?"

"What? The same gun? How is that even possible?" Ortiz didn't answer. Greenleaf just grappled with that for a few moments. Men like Greenleaf don't like surprises, Wren knew well. She and her father had had to explain to clients enough times why their desires violated local regulations, building codes—or the laws of physics.

"I do need to know if you've owned a gun, if there have ever been guns in this house?"

"Own a gun? Of course not."

"What about your father? Your ancestors?"

Greenleaf took a deep breath. "I heard my great-grandfather owned a revolver, but I never saw it and assumed it was given away many years ago. I never saw it, and I personally have never owned any kind of firearm." He paused. "Neither of these murders was committed with a musket ball, were they?"

It was Ortiz's turn to be surprised. "Excuse me?"

"There was a Greenleaf at the Battle of Yorktown, and we have his musket on the wall in my apartment. I don't think it works anymore, though." A hint of a smirk there. Yes, these were the Greenleafs.

"Battle of Yorktown? Really? Which side?" Greenleaf didn't like that, but Wren hid a smile. "No, it was a bullet. May I suggest that you speak with your aunt and her companion to tell them I'm coming, and I'll be along in a few minutes."

Greenleaf gave that a moment's thought, then turned and left. Wren was alone with Ortiz now, and suddenly felt like a fifth wheel.

"Well, I should be getting back to work myself," she said. She assumed the police would take away the dress and shoes, but she didn't want to lose them—original turn-of-the-century clothing. She even thought of asking Ortiz if the Greenleaf family could have them back when he was done with them. But he seemed lost in thought, and Wren doubted he was in the mood for her questions.

Wren didn't know if she should make a more formal goodbye, but after thinking about it, just started walking away.

"Ms. Fontaine," he said. "Would you join me when I speak with Mrs. Ryan and Miss Greenleaf?"

It was the house—Ortiz knew that this had been a seat of power, a symbol of New York that was still powerful. Wren could see that much. The first time he entered it he couldn't stop looking at it—she had seen it in his eyes. A death of a woman in the house and the death of a woman who wanted it.

"Because I'm the expert in the house?" she said.

"Something like that. When I spoke with Mr. Greenleaf after the Lavendell death, I found out his aunt had spent some 90 years here. I want your impressions. Don't ask questions, don't comment, just listen."

Mystified but intrigued, Wren followed him downstairs to Aunt Agnes' suite, and as before, Mrs. Ryan answered the door. Again, no emotion showed on her face. Stephen was standing by Aunt Agnes, still in her chair. He looked unhappy, even worn out, but Aunt Agnes—there was something else. Wren couldn't put her finger on it, but she wasn't upset.

"Mrs. Ryan, Miss Greenleaf. My name is Sergeant Enrique Ortiz. You may have heard that a sealed attic was broken open earlier today, and a long-dead body was found there. It was there, most likely, for more than a century. Since the attic was opened under her direction, I have asked Ms. Fontaine to stay here while I discuss this with you. Can I ask you how long you have both lived in this house?"

"I am 90 years old," Aunt Agnes said, "and I have lived in this house for 90 years. I was born in this house."

"Ah. And you, Mrs. Ryan?"

"Twenty-eight years, sir," she said.

"And before your marriage," said Aunt Agnes. "Mrs. Ryan was born a Murphy. One way or another, the Murphys have been here as long as the Greenleafs. How would we have run our lives without the Murphys?" She seemed amused at that.

"That's very good of you to say," said Mrs. Ryan.

"So you both must know something about the family, the history of this house. The woman we found was most likely a servant. Naturally, this was long before either of you were born. Perhaps a story, a rumor, that came down to you?"

"A dead servant? My goodness, sergeant. I can't imagine how that happened. That's hardly something that could've been hidden. In 1922,

I heard, our butler got drunk on bathtub gin, so they say, but that's as bad as it got, I believe." There was a certain glee. This was doing a lot to enliven her day.

"Thank you. Mrs. Ryan? Any gossip over the years?"

"I don't gossip," she said.

"I'm sure," said Ortiz, with a welcoming smile. "But have you *heard* any?"

Before she could answer, Aunt Agnes jumped in. "The Murphys never gossiped."

"No, Miss, we did not." She turned back to the sergeant. "I know nothing about a body in the attic, sir."

Chapter Seven

The fun seemed to be over for now, and Wren felt a little guilty, realizing that she needed to focus on the job. Would any of this interfere with her work? She knew that legal and environmental tangles can bring things to a halt, and there was no telling what not one, but two, criminal investigations would bring.

"Thank you for your time," said Ortiz. "We will be removing the body and shoes for further investigation."

"Sergeant, if you uncover anything, will you let us know?" asked Aunt Agnes.

"I don't think we'll find out much," said Ortiz.

She nodded. "In my day, they sent unclaimed bodies to Hart Island. Do they still do that? Will she end up there?" Wren heard a teasing tone.

"Very possibly. But it seems obvious she has a connection to this house. If you wish, I can arrange for the remains to be released to your care for burial in the Greenleaf family plot."

Stephen looked surprised at that. And Aunt Agnes—the color drained from her face, and she started to say something, but stopped.

"Thank you again," he said. He snapped his notebook shut, and Wren followed him out.

"What do you think?" asked Ortiz. "Do they know?"

"I don't know these people as well as you think I do," she said. "I can't tell if they're lying." Why had he brought her along?

"I don't need your analysis of these people. Mr. Greenleaf might be lying. Mrs. Ryan is probably lying. Miss Greenleaf is definitely lying. But about what, exactly? Even more important, why? Family embarrassment?" He looked down those marble stairs. "How did people live in a house like this? You seem to know. I wonder if, in a house of such size, something like this could happen without anyone knowing? A servant, if that's what she was, disappearing and no one noting, no one caring?"

"A servant might've run off—if she was unhappy, had a lover, was offered a better job. They would've just shrugged and hired another girl. There was no lack of young girls needing jobs."

"How interesting. A house swallowing someone up. Her employers not bothering themselves with her disappearance, her family...just another mouth to feed." His voice trailed off. He looked at Wren, and she felt his words were aimed at her.

"I love houses like this. But I am also aware of the shortcomings of the society that made such residences possible." She heard the defensive tone in her voice and wondered if Ortiz would laugh at her.

But no. He took her seriously and seemed to consider her comments carefully. "A society that made the Greenleafs possible. But stepping away from politics and sociology, why shoot a girl like that? Shooting is a very deliberate way of killing someone. It's not like strangling in a jealous rage. Why, I wonder? And if the family knew, would they cover it up?"

Yes, they would.

"Ah, well. Not really my problem. Except for the need to find an antique firearm."

Wren thought of Uncle Ambrose again, smirking in that cold room. She also thought about telling Sgt. Ortiz about him but stopped. It was a theory, not a fact, and she could make the argument that it was told to her in confidence as the family's architect. After all, he didn't rise from the dead to kill Karen Lavendell.

"One more thing," he said. "The evening Karen Lavendell was killed. Your client hasn't been forthcoming about where he was. He said he was meeting someone in sensitive business negotiations and needs to protect the other party's privacy. I wonder if you knew. I respect your commitment to confidentiality, but a murder inquiry takes precedence."

That startled her. What was Stephen up to? She knew Wall Street players put together secret deals, but to leave yourself open to a murder charge?

"I have no idea, I assure you. We only discuss issues related to the house."

He smiled and shrugged. "I figured as much, but thought I'd ask. Anyway, I appreciate your insights, Ms. Fontaine. Have a good day—I'll see myself out."

* * *

Wren looked up at the not especially interesting pre-war building, its façade in need of a cleaning but otherwise in good repair. The doorman inside directed her to the 4th floor, and directly opposite the elevator, in a dingy hallway, a young man in a jacket and tie sat behind a desk.

"I'm here to see Conor Ryan."

"You're expected—just a moment," he said. He pressed a button on the phone console, and a moment later, the door at the end of the hallway opened, and Conor's smiling face peered out.

"Come on in," he said. The inside of the office wasn't any more exciting than the outside, plain furniture from a catalog and grey cubicle dividers. Office workers focused on their monitors.

"Coffee?" he asked. "I'm warning you, it's awful."

"I'm fine, thank you."

"I suppose high-end architects like you only drink the very finest java."

"As a researcher, maybe you shouldn't make such assumptions without facts," Wren said. She meant it to come out as a joke, but to her ears, it came out as critical. Conor raised an eyebrow. "Anyway, you're half-right. My father is a terrible coffee snob, but I'm not."

He laughed, and she followed him into an office with a window that opened onto the street. He showed her to a visitor's chair, closed the door, and sat behind his desk.

"I'll go first," Conor said. "I'll tell you what I have, and you'll share what you can. I'm going with the supposition that Karen Lavendell, of PH Hospitality, was trying to buy Greenleaf House."

50

"Yes, I was wondering how you knew about Karen Lavendell. There was nothing in the news about her connection with Greenleaf House. I thought Stephen and I were the only ones who knew. Did he tell you?"

"Fair enough," said Conor. He nodded, as if he were thinking what to say next. "I've known about PH Hospitality for some time, and their interest in the house. Again, my job as a researcher helps me find these things." He smiled and spread out his hands. "See, I'm being honest."

Wren wondered if he could see how fast her heart was pounding. *How did I end up here?* She didn't want to say it, but knew she had to, and to speak slowly and clearly.

"Not entirely," she said. "That was a high-security all-steel door at the entrance. It costs thousands of dollars and is usually found in jewelry stores. It's fitted with the most sophisticated electronic lock. There are probably only two or three locksmiths in this city who sell it. That door is installed to swing in, so the hinges aren't accessible from the outside. I don't know who did it, but it's against New York building codes. And the glass in the window behind you is Riot Glass—almost unbreakable. So who are you, Mr. Ryan, and what is this place?"

Chapter Eight

She folded her arms across her chest and hoped she looked as imposing as her father did when he was displeased with a vendor.

Conor just stared at her for a while, and then smiled. "We've never had an architect visit us here. I probably should've met you somewhere else."

"My father likes working out of his home office in our townhouse, but he meets clients in our midtown office to impress them. You wanted me in your office, on your turf."

"That's a pretty shrewd observation from someone who presents herself as more connected to houses than humans."

"You're right. But that isn't about humans. This is about houses. It's about the power of a house, a room. Have you ever really looked at the Greenleaf House dining room? I mean, really looked at it? It wasn't built just for eating dinner. The size, shape, proportions—it was a throne room, from which the Greenleafs could rule. That's the power of design, the power of architecture."

"You sound like a college professor."

She felt her face getting hot. "There's no reason to mock me."

"I'm not mocking you, Wren," he said, looking serious.

"I'm sorry," she said. "I don't always say...but you're one of the few people alive who understands just how powerful that room is."

"You're right. But about this office...yes, I'm busted. This is not just a corporate research company. We are in the business of secrets here, and I can't tell you more. You're right that I brought you here to get you on my turf, as you say, and I paid the price for that. But getting back to Greenleaf

House—I can tell you that Karen Lavendell died for a secret."

"Do you mean the secret of the family reprobate, Uncle Ambrose?" asked Wren. She meant it as a joke, but Conor didn't take it as such. He frowned—he looked almost sulky.

"I'm sure he did something appalling. Aunt Agnes, the only one alive who knows what he did, won't talk about it. The bar for rich men behaving badly in nineteenth-century New York was pretty high, and the likelihood for any punishment was small. The Gilded Age, I'm sure you know, wasn't as gilded as we'd like to think." He forced a smile. "We'll assume Uncle Ambrose's sins died with him. No, there was a modern reason for her death. Did Stephen tell you his plans for the house?"

"If he had, I still wouldn't be able to tell you."

"So, no, he hasn't. I know things—my job puts me in the way of learning certain things. I can tell you that this house's future is by no means settled. This thing with PH Hospitality has been going on for a while. Stephen is a Wall Street player, and joking aside, he has robber baron blood in him." He wagged a finger. "Watch your back, Wren."

She blinked. "Are you saying I'm in danger?"

"I don't want to be dramatic. I'm not saying you're on someone's hit list. But I can tell you again that this house's future means a lot to many people. So...I've been open with you, a lot more than Stephen has, frankly. What can you tell me about this house?"

"Before I tell you that," said Wren. "I'd like to know why you care so much."

"No one asks Stephen about his interest in the house. It's the Greenleaf legacy, isn't it?" Wren heard the bitterness in his voice. "But it was my home as much as his, even though I didn't own it. I am a descendant of the Murphys who lived in that house and worked there and died there. It's my legacy as much as Stephen's."

Wren waited until he was done, waited in the silence that followed. "You're right," she said softly. "You have the same emotional investment in the house as Stephen does. But, like it or not, it's Stephen's name on the contract. I can't break his trust."

"I'm not asking you to. Let me get specific. Somewhere in that house, there are papers about the Greenleafs. Their heritage and mine as well. If you find anything related to the Murphys, please ask him if you can share it with me. He trusts you. He wouldn't have hired you for his house otherwise. OK?"

She considered that. Meanwhile, he hadn't brought up the body in the attic. Had he heard yet?

"It's a deal," she said. "If I find anything key, I will ask, but I need you to be specific. I'm guessing you expect to find something. I know how researchers work."

He gave that some thought. "All right. I'll tell you. When I came to work here, they did a major background check on me. They want to make sure there is nothing problematic in anyone's past. The wise men here found a member of my family who disappeared toward the end of the nineteenth century. Police were called, but nothing happened. Her name was Fiona Murphy, and she was a servant. I asked my mother, who said she was a nursery maid. That wing where Aunt Agnes and my mother live now was the nursery wing. But you probably knew that. Anyway, Aunt Agnes never left it. She just carved out her own space. I assume you saw the portrait of Uncle Ambrose in that little room?"

"Yes—I thought he had an…odd expression."

"Like he was smirking? I remember that portrait since I was a child. I had always wondered about him. Why was he stuck in that out-of-the-way room? You know, I asked my mother about him. She knew everything. The Murphys knew everything, and my mother has been with Aunt Agnes long enough…the old girl just talks…and talks….and talks." He seemed lost in himself. "You see, I had always known something was up, things about my family's past my mother wouldn't talk about. My mother can keep her mouth shut, but she's a terrible liar—I knew there was something about Uncle Ambrose. I knew that there was something she—and the Greenleafs—were hiding. But I didn't really look into it until the investigators at my employer, Sapiens, told me about the missing Fiona Murphy. They asked me if I knew about it, but I told them, quite truthfully, I did not. That was the end of it, from their viewpoint, but it got me thinking over the years, looking up stories about Ambrose. He was a bit of a hellraiser—lively parties, gambling dens, seen around town with actresses. I heard he was sent away and died abroad." He smiled, but it was brittle.

"Do you know why Ambrose's picture is in that out-of-the-way room in the children's wing?" he continued. "It was a joke. It was to insult him, to mock him, not that they cared about anyone he hurt, but that his behavior was common. No worse, it was *inconvenient*. I had always wondered, always suspected what they had done to Fiona. But now I know. That room belonged to Fiona. Until Ambrose raped and killed her right there. And now you've found her body, which the Greenleafs stuffed in the attic."

"How do you know that?" she asked, after a long pause, realizing that Conor was expecting a response.

"It fits entirely," he said. "We know he was wild. Fiona was young and available, and who would care about anyone assaulting an Irish maid? Why did that portrait end up in her room? This was the nursery wing. It was probably Fiona's room, and this was some sort of joke. I admit, it was some guesswork, but I knew in my heart. That body must be her, mustn't it? It all hangs together—Ambrose killed her, and his brother Benjamin covered for him. But there's more. Why have they been so nice to me? Aunt Agnes knows, I'm sure, although I don't think Stephen does. It's generations of guilt. My education was blood money. And you know what else? My mother knows. I am sure my mother knows but is staying silent out of respect for the Greenleafs."

She heard the anger and contempt, which she hadn't gotten from him before.

"My father told me, when I started the job, that I had to be careful with the Greenleafs. That because of their history and their position, they were not like other families—"

"Exactly my point!" said Conor. "A family like that would stop at nothing."

"You didn't let me finish," she said. "I was going to say that they were not like other families, and neither, apparently, are their servants. An obsession with the past."

He looked taken aback at that, and she wondered if he would get angry at her and, if so, would that be a good enough excuse to leave. But after a pause, his charming smile came back.

"You're a surprising one, Wren. But we're alike—a passion for research. That's what I'm paid for here. I'm very good at it, and I expect you are too. My theory fits the facts. I just have to give some thought to what will happen next."

"I assumed you'd find out about the body but didn't want to be the one who told you. Did your mother call you?"

"No. It was Stephen, actually, not long before you came. He knows I've long had an interest in the house. He knew I'd hear what happened and asked if I wouldn't discuss it widely. He said he needed to keep a low profile until his plans for the house were finalized, whatever those plans are."

"You referenced Stephen's plans. So this is not just about the home's history. It's about the present. But you seem interested in the past."

Conor grinned. "Nicely put. Stephen told me what the police uncovered—one gun, two murders, a century apart. I want to know what happened to my ancestor. Stephen wants to pull off some sort of deal with this house in the present. A pair of murders with one gun connect us. Papers I'd like. Secrets that Stephen is keeping. And you have a stake in keeping this project on track, too."

He was right, but she didn't know what to say. A century's worth of motives, and it wasn't clear who was being honest. But Conor seemed to read her. He smiled.

"I see I've given you a lot to think about. We can talk later, if you want. Anyway, I'm done for the day. We'll walk out together." They didn't speak again until they were on the sidewalk.

"Thank you, Wren. I want you to know I don't mean this to be adversarial. You want a perfect restoration. Stephen wants to close a deal. I want a resolution for Fiona. There's no reason we can't all get what we want."

"But Aunt Agnes. What does she want?" asked Wren, and she felt pleased to leave the self-assured Conor speechless, at least for a moment.

He eventually grinned again. "Oh, Wren, you and I both know there's no getting Aunt Agnes what she wants. Again, it's been a pleasure."

Wren walked absently to the subway. Could she trust Stephen? Conor? Well, she could understand buildings, at least. She knew rooms, how places people lived affected, and reflected their owners. She'd love to see Conor's apartment! But for now, she knew his office. She saw a man who lived behind bulletproof glass and doors that could resist a battering ram. Fearful. Even paranoid. Did his job make him that way—or did he pick his job because he was always that way? The resentment growing up as the son of a servant, always feeling belittled and talked down to. Was that what drove him?

* * *

Wren told her father about the body in the attic, which was relevant to their work on the house, but not about her conversation with Conor, which she mentally filed as "just business as usual." She didn't want him to think she needed his help in managing an increasingly complex job, but realized she'd have to start keeping a list of what she was keeping a secret from whom—they didn't teach that in architecture school.

"And the police seem to think the same gun killed both women The police aren't delaying the work?"

"This is not apparently a crime scene, and clearly not something like an old cemetery of historic interest, so we should be fine to go."

Ezra nodded. "Be careful," he told her before turning back to his work.

"Is that my father's advice or my partner's?"

He didn't bother answering.

Wren settled herself in the kitchen, poured herself a cup of coffee, and cleared off the table. Two nasty surprises now. She didn't like that. She liked an orderly world, with predictable buildings. Even the problems she faced in her job were predictable, like rust and water damage. As a little girl, Wren loved arts and crafts time in school—but her mother was called in when she refused to participate in fingerpainting. "Too messy," she had told her mother.

"I don't blame her," said her father.

So what was happening here? Sergeant Ortiz had said the family was probably lying. Someone had shot that poor girl and stuffed her in the attic, and that meant the family was involved. Guns in those days were expensive and hard to come by. A shooting in a mansion meant it was planned—no one left guns just lying around, and they were very loud. She had never held a handgun, but she was familiar with the 19th century.

Did Sgt. Ortiz know about old handguns? Did he care? Yes, two murders with one gun, but Ortiz was probably thinking more about Karen Lavendell than the woman in the trunk. And so, probably, was Conor.

Conor seemed to know about PH Hospitality, so she figured she needed to get up to speed on them and began researching them. It was a privately held company, well-funded, and its senior managers—including Ms. Lavendell—also owned a piece. They had been quietly successful, turning grand old homes into inns and small hotels.

But not without controversy. There had been lawsuits—angry contractors, who said they had been pushed hard to cut corners. And many accusations of shoddy work—making a big deal of 'honoring the classic homes' while using panels purchased from Home Depot. Also, they raised some hackles among purists, chopping up old houses with no regard for their history, only for what worked commercially. Maybe Lavendell would've made a show of trying to hire the Fontaines, but as she thought, only to get an inside track on buying Greenleaf House.

She thought of the Greenleafs and the Murphys who served them. Not just in the 1890s, but today. Conor had made a good case for why the house was as important to him as to Stephen, but he was an accomplished liar, and his attachment to the house seemed sentimental, not financial. He had no monetary interest—that she knew about, anyway.

Look at me, finally giving the same attention to people as I do to buildings. Progress.

But Stephen and PH Hospitality certainly had financial interests. PH Hospitality was a well-funded private corporation. But who was backing Stephen? Wren knew to the penny what the renovation was costing—he wasn't doing this on his own. A bank was guaranteeing payments, but Wren knew there must be a group writing the checks behind the scenes. What did this have to do with Karen Lavendell's death?

Or Fiona Murphy's? Wren thought of Uncle Ambrose's portrait in the forgotten room. Had he killed that woman in the trunk? She didn't want to think so. Was she falling for the "bad boy"? To be fair, her first crush was a figure in a pre-Raphaelite painting, a cold beauty, but a beauty nonetheless, with the confidence that came from perfection. If Wren was going to share the Georgian masterpiece of her dreams with anyone, it would be with someone like that. Had anyone felt that way about Uncle Ambrose? She shook her head. There would be no understanding that.

Or understanding Aunt Agnes. She had been enraged at the thought of Ambrose's secrets revealed, but not about the body. And she certainly hadn't been surprised.

Chapter Nine

Wren knew the next morning she'd need some assistance—and just who could provide it, after her morning's work.

She showed up at the usual time the next day at Greenleaf House, and Bobby and his crew were already there.

"Got up on the roof and it looks pretty good, considering the age. The roofer will be coming later today."

They went over the next steps during the morning, walking through the next rooms they had to work on, and then grabbed a quick lunch in the remains of the kitchen with the crew.

"Are you settled then today? I have some errands to run," she asked.

"We have our marching orders, Chief," and gave her a salute.

"All right then, I'll leave you to it. I'll be back later."

Wren made two purchases on her way and put both in her bag, then caught the subway uptown. Prof. Lavinia Suisse lived in a rambling old apartment near Columbia, and Wren had always loved it as an undergraduate. The rooms were a delightful architectural contrast with her family's Brooklyn townhouse, and despite her obsession with order, she somehow found the delicious untidiness of the place a welcome change from the bare, meticulous perfection her father had imposed.

Wren buzzed, and Lavinia let her up and greeted her at the door. In the twelve years Wren had known her, some grey had crept into her hair, but otherwise, she hadn't changed, still brisk, and she gave Wren a hug and a kiss on the cheek.

"Wren, Wren, Wren, always good to see you. Not surprised, though. Word is out about you and the Greenleaf House. Can't say I'm not jealous, getting to go to work in that house every day."

"If I'm not interrupting anything…." Wren ventured.

"Stop being so damned self-effacing. You think I'd be too shy to tell you to get lost if you were bothering me? Come on in. Angela is here but is going out shortly."

Angela was just coming out of the bedroom and lit up at seeing their guest.

"Ah, my dear, glad I caught you." She also gave Wren a kiss. "Always a pleasure seeing our flower girl."

"Bridesmaid, actually," Wren reminded her—yet again.

"I'm so sorry, no offense, but you were so young."

"She's still young," said Lavinia.

"Of course." Then Angela's eyes narrowed as she saw Wren's bag. Surgeons are like architects, Wren had found. They don't miss much. "You didn't bring Lavinia any more alcohol, did you? It's not good for her."

"Don't be such an old lady," said Lavinia.

"I want us to live to be old ladies," said Angela.

Wren pulled out a box of fine tea. "Just caffeine."

"I guess you have 'group' business? Have fun, you two."

Lavinia cleaned books off her couch, and they took a seat.

"And here's your real gift," Wren said and pulled out a bottle of Glenfiddich.

"Oh, you are clever," said Lavinia and laughed. "And I thought you were too good to be sneaky." She grabbed a couple of glasses from the sideboard.

"Light for me," Wren said.

"You've never been much of a drinker." She poured two glasses.

"How's your father? Our teaching schedules don't seem to mesh right now, so I haven't seen him recently."

"Doing well, working too hard, as usual."

"Like father, like daughter. So, I don't think it's group work that brought you here. How can I help my favorite former student?"

"The Greenleafs," Wren said.

"The house? I'm a history professor. You're the architect."

"Not their house. The family itself. This comes under your area of expertise."

She nodded. "An interesting family. Rather, interesting for not being interesting. They were wealthy and prominent without actually achieving anything. They had various businesses, shipping, and so forth, but nothing long-lasting and no political ambitions—they just ruled New York, so to speak, from that lovely house. Nevertheless, there are some notable points about them—just let me get my notes. Now, where did I leave my laptop?" They finally found it under a pile of student papers on her huge desk. "I know about them off the top of my head, but my notes will give me more. I really have to finish this book someday." It was going to be her magnum opus, The Great Families of New York.

She scrolled through her notes. "So the family goes back to the 17th century. But I'm guessing that you're really concerned from the time they lived in Greenleaf House. That would be Benjamin Greenleaf and the former Susan Vanderwerf, and he built this house for her in 1895 as a wedding present. Now, the really interesting one in the family is Benjamin's bachelor brother—"

"Ambrose," Wren said.

Lavinia looked at her with surprise and smiled slowly. "You've started without me," she said. "You *are* good."

"There's a portrait of him in Greenleaf House. Just between us, Stephen Greenleaf told me Uncle Ambrose had done something horrible, but he doesn't know—or won't tell me what. His 90-year-old aunt, who has lived there her whole life, became apoplectic when his name came up. And I've gotten a hint why...." She told her about the body in the attic and its connection with Karen Lavendell and her lunch with Conor. "I was asked to keep it quiet, but I know you aren't going running to the Post."

"Jesus Christ, Wren, you've really landed in it. Two murders seemingly connected over a century apart. Let's see what we can find, with the promise that I get first rights to the account for my book. Anyway, Ambrose was quite a figure in the era, so I'm not surprised that he was involved in a secret family scandal. He made himself notorious, even by Gilded Age standards. Wild parties that were covered up by paying off police and judges, liaisons with actresses that he barely bothered to hide. Now, let's start with a look at the house."

Lavinia called up the Census data. The Bureau declassified data after 72 years, so the 1900 Census was available.

"Here we go. In 1900, there are three adult residents in the family: Benjamin and Susan Greenleaf and brother Ambrose. The Greenleafs went on to have two children, Caleb, who would go on to inherit the house, and his little sister Laura. If I remember right, she eventually took her substantial dowry to England and married an impoverished Earl in the 1920s. But they hadn't been born yet."

"I thought that odd—it took about six years for Susan to get pregnant."

"Who knows? Fertility issues. Miscarriages. Maybe Benjamin wasn't doing his job. Now, of course, the Greenleafs had a slew of servants. Back in the day, the Census Bureau had to give specific instructions to make sure live-in servants were counted."

Lavinia scrolled down the list—they had a butler, cook, undercook, an assortment of maids, a couple of footmen, and a coachman.

"A number of Murphys," Wren said. "Including Kevin Murphy, 27, the coachman, and Fiona Murphy, twenty-five, maid. Probably brother and sister. Anyway, Fiona is the one Conor is sure is the body in the attic and that Ambrose killed her."

"And Conor's mother is Miss Greenleaf's companion, a Murphy before she married."

"Exactly. She has been with the house for decades in one capacity or another."

"So you think they know something?"

"The police are sure they're lying."

"I wonder if anyone stuck around." She jumped to the 1910 census. Benjamin and Susan were still there—now with their children. "Now this is interesting," said Lavinia, opening another database. "As we noted, the Greenleafs didn't have their first child until 1902, but Fiona had been listed as a *nursery* maid in the 1900 census. Maybe they hired her in anticipation—again, perhaps a miscarriage. Since she was the coachman's sister, she was on hand, and they wanted to be prepared with someone they already knew and trusted. Of course, she'd have been assigned other duties meanwhile, no doubt. "

"Miss Greenleaf now lives in what was the nursery wing, according to Stephen Greenleaf. Presumably, Fiona would have a room there. Perhaps the room where Ambrose's portrait is now displayed."

"Curious," said Lavinia.

Whatever happened, Fiona was gone by the 1910 census, although Kevin was still driving the coach. Did Fiona have a new job? Married and raising her own children? Or stuffed into a box in the attic? The truth was that servants, especially junior ones, could have had any reason to leave. But Ambrose was also gone. Wren wondered where. Had he married as well and set up his own household?

"Ambrose, if I remember right, departed for foreign shores. Let me look at his obituary. People like the Greenleafs always got an obituary."

"It was Stephen's belief that he would end his days in an opium den."

"He wouldn't be the first," said Lavinia. "Ah, here we go, the Times in 1945. 'Greenleaf Scion dies. Ambrose Greenleaf, seventy-three, was reported dead in Buenos Aires, Argentina, where he had long made his home. He had managed various family interests there since about 1900 and was not believed to have been back to the States since. According to the family attorney, he never married or had children. He is survived by his brother and sister-in-law, Benjamin and Susan Greenleaf, of New York, a nephew, Caleb Greenleaf, also of New York, a niece, Laura, who since her marriage has been Countess of Haverton, and several great nieces and nephews. His estate has been left entirely to his niece, Lady Haverton."

"So he moves to South America for the rest of his life," Wren said. "Conor told me he had gone abroad. But it's not clear if he wanted to do so or was being exiled for whatever horrible thing he did."

"Like killing a maid?" asked Lavinia. "Let me see what my notes are on dear Uncle Ambrose...here we go." She clicked open the Ambrose file. "Buenos Aires was a lively town back then. I'm sure he fit right in. There were reports from our consular offices. It seems Ambrose made them a little nervous, with some extracurricular business deals. Numerous trips to Bogata, which was the scene of a lot of political unrest...with hints of arms smuggling."

"Just greed? Weren't the Greenleafs wealthy enough without breaking the law?" Lavinia gave her a look. "Okay—without breaking the law to that extent."

"Well, let me see...my research so far has been more about social history than financial, but I think I have some notes here about that because I wondered about him down there...here we go. The Greenleafs, like many families of the era, had ways of tying up their money, and here was the deal with Ambrose. He had an income, a limited income, from a directorship in the family business. But it was at his father's, and then his brother's, discretion."

"Right-of-the-firstborn, or just because his own family didn't trust him?"

"Could be a bit of both. But the bottom line was that he had to remain in his brother's good graces, or he'd be left with very little money."

"So he may have been feeling desperate, if he did something that would alienate the family. But although Aunt Agnes was enraged when Uncle Ambrose's name came up, she didn't seem surprised or upset by the body in the attic. Maybe, they're not connected. Or not in the way we think."

"Where does that take you?" asked Lavinia.

"That Ambrose was involved in something shameful that Aunt Agnes wants hidden, but he wasn't necessarily the perpetrator. She doesn't believe that body can be connected to Ambrose, that it's part of a secret so well hidden it can't cause a scandal. But Ambrose's secret may be more accessible, and she doesn't want anyone looking in on that. Or...it may simply be that Aunt Agnes cares about family, no matter how awful, and doesn't care about anyone else, no matter how innocent. How terrible, if that's true."

"Old houses have old secrets," said Lavinia.

"And new ones," said Wren. "I told you that the police think that Mrs. Ryan may be lying. She's not the only one. I haven't given you the full story on Conor. We met again. This goes beyond a simple family history." She told Lavinia about their conversation and their deal.

"Oh Christ, this gets even stranger. This—secret agent, whatever Conor is, seems to have an interest, maybe even a stake, in what happens, and I agree he's not to be trusted. So what do you think?"

That was always the most exciting, and frightening, question from Lavinia. Nothing was better than pleasing her with an answer. Nothing was worse than disappointing her.

"I think…that there is only one secret, just like there is only one murder weapon. Conor and the police seem concerned with the modern one. You and I are interested in the historical one. But it's part of the same secret. Conor is obsessed with the past, and he's been researching this house. He's a research professional—like you, if not as experienced. I'm wondering what he's already found out, but hasn't shared with me. I agreed we'd share information, as long as Stephen agreed, but now I'm wondering.… He's playing it close to the chest. He's a trained keeper of secrets, a skill he first learned from his mother."

Lavinia nodded. "I agree. We forget just how much servants know. In the days when the Greenleafs ruled, they were surrounded by servants and were so used to them, they forgot they were there. The servants picked up a lot, and gossip was passed along downstairs just as easily as it was upstairs. How much do you think this Conor knows—about either murder?"

"Not as much as he'd like to know. But there's something shrewd—something sharp about him—the nature of his job, no doubt. And I get a sense there's more than just family curiosity about him. He's playing a long game."

"Yes. But you have knowledge too, Wren. You're the one going through this house every day. He was wise to ally himself with you and take a bet you would convince Stephen Greenleaf to share whatever you find."

"Thank you. I'll see what I can do—the family seems to like me. Aunt Agnes at least approves of me. She was only fifteen when Uncle Ambrose died, and as he was out of the country, I don't see how she could ever have met him. But she may have heard a lot of family gossip about him. I'll see if she's willing to share. And now there is one other thing.…"

Lavinia raised an eyebrow, like she did when Wren was her student and expected something from her, and Wren wanted so badly to make her happy.

"Why did Ambrose leave his estate to his niece but not his nephew? It's hard to imagine that he had formed an attachment to them—they were so young when he left. So why one and not the other?"

"Good point," said Lavinia. "He probably didn't have much to leave. He was no doubt a spendthrift living on whatever his brother gave him. So, what he left his niece was more symbolic than anything. But why? That will require more work." She smiled. "I know you well, my dear. You want your books and your archives and your big homes with empty rooms you can walk through. Talking to Conor and Miss Greenleaf is something of a chore for you. And yet, you like the group."

Wren struggled for words. "I can be someone different there. It's a game, really..." Lavinia looked at Wren with kindness. "You think too much and get self-conscious. You don't have to slip into another world. You can do fine in this one."

But for so long, she hadn't been able to. If Lavinia hadn't come along... where would life have taken her? She wouldn't be working in Greenleaf House, partner in the finest firm in New York.

She wasn't a college student anymore, she reminded herself. She wasn't Lavinia and Angela's young bridesmaid. She was a partner in one of the most prestigious architectural firms in New York.

"You've never been afraid," Wren said.

Lavinia laid a hand on her shoulder and smiled wryly. "You didn't notice what I was feeling the day Angela and I got married? Walking down the aisle for the first time at my age? But this isn't about fear, Wren, or about incompetence. You're not a coward, and you're not incapable. It's about discomfort. And you can get more comfortable."

Wren's heart warmed. She was right.

"Now, let's think about whom else you should talk to. Who else has a connection to that house?"

"It wasn't just a Greenleaf House, though, was it?" Wren said. She remembered what she had told Conor. "I mean, we always think of the man's name, but back especially then, it was the woman who made the house a home. Aunt Agnes may not share more with me, but let's think of the other side of the family. Susan Greenleaf was a Vanderwerf before her marriage. Are there any Vanderwerfs left?"

"They're still around. Their money, and influence, disappeared about the time the Greenleafs' did. No stupendous mansions for them, but they had some nice townhouses over the years, and there's a two-block street named for them near Trinity Church." Some more clicks on the computer. "Here we go, still some descendants left in the city, including one about your age—looks promising. Hadley Vanderwerf—she seems to run Vanderwerf Events Planning, which 'promises lively events for the discerning.' See if there are any stories," advised Lavinia. "Maybe all those years ago, Susan confided something to a sister, and it was passed down on the distaff side."

"How far down?" asked Wren.

"Hmm?"

"We get lost in history, in what happened a century ago. But someone connected to this house was killed this week. They must be related."

"Yes. What does that tell you?"

"That I need to be careful," said Wren, a little tentatively.

"Was that a statement or a question? Anyway, you've never been reckless, and fortune favors the prepared. You're not going to run away from Greenleaf House so let's figure out what happened in the 1890s. And what's happening today."

Wren nodded and took down the contact information for Hadley Vanderwerf. Lavinia was right. She needed to remember that houses were just houses until people lived in them, like her father had said. That's what made them homes. And Fontaine Partners was in the home business.

And that she was not going to be a coward.

"You've been wonderful," Wren said and gave her a kiss on the cheek.

"Group meeting is coming up," she said. "I'll see you there?"

"Of course. And you'd better hide the scotch before Angela comes home. I don't want to get in trouble with her."

Chapter Ten

Wren had lost time meeting with Lavinia, but more than made up for it with renewed energy for the rest of the day. Today, she and Bobby tackled what had been the master bedroom. Wren had been sad the first time she had seen it, and saw Bobby was shaking his head too. It must've been grand once, but now the deep red wallpaper was peeling off, and the once-thick cream carpet was worn down and stained beyond redemption. A few generic landscapes decorated the walls—Wren doubted if they were worth anything.

"When was the last time they upgraded this?" he asked.

"I'm thinking, never. The couples just kept living here." She thought of Stephen's late parents. Were they like Aunt Agnes, just watching the place fall apart but dreaming of better times, as they closed off rooms, as staff disappeared? It was sad—to Wren, it was like watching a person slowly die.

But then she brightened. A house could be brought back, even one that appeared terminally ill—she was the one who could do it. That was the thing about homes, rather than people: They could be managed. Wren looked at their plans. "This is marked master bedroom, but there's a similar room adjoining it, with a connecting door." It opened into a closet that provided a short hallway to the next room. It had the same layout, a mirror version of the first, but it was indifferently furnished, not looking as if it had been much lived in. A dresser, a bed, and a pair of night-tables, none of it as fine as the main bedroom. Someone had ripped up any carpet years ago, and the wallpaper was long gone, but the walls still needed a paint job.

"His and her bedrooms," Wren said.

69

"Yeah, go figure," said Bobby. "All that money and you don't even sleep together every night." Wren knew Bobby and his wife, Rosa, had five children—no separate bedrooms there.

"This was probably his, as the elaborate one also contains a boudoir on the other side where the lady of the house could get huffy in private. It comes from the French, meaning 'to sulk.'"

"Rosa just uses the home office," said Bobby. "We all know to leave her alone when she's in there." Wren walked around the nearly bare room, and every sound echoed the way it does in under-furnished rooms. This was the "good" side of the house—where the master and mistress resided, along with principal guest bedrooms.

Wren heard Bobby shuffle his feet—fair enough. He wasn't making money when he stood there watching her think.

"All right—let's see what we can do. We're supposed to be adding a new bathroom here...."

The rest of the day was profitable, and after lunch, all Wren had to do was some paperwork, which she could handle at home. But first, she wanted to take another look at the portraits in the "ancestor hallway." Benjamin was handsome in a standard way, fair-haired, with high cheekbones, a hint of a smile. Yes, he was dreamy, but also had the confidence that came from being one of the richest men in one of the richest cities in the world. He was sitting in a comfortable chair, and his wife stood behind him, an effective pose when the man was much taller than the woman. If he was blandly attractive, Wren saw now that she was far beyond that.

Yes, there was definitely merriment in her eyes, and something playful around her lips. Wren doubted if the artist would've invented that if it wasn't there. She was younger than her husband, maybe only around 20 to his 30. Was he proud because he had landed such a beauty? Did one of them, or the smirking Uncle Ambrose, know who the woman in the attic was, and how she came to be there?

Her phone rang.

"Is this Wren Fontaine?...Hadley Vanderwerf. You left a message for me earlier today, something about my family?"

70

Wren had planned her response—she knew she was no good at winging things like that. "I'm an architect and supervising the renovation of Greenleaf House. The original mistress, Susan Greenleaf, was born a Vanderwerf, and I'm looking into the history of the house to assist me. I thought, as a Vanderwerf, you might be able to help me."

"Ooh—that sounds interesting. I heard they were going to do something with that pile. What's it going to be—a girl's school or an embassy?" She didn't wait for a response. "I have some time around 11:00 tomorrow. Does that work for you?"

"Ah...yes, thank you." She could get some morning tasks done at Greenleaf House, and it was a quick trip to Hadley's office in the east 30s.

"Fine. Thank you for the quick appointment."

"I don't have pictures or plans or anything like that, although there's probably something in someone's attic, but if you're working for Stephen Greenleaf, you probably have all that. If you're calling a Vanderwerf, you probably want to know about Aunt Susan. You want to know if I have any stories about her. Oh yes, I have plenty—she was a piece of work."

* * *

Vanderwerf Events Planning was located in one of the pre-war buildings that still remained on the East Side, below 42nd Street. It didn't seem posh enough for an events planning firm, which Wren thought would gravitate to a sleeker building. Still, when she got out of the elevator and opened the door into the reception area, she gave them marks for working with what they had: they had ripped out the drop ceiling to expose the wires and ducts and kept the furniture simple—glass and metal, with gray carpeting. Five employees worked in an open plan, and there was one separate office with glass walls. Wren assumed that was Ms. Vanderwerf's—she was facing away while she talked on her phone.

There was no receptionist, so Wren just stood there for a while, and eventually, a young man saw her and came over.

"I'm here to see Hadley Vanderwerf," she said. "I have an appointment."

"Oh, sure," he said, and Wren assumed he wanted her to follow him. He rapped on his boss's door. She swiveled around and motioned for Wren to come in while still talking on the phone. Her guide left, closing the door behind him. She took a seat while Hadley talked and laughed. Photos of her with a variety of B-list actors and musicians adorned the wall behind her. No doubt these were Vanderwerf clients, the sort-of-famous.

Wren studied Hadley while she talked on the phone, with an architect's eye for how people adorned themselves. Could she tell something about the person from her...architecture? Hadley's perfect blond bob had probably cost more than Wren spent on grooming all year, and she was dressed in clothes far more dramatic than Wren would ever have the courage to wear, bright and lively and unconventional. Wren clutched her fine leather bag, thought about what her father said about making a good visual impression, and suddenly felt fifty years old.

"...listen, I have an appointment, must go, love to Denny...."

Ms. Vanderwerf hung up and sighed. "Asshole," she said. "But I guess you have your share of them too, in architecture. You're Wren Fontaine, right? Can I get you a cold water?" She had a small fridge at her feet, and before Wren could say anything, she had handed her a brand of bottled water labeled in some sort of Scandinavian language. Wren suddenly felt self-conscious, as if she were back in high school, as Hadley quickly looked her over with sharp eyes. She felt she knew Hadley, one of those beautiful and poised girls she had feared in high school and envied in college, always knowing and saying the right thing. Always secretly judging Wren for being a teacher's pet. Then she brought herself up short: *Who's judging who now?*

"So you're working on the Greenleaf House? Is there going to be a big celebration when it opens? We could do something really smashing."

"Uhh...I'd have to ask Stephen Greenleaf...."

"We should all meet. I'm family—rather distant. I've never actually calculated. You're no doubt here about Susan Greenleaf, nee Vanderwerf. She was quite a girl, I heard tell, and lived a long life. You heard about her and want to learn more. Right?"

"Oh...yes," said Wren.

She smiled, a little triumphantly. "That's some place, Greenleaf House. I've passed by it but never went in. I suppose I could've introduced myself as family, but it never really occurred to me."

"You've never met Stephen Greenleaf?"

"Probably, but not that I remember. It's the kind of thing where we get together for funerals and weddings and meet in passing. I'm sure he was at my christening at St. Thomas. Everyone turns out to welcome a new generation—or see one out. Anyway, my branch is descended from Susan's brother, Anson. His granddaughter was Myrtle Vanderwerf—so Susan was Myrtle's great aunt. You never see that name anymore, do you? Anyway, as a girl and young woman, my great-aunt Myrtle knew her great aunt Susan very well. Susan lived into the 1950s, and they say she was clear of mind to the end when my Great Aunt Myrtle was in her twenties. And likewise, I was close to Aunt Myrtle, who liked me because she had no daughters, and she was around until about four years ago, so I knew her well."

Wren felt a little thrill. This was someone who had a connection to Susan—a connection separate from the Greenleafs. But what to say next? Family was family, but Stephen would not thank her for bringing unwanted attention to his house, even if the Vanderwerfs were technically his relations.

"Something came up. In researching the house, we found some aspects of it had to do with decisions Susan Greenleaf made. In trying to rehabilitate it, it would help to know more about her."

Hadley gave her a cheeky smile, and green eyes flashed. She bet Hadley entered into every conversation with joy, brimming with confidence. Wren had confidence in her work. But Hadley, she was sure, had confidence in...everything.

"You discovered something shocking about Susan, didn't you? Aunt Myrtle told me a lot, but I'm betting you discovered something new. However, you can't tell me, can you? Is there architect-client confidentiality, like with lawyers?"

Hadley seemed to read her well, and Wren took another glance at the pictures on the wall. Setting up parties for those glittering, ambitious actors and singers meant she could read people. Just like Wren knew how houses were put together, Hadley, she guessed, knew how people were assembled.

Hadley laughed. "It's OK. I understand. You want to know about late Aunt Susan, even if it is through Aunt Myrtle and me."

"If you're not too busy…" said Wren, then cursing herself for being self-effacing again.

"Oh, I know we look busy here. Well, we're not. Not as busy as we should be. We're always one small step ahead of the creditors. I'm only here because a family inheritance is keeping me afloat."

"I thought the Vanderwerf fortune was pretty much gone," said Wren. Hadley's eyes narrowed, and Wren felt warm under her gaze.

"So you checked us out. I've never met an architect, but I bet they plan very, very carefully. Yes, the Vanderwerf money is mostly gone, but there's still a bit left. And I got something through my maternal grandmother, if I don't blow it all here. But you want to know about Susan. I wonder if you'll understand. I bet you've always been a good girl, Wren." Yes, she was. Everyone always talked about her like that. Maybe she should've called the client a "pompous bourgeois vulgarian" to his face…

"I'm afraid I was never given the opportunity to be a bad girl," said Wren. Hadley just looked at her for a few moments—and then burst out laughing.

"Oh, that's a good one! I like that a lot. Anyway, I'm working with a new band that's leading a second wave of emocore. I'll introduce you. Plenty of chances to be a bad girl."

Wren had no idea what emocore was. And at thirty, she wasn't going to fall back on her teenaged excuse of work to avoid the cool kids' parties. Still, Hadley didn't seem to expect an answer. She just rolled on. "But Susan wasn't a good girl. Not at all."

Chapter Eleven

It took Wren a moment to find her voice. "I'm not naive. I know this wasn't some costume drama."

Hadley laughed again. "No, you're not just a fangirl. I can tell that much. You see things clearly. Aunt Myrtle loved talking about Susan. It was quite the marriage of its day. Two of the wealthiest, most distinguished families in the city united. Have you seen a portrait of Susan?"

"Yes. There's one of her and Benjamin at Greenleaf House. She was stunning. But more than that. It sounds silly—but I saw some mischief there."

"Not silly at all. Yes, she was stunning. And mischievous. My parents also have a portrait, painted when she came out. I was fascinated with it as a little girl…wondering what such a beautiful woman, in such beautiful clothes, was thinking about. Such a lovely girl got a lot of attention, and I think she *knew* how beautiful she was."

"You wanted to be her?" asked Wren.

"You're a quiet one, but sharp," said Hadley. "Oh yes, I wanted to live in a big house, wear fabulous clothes, and have parties with my friends every night. You're the old house expert, Wren. Isn't that what you want?"

No, not exactly. Yes, she wanted to wear a Gibson girl dress and sit at the dining room table with linen and silver, but in her fantasy, she was always by herself.

"Something like that," she said.

"Well, let's hope we can persuade cousin Stephen to throw a party. But back to Susan. Benjamin Greenleaf had rivals for her hand, and apparently, his younger brother Ambrose was chief among them—you know about Ambrose, of course. I can see it in your face. Did the Greenleafs tell you about him?"

Wren thought carefully. She decided she could go as far as to reveal Aunt Agnes' rage.

"Just between us?"

"Of course," said Hadley. Those eyes sparkled. It occurred to Wren she was indeed related to Susan.

"Stephen Greenleaf says he has no idea what Ambrose did—no one ever told him. But I think his Aunt Agnes Greenleaf, who still lives in the house, knows what he did. She became so furious when Stephen just mentioned his name. I thought she'd have a heart attack."

"Oh my. Ambrose would be amused if he knew his name still roused such strong emotions after all these years."

"There's a portrait of him, alone, in a long-empty bedroom at Greenleaf House. I got the sense he was smirking at me."

She thought that would provoke another laugh, but Hadley just nodded. "I've never seen a portrait of Uncle Ambrose, just a grainy photograph from Susan and Benjamin's wedding. But I can understand the smirk. He was sleeping with his brother's wife. Did I shock you, Wren?"

But Wren shook her head. Hadley was trying to shock her, but...no. She was shy, but not naïve. "Surprised, but not shocked. 'Sexual intercourse began / In nineteen sixty-three / (which was rather late for me) - / Between the end of the "Chatterley" ban / And the Beatles' first LP.'"

Hadley clapped her hands. "That's marvelous. Who said that?"

"Philip Larkin, an English poet. But they were no more averse to sex then than people are now. They just had to be more careful. I guess Susan told this to your great aunt Myrtle?"

"Yes, after both brothers were dead. It seems Susan had wanted Ambrose. He was fun, exciting, adventurous, and Benjamin wasn't."

"Then why didn't she just marry Ambrose? Or did Benjamin get all the money?"

"Oh, I'm sure Ambrose would've had a piece of the family business, and she would've had a substantial dowry. Even if they didn't have enough for a house like that, they could've had a good life. That's the thing about families like ours—we're often broke but never poor. But the qualities that made Ambrose a wonderful lover would've made him a terrible husband. That's always been the way of the world, don't you think?"

What could Wren say? She never could figure out how her solemn father persuaded her beautiful and romantic mother to be his wife.

"I don't suppose I've ever given that a lot of thought."

"But I bet Susan knew the difference. Aunt Myrtle knew it. I know it. What do you think Susan decided?"

Wren gave that a lot of thought as Hadley watched her with curiosity.

"It seems that Susan wanted to have her cake and eat it too. Considering all she had, and that she wanted even more, I'm guessing she was remarkably greedy."

"You got that right. Myrtle was fascinated with Susan, and she came to the same conclusion. Still, there's all kinds of greed. I bet you've done at least some basic research on the family. They ruled New York, and they did it from that remarkable house. Money—well, they all had money. But to rule from Greenleaf House."

Wren thought about that portrait again. Susan, with limitless wealth, impeccable social position, staggering beauty—mistress of the greatest house in the greatest city in the world.

"Did Susan brag about this to her niece Myrtle? Or confess it?"

"I definitely got the sense it was bragging. I don't believe she had any regrets about her behavior on her deathbed."

Yes. An old lady, those grand years of her youth wiped out by two world wars, the great families becoming less relevant every day as the descendants of immigrants took over the bureaucracies, businesses, and universities, friends dying, and nothing to do in that big house but reflect on when she was beautiful. When she was important.

"So tell me, Wren." Hadley leaned over her desk. "What about this interests an architect? Can you share that much with me?"

"We're figuring out the bedrooms," said Wren. "Residences like Greenleaf

House generally had two master bedrooms, one for the husband and one for the wife. But I'm wondering if they shared a room and gave the other master room to Ambrose, because he merited an important room like that? It would make it easier to visit if Benjamin was out of town."

"Oh yes—that was his room. Aunt Myrtle delighted in the details. Apparently, back then, the Greenleafs had a variety of businesses around the country, and Benjamin would make trips to check up on them. Ambrose was supposedly in charge of keeping an eye on the New York end of things while his big brother traveled. That's presumably when she got together with Ambrose. With adjoining bedrooms, it was that much easier," said Hadley with a smirk. "According to Myrtle, the door between the two bedrooms was kept locked—to ensure privacy between the rooms, not only from the residents but the servants. Susan wore the key around her neck, under her dress, and would unlock the door to visit Ambrose when Benjamin left. Although—and again, this is courtesy of Aunt Myrtle—the first time they made love was in the conservatory." Hadley clearly found the story delightful—and titillating.

"You don't think Benjamin knew?" asked Wren.

"I'm guessing that Benjamin wasn't the sharpest knife in the drawer."

"Perhaps in some areas. But he built that magnificent house."

"I thought some nineteenth-century architect built that."

"Yes, the technical ends. But there is a vision there. And it didn't come from the original architects, who did plenty of fine homes, but absolutely nothing like this. Benjamin had magnificent volumes on architecture and decoration, worth a mint even in his day, which Stephen rescued some years ago from Benjamin's private study. He was definitely involved in this house—this was his unique vision."

"Interesting. I can read people. I'm very good at that. But you can read houses." Those eyes seemed piercing now. Wren had thought that Hadley might be a lightweight, but she was smart. Even wise.

"Yes, I'm better with buildings than with people. I guess I don't understand. I'm an only child. And I'm single. But I'd like to think I could trust a brother and a wife," said Wren.

It just came out. Hadley's frank tone seemed to invite it, but she regretted it right away. Her tone was harsher than she meant it to be. She wondered for a moment if Hadley would take that as a rebuke or laugh at her for being stuffy. But she just stared with her green eyes.

"As I said, Wren, you're a good girl," she said softly. "And Ambrose was a bad boy. Maybe his love for Susan was one for the ages, but Aunt Myrtle said he had a reputation for womanizing going back to his college days. She told me he was caught promoting an underground network of bare-knuckle boxing, and the family sent him down to New Orleans, where they had some shipping interests, but he got involved in smuggling and allegedly became engaged to a Creole beauty. So he was dragged back home again, until his final exile to Argentina. They say he never came home. As for Susan…." Hadley shrugged. "I think she had a quiet life after that. Planning parties and charity committees. Maybe Aunt Myrtle exaggerated, but she said Susan had a breakdown after Ambrose left for good and was sent, without her husband, to family in the country. To take the waters in Saratoga, or something like that." She cocked her head at Wren. "Are we off topic? I'm not sure this is what architects need to know."

"Background on old houses is always welcome," said Wren. "And it seems Susan loved Ambrose not despite his behavior, but because of it. Good girls have the option today to settle down with bad boys. But not back then. Not if you want to be mistress of Greenleaf House."

"Of course." Hadley glanced up at the pictures. "My business is based on bad boys. I'm living the dream of so many 16-year-old girls, hanging with musicians and actors. Only, half of them are wired on heroin or coke, and they have the emotional maturity of third graders. It gets tedious sometimes." She flashed those eyes at Wren again. "I bet you never fell for a bad boy, did you?"

The conversation was getting dangerous, professionally and emotionally. Hadley clearly knew this was about a lot more than renovating a mansion.

Wren stood. "You've been very generous with your time. Thank you."

"You're welcome." She paused, and Wren watched her think about her next words. "I'm sure you're a super architect. I know enough about Stephen

Greenleaf to know he would only pick the best for that ridiculous building."
It's really my father he picked. But no, no self-effacement here! "However, you
won't understand Greenleaf House unless you understand us. If you'd like, I
can help. If you weren't born one of us, you'll need some explanations. This
isn't Downton Abbey. At the end of the day, we weren't very nice. Anyway,
we should talk again." She handed Wren a business card from a glass holder
on her desk. Wren reached into her jacket pocket and handed Hadley one
of hers.

"Again, I appreciate your help and will keep what you said confidential."

"Oh dear lord, no need for that. No one minds anymore, and everyone
involved is long gone. I was even thinking about writing something about
it."

"You're not afraid of embarrassing the family?"

"Because of a century-old infidelity? What are they going to do—blackball
me at the Junior League? Cancel my Mayflower Society membership? My
name is at the door of the hottest places in Manhattan—they certainly aren't
interested." She looked a little embarrassed at her outburst. "Anyway, I
appreciate your offer. But no one cares anymore. At least none of the
Vanderwerfs."

Oh, but I'm sure Aunt Agnes still cares.

"You really did help me understand the house better."

"But we didn't talk about the furnishings or anything like that. I guess I
thought you'd want to know what kind of curtains Susan liked, and we just
got sidetracked."

"I can look those things up," said Wren. "I wanted to know about the
house's personality. Houses are like people. They have personalities." Wren
enjoyed her turn surprising Hadley.

"I'm glad I could help. I'll see you out." She walked Wren to the front door.

"I really meant that, about helping. That wasn't just being polite. If you
have some time, and are interested, we could talk more about Susan and her
family over dinner some night. I'll call you?" She looked almost shy.

"Yes. Thank you. That would be nice." She forced her voice to be even.

"Your name is Wren. Like the little bird?" asked Hadley, with a half smile.

Wren blinked. "Yes, just like that."

* * *

Outside again, Wren had to take a few minutes to breathe. Susan, the beautiful Susan, lived a dangerous life. Did Aunt Agnes know that? Wren guessed she did. But it didn't seem to explain the body in the attic. Still, the Greenleafs and Vanderwerfs were wealthy enough to afford multiple scandals, she thought wryly.

And Hadley. Wren looked at her card again—the post-modern design with the latest font. Her father would loathe it. But her father's opinion wasn't relevant here, was it? She smiled briefly and put it in her pocket.

Chapter Twelve

In very different ways, her meetings with Hadley and Conor had left her wrung out. More...people. She wanted to go back to the house, to something she understood.

Susan Greenleaf rattled around her head—she thought she could understand her, to a point. She fell in love. Or at least in lust. People did that. Still to have so much and still put it all at risk. *Mistress of Greenleaf House, that should be enough for anyone.*

What about her descendant, Hadley? Did Hadley really want to see her again, or was she just being polite? Or did she see Wren as a way to reconnect with her cousins, the Greenleafs. Beautiful Hadley with her perfect haircut. She should've asked her where she went. But that was the thing about girls like Hadley: they never had to ask. They just...knew.

She forced herself to think about Karen Lavendell. Wren had so wanted to believe that it was just a random robbery gone wrong, but not if she was killed with the same gun as the woman in the attic.

* * *

Bobby and his crew were keeping busy, along with a plumber in the kitchen and the roofer with a truck full of copper.

"Mrs. Ryan periodically comes down to see what we're up to," said Bobby.

"Making sure you're wiping your feet on the doormat?"

"At first, but now I think it's boredom and curiosity—and she reports back to madam upstairs. Still, we're getting along. I figured she goes to church

Sundays. I mean, just look at her. I asked her about it, and it turns out I have an aunt who's a fellow longtime parishioner, and we talked about the shortcomings of the priest—"

"She criticized her priest?"

"Oh yeah. But I think I rose a few notches in her estimate. Anyway, she asked if you could give Miss Greenleaf a report on your progress and plans. Actually, the word used was *precis*."

Her heart sank. "Miss Greenleaf wants to see *me?*"

"Yes. Mrs. Ryan said Miss Greenleaf was curious about our next plans, and I said we would be working on the closed-off wing—the ballroom and library and a few other minor rooms. Mrs. Ryan was back within the hour, asking if she could speak with you at your earliest convenience." He grinned. "I wasn't blessed with the details: I'm just the help—you're management."

They walked through the near-empty hallways to the double doors that led to the largest room in the house, the ballroom.

"When we did the walk-through with Stephen, he said this room had never been opened in his lifetime. There's a valuable chandelier and other accents, and they wanted to keep them safe from any workmen or cleaning services over the years. But I have the key on this ring...." In a few moments, they were in and looking around.

"Ah. It's in pretty good shape, actually," said Bobby. Because of its position, it had been spared damage. The royal blue curtains were falling apart, but the scrollwork and gilt just needed a little touch-up, and the black marble pillars lining the room only wanted some cleaning. Best of all was a ceiling scene, garlands against a pale blue background—green leaves. A little visual pun from Benjamin, but understated. The grand chandelier was casually covered with old bedsheets.

"Before you start work, take it down entirely, so there's no chance of damage. I doubt if Stephen wants it to remain anyway—too imposing. Maybe he can donate it to a museum."

Still, the room was ornate, with no money spared in giving attention to every decorative detail. But it was not nearly as baroque as similar rooms in other houses. She assumed it reflected Benjamin's tastes, relatively austere for the 1890s. Had his bride wanted something…livelier?

Wren thought about the events that room had seen—the long dresses and white ties giving way to tuxedos and short dresses in the Roaring Twenties, a scaling back in the 1930s, then the War, with all the men gone. Had it ever been used again?

"I'd have thought he'd want to divide this up, but it's staying as is, with some rewiring," said Bobby.

"Again, he was cagey about plans for the house, but he told us he wanted to keep this room flexible for business meetings, presentations, receptions. That's why he asked for outlets not just around the walls but in the floor. It's a shame. The floor is still in good shape."

"They have some very good portable dance floors now," said Bobby.

"It won't be the same." Wren got a dreamy look and, for a moment, was back in the home's heyday. "I don't think anyone will ever waltz here again."

* * *

They went over the details for the ballroom, and then Wren sighed and made her way to Aunt Agnes' suite. As she walked, it occurred to her that although she didn't want to betray the Greenleafs by discussing them with the Vanderwerfs, there was no reason not to discuss the Vanderwerfs with the Greenleafs. Hadley hadn't wanted privacy at all, hadn't even thought it necessary. In fact, Wren thought Hadley might find any responses Aunt Agnes would have amusing. She'd tell her when she saw her next, realizing, with that thought, that she would see her again, smiling at the thought.

Meanwhile, it occurred to her that her conversation with Miss Greenleaf could be a two-way street. If Miss Greenleaf wanted information, perhaps she would share what she knew about old secrets—and maybe even new ones.

She knocked, and the unsmiling Mrs. Ryan opened the door.

"I heard Miss Greenleaf wanted to see me," she said, and without speaking, Mrs. Ryan showed her into the sitting room. Aunt Agnes was playing solitaire on a low table.

"I understand that you had some questions about our progress," she said and took a chair opposite the old lady. Mrs. Ryan stood by.

Aunt Agnes just kept playing the cards.

"I understand that you will be working on the ballroom and library," she said. She stopped playing cards and looked closely at Wren.

"The ballroom needs extensive rewiring and some maintenance work, but it's generally in good shape. We won't have to do too much. I have to do more work on the library. We will have to empty the shelves and pull them all down. The walls will need, at the very least, some inspection and probably reinforcement." She saw some concern in Miss Greenleaf's face. "Don't worry, we'll put everything back exactly as it was. You won't even know anything has changed. All this will be done in the coming weeks."

Aunt Agnes put down her cards and met Wren's eye. "Thank you. I have a sentimental attachment to that part of the house. I haven't been in the library or ballroom in about 70 years, the last time they were used. In 1947 I made my debut in that ballroom. Drinks were served in the library, where the older guests could rest and talk away from the music."

"That was important, to have that space?"

"Of course it was," she snapped. "You've seen this house. You must realize it. It was designed for comfort, not just for the people living there, but for the visitors, for those at the balls. There's a reason for everything."

"Of course," she gave what she hoped was an accepting smile. "I've only been here for a few days. You've been here for nine decades. I'll need a little time."

Miss Greenleaf stared at her for a few moments, then smiled. "That's reasonable enough," she finally said.

"Anyway, it must've been a lovely party," said Wren.

"In fact, it was sad. So many men who should've been there were dead. Everyone else was exhausted. The good families...it wasn't like before. We had always had a grand New Year's Eve party here, with full orchestra, women in sable. Even in the 1920s, times had changed, but they brought in champagne...." She looked at Wren and smiled slyly. "Surely you didn't expect Greenleafs to let something as silly as the 18th amendment stop them.

Jazz bands played here. F. Scott Fitzgerald and Zelda came once. It was different, but still glamorous."

That was before Aunt Agnes was born, but Wren remembered what Stephen had said, as if she remembered a time in the house before she even came on the scene. As if she were part of the house.

"I'm sure," said Wren.

"After the party, the servants came in—the few who were left. My father had them empty the room and cover the chandelier. He knew it was the last time—even if he kept it to himself. When they were done, he locked the doors, pocketed the key. We took photographs in the library beforehand—and he locked that room up at the same time. That was it. That was the end." Her eyes were glassy. Wren felt a little pang—she wanted to remember when she last saw those rooms, when she had been young.

"Would you like to see those rooms again?"

"Is the library ladder still broken? There were no workmen or materials to fix it during the war, and afterward, no one got around to it. The room was shuttered anyway."

"We're arranging for it to be fixed, probably with original materials. It would be very dangerous to climb on it now. But I could take you on a walk-through, if you want."

"No, but thank you for the precis."

She went back to her cards. Wren assumed she was being dismissed—but Wren knew that here was a Greenleaf who had as much stake in the home's future as her nephew.

"As long as I'm here," said Wren. Miss Greenleaf looked up, curious. She was at a point in life when few people wanted to talk to her.

"I want to know how this house was used. It will help me figure out how to bring the house back to its peak. I see there are two master bedrooms. I know very often a married couple would have their own rooms, but some old plans I have indicated that the second room was for Ambrose Greenleaf. Being able to confirm that will help us decide how to refurbish it—as a masculine or feminine room."

She wondered if that would upset Aunt Agnes. Indeed, the old lady looked at her closely, then seemed to decide that her question was genuine, not an attempt to delve into a family scandal.

"I don't know if you will understand, but married couples in the right families had separate bedrooms. Ambrose had one of the principal guest bedrooms nearby. But he was apparently restless, found some opportunities overseas, and never came home. My grandmother had a fine old desk in her bedroom, where she ran a lot of charities. If I was a good girl, I could visit her there, and we'd have lemonade and sandwiches in her boudoir."

"Ah—so the room has changed over the years." No doubt it found yet another purpose after Susan died, and Agnes' mother became mistress of the house. "Thank you, that helps me understand the stages that room went through as we refurbish it. I will talk with Mr. Greenleaf about how he'd like to prepare it next."

"I'm pleased I was able to help," she said. "I haven't discussed those times with anyone. Mrs. Ryan—you're sick of hearing me ramble, aren't you?"

"Delighted to listen to your stories, Miss Greenleaf," she said drily.

Wren took a breath. *Don't quit now. You may not get as good a chance again to ask about Uncle Ambrose, about the man who may have killed a woman and put her in the attic.*

"Yes, you've been very helpful. Mr. Greenleaf's memories do not go back as far. I was a little nervous about asking you, however, as it seemed the other day you were very reluctant to discuss your Uncle Ambrose."

Aunt Agnes stared at her, as if trying to force her to turn away. When that didn't work, she said, "I think he got involved with a chorus girl. The family had to pay her off. Mrs. Ryan—remember chorus girls?"

"Before my time, miss," she said. Aunt Agnes was smiling, not even pretending she was telling the truth.

"It's still a sore point in the family. My nephew likes to tease me about it. As you can see, I wish he wouldn't."

"Thank you. I should be getting back to work now." She steeled herself. "Just one more thing. I know when we first met, you said you were nervous that we were going to turn this house into a hotel. I want to assure you again that I have not been engaged to do that. I don't know what gave you that idea."

Those sharp eyes flashed…but not at Wren, over her shoulder, at Mrs. Ryan.

"That was Conor. He told me that company, that, what was it again, PH, something—"

"PH Hospitality," said Wren.

"Yes. Conor said they wanted to buy this house and make it a hotel, didn't he, Mrs. Ryan?"

"I believe that's what he said," said Mrs. Ryan, a little reluctantly.

"I don't understand business. But Conor said they might offer Stephen so much money that he wouldn't have any choice. We didn't like that. Conor loves this house like I do. He said Stephen wouldn't listen to him, but might listen to me." She turned back to Wren. "Stephen never tells me anything. Conor told me the hotel people would destroy the house. Memories and… important things." She looked sad, and her eyes went down to her lap. It was quiet for a while, and Wren felt awful about pushing Miss Greenleaf further, but she needed to know.

"Did Conor tell you anything else about PH Hospitality?"

"Yes. We were very nervous, and I was thinking about how to address this with Stephen. But then he told me that the lady from the company had been killed, and Conor said that everything would be all right because, by the time the company got a new lady, Stephen would be done with whatever he was doing. I'm sorry she's dead, of course. Christians don't rejoice in anyone's death, do they, Mrs. Ryan?"

"No, miss."

"But I am glad that this house is safe now. I don't entirely trust my nephew, but I know he wouldn't destroy this house. I wish he would tell me more about what's happening. It was nice of Conor to take such a close interest. He's a fine boy, Mrs. Ryan."

"Thank you, miss."

Chapter Thirteen

Wren had to take a chair in the hallway just outside Aunt Agnes' suite to gather herself. Conor, a man who dealt it secrets and lies. Would he actually kill if he thought it would save Greenleaf House? Perhaps. But Wren didn't think he'd kill purely out of sentiment. What did Aunt Agnes say—"memories and important things." What important things? Conor might kill for that.

"Memories and important things." Two dead women connected by one murder weapon. And that was the only thing Wren was sure of—there were many pieces here, but actually only one crime.

Miss Greenleaf and Mrs. Ryan. Sitting in their echo chamber day after day, week after week, year after year, with almost no company but each other. She had thought it was a joke, thinking of Mrs. Ryan as Mrs. Danvers, but after all this time, Miss Greenleaf may not have been the only one living in the past.

Both of them could be lying at this point. Even worse—lying without even realizing what the truth was anymore. Never mind what Conor and Stephen were telling her. Even Great Aunt Myrtle—they only had her word on how Susan had behaved. Wren felt she was even further behind. She wished she could just stay with houses—they never lied. Those once-beautiful bedrooms, so generous in size, and no doubt accented by carefully chosen wallpaper and furniture—even the hardware on the doors.

Wren stopped. Indeed, houses didn't lie, and she searched back over her memory, and then almost ran to the master bedrooms. She headed straight for the connecting doors. The hardware, the doors—they were original to the house, the ones that Susan and Benjamin—and Ambrose—used when they first moved in. She'd stake her reputation on the time period.

She smiled. Her memory had been right: There were locks on the main bedroom doors that led to the hallway, but no locks at all for the connecting doors between the bedrooms. The romantic story of the key around the neck Hadley had told her was false. Aunt Agnes may have been mistaken about which room belonged to Ambrose—or she'd been lying. So might Aunt Myrtle. Wren now had proof of lies, but who was lying?

Still more questions, but Wren felt a certain pleasure. She caressed the door—walnut, beautiful and expensive. No corners were cut here—no veneers over cheap wood. Everything here was true—the house didn't lie.

Feeling very pleased with herself, Wren went to find Bobby and found him and his crew progressing nicely. The kitchen had been stripped out entirely, and Wren enjoyed the behind-the-scenes view of the house. Like the solid walnut door, the walls were not just a veneer. They held up a house built to last for generations.

"I see you admiring the lath and plaster," he said. "They stopped using it before you were born—heck, before *I* was born. My father taught me how to do this."

"Quieter and more flexible than drywall. And as we both know, better for rounded walls and more fire resistant. Also, more expensive, for which you'll be billing us."

"Which you'll be passing on to the Greenleafs." He grinned. "You were the ones who wanted it perfect."

"The house deserves nothing less," said Wren, but she was looking at the opened walls, not at Bobby, and she wasn't smiling. Bobby shook his head. *Just like her father.*

"Listen, we have some more things to go over. I'll send the boys home at the usual time, and if you want to stay late, we'll go over the next stage together."

"Thanks—but I don't want to keep you from getting home."

"No problem. Rosa is going out with her sisters tonight, and I'll grab a pizza and beer with a friend who works nearby. I'd just be hanging around here anyway."

Pleased for the chance to get ahead, she spent the rest of the day reviewing the house and her earlier notes. At 5:00, she heard the crew leaving through the front door, and a few minutes later, the doorbell rang. Did one of the workmen forget something? Bobby had the opera going again and probably wouldn't hear it, so Wren decided to answer the door herself. From the foyer, she saw Mrs. Ryan at the landing above.

"It's probably just one of the workmen who forgot something," she called up. Mrs. Ryan pursed her lips before leaving. *She* wouldn't have forgotten anything.

But it wasn't a workman. It was Sgt. Ortiz.

"Oh! Did you want to speak with one of the Greenleafs?"

"No, as a matter of fact. I came to speak with you." He smiled. "And for a chance to see this house again. Do you think when you're done with it, it will be open to the public?"

"I don't know Mr. Greenleaf's plans. You'll have to talk with him."

"Of course. But that's what this is all about, isn't it? Mr. Greenleaf's plans. But no one wants to talk about that. The PH Hospitality people just say they were having exploratory talks, and I have no way to force Stephen Greenleaf to say anything beyond his plans are still in development. You seem to be front and center here. I've asked about you, Ms. Fontaine. You're gaining quite a reputation in your field. You're meticulous. You notice things—that is, you look at a house and see things. I'm wondering what you've seen here?"

Wren colored a little. "Are you just flattering me, sergeant?"

He shook his head. "No point in that. I'm being honest. I need some help here."

Wren looked at him for a while. She heard her father's voice: "You're a partner now. You can't just do the fun parts of the job." *But even the tedious parts could be made fun.*

"Could you come with me?" she said. "I want to show you something."

Wren grabbed the keys and led Ortiz to the ballroom.

"My God," he said. "I've never seen anything like it."

91

"You haven't seen anything like it because there isn't anything like it. This isn't the most aesthetically pleasing room in this house, but from an architectural perspective, it's the most impressive. Do you know what's involved in creating a room this big and completely open? Every physical aspect must be in perfect harmony. You cannot know just part of it."

"Fascinating," said Ortiz, continuing to look around the room before landing his eyes on Wren. "But I'm assuming that you didn't bring me here just for an architecture lecture."

"I wanted to let you know that I see that everything that happens *in* this house and *about* this house is related. In the same way that the beams and arches of this room are connected. You are solving a murder. I am trying to make sure this job goes smoothly. The connections. I will share if you will."

He looked at her wryly. "I checked with the D.A, Ms. Fontaine. There is no such thing as architect-client confidentiality. You have to tell me what you know, deal or no deal."

"I've told you everything I *know*. I thought we'd share what we *think*."

"It sounds like you're trying to manage me. Like I was a client."

"Our firm's clients tend to be wealthy people who have strong feelings."

"I bet you're good at it," he said.

"I'm awful at it. My father is good at it, and slowly I'm learning."

Ortiz laughed. "Oh, what the hell. Here's where we are. As we thought, ballistics shows that the same gun killed both Karen Lavendell and the mystery woman in the attic. We're not spending too much time on the attic death. But there's clearly a connection. And maybe if we solve the old one, I'll get a lead on the new one. So do you know anything about her?"

"No, nothing about her. But I've been doing some research. And I can tell you there was a rumor that Susan Greenleaf, the first mistress of this house, was having an affair with her husband's brother. But nothing anyone can prove. Perhaps it was just an infatuation that was misunderstood and exaggerated over the years."

She thought Ortiz would be scornful, but he was thoughtful about it. "Things like that can rankle for years, even generations. Do you think Karen Lavendell researched the house, found out about it, and someone wanted her shut up?"

Wren thought what Hadley had said, who would care after all these years? It was nothing but scandalous, and entertaining, gossip to share during a family reunion. But Aunt Agnes would care.

"Families like this are very different, even from the wealthy today," she said. "It wasn't just about money, it was about position, and that was something that couldn't be bought. Many scandals could be covered up—but there were some that couldn't." She thought about what she knew of the Gilded Age, and what her father had told her about their descendants. "Something that seems silly today still may mean a lot, not just to Agnes Greenleaf, but even to a modern man like Stephen Greenleaf."

He nodded.

"And then there are the servants," said Wren. She didn't owe Conor secrecy from the police. "This was their home as much as the Greenleafs, only their names weren't on the deed. Conor Ryan, the son of Miss Greenleaf's companion, Mrs. Ryan, is obsessed with this house. I've spoken with him. He's close with Miss Greenleaf, and she dotes on him the way she doesn't with her actual nephew, Stephen. He told her PH Hospitality was a threat, to see if she could use her influence with Stephen to block them. And he told her that when Karen Lavendell died, it was unlikely the firm could regroup in time to thwart any plans Stephen had."

Ortiz listened closely, waiting until she was done to talk. "So you're saying that Conor might've killed Lavendell for the sake of the house? To please Miss Greenleaf?"

"I'm not a detective," said Wren. "I'm just telling you what I heard from him."

"Yes. And thank you very much." He seemed to consider something. "I can tell you that Conor Ryan does not have an alibi."

"And as you probably found out, he has an unusual job."

Ortiz smiled. "Exactly. You are a bit of a detective, after all. But I suppose fixing up a house like this requires some detective work."

"I suppose."

"You've been upfront with me. So I'll return the favor. Do you know an

Andrew Heppenstall?"

Wren smiled. "Everyone knows Heppenstall."

"Tell me about him."

"He's an obsessive preservationist, would like every building older than 50 years frozen in time, utterly untouched. He's always making a scene with homeowners and politicians about some building or other."

"I thought you'd approve of him, but you sound dismissive."

"He's a fanatic. He frowns on even adding modern plumbing and electricity. He also doesn't differentiate between houses like this, of genuine historic and artistic importance, and other houses that have nothing to recommend them except their age. Still, he has his supporters, even among architects and professors, although they're quiet about it. Why are you interested in him?"

"I found out he's been bothering Stephen Greenleaf for months about his plans for this place. He wasn't happy about it."

"He didn't tell me."

"He only admitted it reluctantly to me when I found Heppenstall had been threatening PH Hospitality for years, and they told me he had admitted to them he was threatening Greenleaf as well. But Greenleaf seems to want to play everything about this house close to his chest. Anyway, he was deluging him with phone calls and emails, begging him to leave this house pristine." He gave her a wry look. "Would he approve of you?"

Wren laughed. "Not entirely. He'd know I'd have the greatest respect for homes like this, but we're going to have modern plumbing and wiring, air conditioning. Wi-Fi."

He nodded. "You said 'fanatic.' Do you think he'd kill to save this house?"

"Do you think he killed Karen Lavendell to make sure PH Hospitality never got its hands on this place? I always thought he was kind of crazy but not a murderer."

"Who knows? But it doesn't seem he was guilty of this particular murder. He spent the whole evening with dozens of witnesses delivering a presentation at Fordham in the Bronx. Even at the outside, she was dead hours before he wrapped up there. Does he have…followers, disciples?"

"He does lead a small organization, the Society for Building Preservation, but he's not a cult leader. Have you met him?"

"Briefly, to discuss his alibi."

"You must've seen what he's like—how awkward he is. Even people who agree with him don't like him. I wouldn't think he'd be the kind of man to inspire someone to kill on behalf of the cause."

"I suppose. He did seem awfully nervous, though. It's funny. I come up against so many obviously guilty suspects with no alibi who can look me in the eye and swear they're innocent. And here's Heppenstall with a cast-iron alibi but looking nervous as hell."

"He probably wished her dead."

"I'm sure. He managed to tear into her even while I was questioning him. He's anxious about something."

"Probably about the fate of this house," said Wren.

"Really?" he looked around again. "You know, I can almost believe that."

Chapter Fourteen

Wren and Bobby finished a little before 8:00, and they walked out together.

"Call an Uber," said Bobby. "I'll wait with you."

"I've been traveling the city since I was 10. I think I can manage."

"It's after dark on a quiet street, and we already have at least one murder connected to this house."

Being protective was in Bobby's nature; it didn't help that he still thought of her as the little girl recreating Monticello with Legos. "For God's sake, why would anyone want to kill me? Anyway, there's a diner off of Columbus with a cold seafood salad plate. I can review my notes, and the subway is close by."

The deli was just around the corner from where Bobby was meeting his friend, so he reluctantly agreed. Still, he saw her into the diner before meeting his friend.

The seafood salad was as good as she remembered it and, absorbed in her notes and fueled with plenty of coffee, it was after 9:00 before she paid and left. On her way to the subway, she realized she was tired and decided to call for an Uber.

It was an odd time. The dinner crowd had long left, and the late-night denizens had not yet arrived after theater and movies, so she had the street to herself. But out of the corner of her eye, she saw a figure approaching her. He was walking past a bank that was closed, so he was in the shadows, tall and broad.

She was used to the city and to traveling late in the evening, but there was something about the figure's approach that made her nervous, a deliberate pace, not someone strolling along. Or was all the talk about Lavendall's death and the body in the attic just making her paranoid? Was Bobby's warning getting to her?

Wren looked around. There was no one nearby and no way to get back into the restaurant before their paths crossed. She could try to jog across the street, but the light was against her, and traffic was moving quickly. Should she just run? Could she outrun the figure? Wren saw a group of people about a block away. Could she make it there?

She decided to run—it was her only option, and she was suddenly nauseous as her heart began pounding. He was almost there—she looked once more for someone, for anyone, nearby—and then he spoke.

"Ms. Fontaine?"

She was right. He knew her. This was the man who had killed Lavendell. Running wasn't an option. He was going to shoot her too.

Then a shadow passed by her and went straight to her assailant. An arm reached out in the dark and landed on the man's shoulder. She couldn't immediately see him but recognized his voice.

"Is there a problem here?" Bobby led Wren's stalker closer to the streetlight.

"Hey, what are you doing?" protested the man. "Who are you?"

"I was just going to ask you that myself," said Bobby.

Wren was trying to catch her breath and keep her dinner down when she recognized her would-be assailant.

"You're Andrew Heppenstall. We've met before. Why are you stalking me?"

"I wasn't stalking you. I just wanted to talk to you. I stopped at Greenleaf House thinking you might still be there, because the work van was still in the driveway. The housekeeper said that your contractor had mentioned he was meeting someone at the bar on the corner, and I thought I might find both of you there. By the time I got there, I saw you leaving...I'm sorry." She got a better look at him now, looking as she remembered him, large and ungainly, sloppily dressed.

"It didn't occur to you to just call me and make an appointment? You

97

scared the hell out of me."

"I'm so sorry." He genuinely meant it, she saw. Sorry and confused. Wren recognized another socially inadept introvert. He seemed especially confused this evening, looking back and forth between Wren and Bobby and not knowing what to say first. He fixed his glasses, sliding down his nose. "But I have some important things to talk to you about. About Greenleaf House. Please."

Wren looked at Bobby. He shrugged. "You want the contractor too? That's me. If the boss is OK with it, I'm going to join you. I was at the bar across the street. We can go there now."

"Mr. Heppenstall, this is our general contractor, Bobby Fiore. We're both interested in what you have to say."

The Shannon Bar was only half filled, a few businessmen still looking for an excuse not to go home. They found a table. "I'm at my limit," said Bobby. "But don't let me stop you." He ordered a black coffee, Wren ordered a tea to settle her stomach, and Heppenstall blinked, thought it about it, and ordered Canadian whiskey.

The waitress looked annoyed at the small order but brightened when Bobby ordered a plate of mozzarella sticks.

"I just have to…be right back," said Heppenstall, and left for the men's room.

Bobby shook his head. "What a nut. Who the hell drinks Canadian anymore?"

"What were you doing here?"

"My friend just left the bar, and I was about to leave myself when I noticed you on the street. And then I saw him come towards you. It was just luck. "

"I'm glad you came along, although he's probably more awkward than dangerous. One of those obsessive preservationists who was fighting with PH Hospitality. "

Heppenstall came back as the drinks and mozzarella sticks arrived. Bobby happily dug into them as Wren and Heppenstall refused. He gave them a "more for me" look.

"It's late, and I'm tired. What did you want to talk about?" asked Wren.

He took a gulp of his whiskey. "You know, the police are after me. They came to me after Karen Lavendell died. Because they thought I did it. That I hated her. Well, it wasn't her. It was her whole stupid company. The shoddy work—the destruction of some of the finest houses—"

"Yes, we know about PH Hospitality's reputation," said Wren. "But what did you want to speak with me about? I don't work with them."

"We had some exchanges—and things got...I threatened legal action under various preservation laws, and they threatened right back. It got worse from there. But I didn't kill her. I mean...no, I didn't kill Karen Lavendell. It wasn't me. I told them that."

"Sergeant Ortiz told me you had an alibi. You couldn't have killed her. And why tell me this anyway?" Wren had had enough with people for the day and didn't need one more, especially one who was crazy.

"I was giving a talk at Fordham. Dozens of witnesses." He finished his whiskey and tried to focus. "I wanted to talk to you about your plans for Greenleaf House. I know about PH Hospitality, but I also know about you and your firm and its reputation. That house is a citywide treasure, no, a national treasure. I'm assuming you'll be respecting the house." He made it almost a question.

"I can't discuss the details, of course, but I can tell you that we are keeping to the spirit of the house."

"It should be a museum—but I don't suppose Stephen Greenleaf wants that. He wouldn't really talk to me, though, but I understand that at least that magnificent ballroom will remain? I know it hasn't been used in decades, but I know it's one of the finest rooms of its kind. And the library. The system used to support the weight of the books—"

"Yes, I know about that," said Wren. "We'll shore it up, and I can at least tell you that with some modernization, the ballroom will stay as is."

"Of course, of course—I'm sorry. I'm just so glad it won't be divided up, and that magnificent fireplace will remain. That's real Calacatta marble, I've heard. The bathrooms are falling apart, of course, haven't been updated in decades, but it may not be possible—or even desirable—" he gave an awkward laugh "—to get plumbing to 19th century standards, although it was a lot more modern—"

"Yes, we know," said Wren. She and Bobby met each other's eye: *he knows an awful lot of details.*

"Again, I'm sorry—I'm used to talking to laypeople. But I'm rambling."

"You must've realized that the house was Benjamin's special vision—"

"Of course! I know about the Greenleafs and their love of the house. Did you know about the Colombia connection? I don't know the details, of course, but that is essential to the future of the house...." He stopped, as if realizing he was saying too much.

Colombia. Ambrose and his alleged gun running in South America. Had that been important? Whatever crimes Ambrose had committed in South America could no longer be relevant, could they? Had it helped pay down the debt for the house? Why else would an obsessive like Heppenstall delve into that? But a moment later, he was off and running on something else.

"Anyway, never mind that. The ball is in Stephen Greenleaf's court, for now, anyway. What I really wanted to talk to you about was Stephen Greenleaf's plans for the house. "

"If you want to know what we're doing, you're wasting your time. We can't share what we know."

"But it's just us here. We're on the same side. All we care about is preserving Greenleaf House. He wouldn't sell to PH Hospitality or someplace like it if, well, a better option isn't available?"

Wren just looked at him. She knew she could be naïve, but he seemed delusional, that they belonged in some special club whose bonds trumped all professional rules and customs. She didn't know what to say.

Bobby had been listening in his quiet, patient way, as he did when she explained how they would handle a new wall. He now filled the silence.

"I'm just a workingman, Mr. Heppenstall, and my main concern is the safety of the people on the job, and that includes my boss. No one has ever been killed or even seriously injured on any job I've run because I'm careful. We already have one dead person."

"But I told you, I have nothing to do with that. My—that is, others in my group, we look for legal means to preserve houses." His gaze fell into his lap.

"We don't murder people to preserve houses."

Bobby didn't say anything. He just glared.

Heppenstall looked down. "I know. I'm sorry. My enthusiasm gets away from me. I am sorry I startled you this evening. I meant no harm—I never meant any harm. You must know that." He looked very dejected, and Wren actually felt sorry for him. He was someone like her, she felt, but even more so. More comfortable with houses than people.

"I'll go now," he said. He fumbled for his wallet.

"It's on me," said Bobby. "Actually, I'll bill Miss Fontaine, and she'll pass it along to Stephen Greenleaf."

"Oh...ah, yes. Thank you," he said, trying to figure out if it was a joke. "Good night, then." He half-smiled and left.

Bobby absently ate the last mozzarella stick. "What a nut. I hope he paid attention and keeps away."

"It was odd," said Wren. " The house has rarely been photographed, and not recently, and no strangers admitted, and yet he seems to have known so many details."

"If he's that obsessive, he did a lot of research."

"The state of the bathroom would not be something he could likely research. How did he get in? Or did someone tell him about it? There were only three people who could've given him access or information—Stephen, Mrs. Ryan, Miss Greenleaf. But none of them seem likely, do they?" She saw him smiling. "What's so funny?"

"You always know what's right or wrong with a building. Now, you know what's right or wrong with a person. Anyway, speaking of buildings, there are some odd things about the house."

"A structural problem?"

"No. Not exactly. Listen, it's late. Let me give you a ride home. Brooklyn is scarcely out of my way, and I want to run some things by you."

She didn't argue, preferring a ride with Bobby than with an anonymous driver.

"Anyway, this is what I wanted to say. I've been getting on with Mrs. Ryan. I think at first, she wanted to make sure we weren't breaking anything, but then it was more about curiosity and a chance to get away from Miss Greenleaf. We talked about church, how terrible today's generation is—" Wren laughed. "And I thought I'd cement the goodwill by offering to fix that ancient medicine cabinet so it would be a lot easier to use until we were ready to redo the entire bathroom. It only took a few minutes, but I had to open it—it was full of various prescription-only sleeping pills for Miss Greenleaf. Believe me, I know what they are—I had an aunt like that." He grimaced.

"Lots of old people have trouble sleeping," said Wren.

"Perhaps. But there were several powerful prescriptions there. My aunt had certain demons that kept her up. I'm wondering what demons Miss Greenleaf has, living her entire life under a murdered family servant."

"I'm sure she knew," said Wren.

"Yeah. And there are other things. You and I talked about the broken rolling ladder. The rail is cracked. It still rolls, but put an adult's weight on it, and it would all collapse. Mrs. Ryan said Miss Greenleaf wanted to know when it would be repaired."

"Yes. Aunt Agnes asked me about it as well. Can you repair it? Or will it have to be replaced?"

"A supplier I know pulled a rabbit out of her hat and found a manufacturer who can send us some hardware that will let us use the original ladder. But it will actually be cheaper to get a whole new ladder, and there are some excellent options—"

"Buy the old hardware," said Wren.

"I was a fool to ask," he said, laughing. "You're the boss."

"Miss Greenleaf was interested in the ballroom as well. These were rooms that were central to her debut, the last gasp of this house as central to society. The ballroom and the library were the principal rooms shut up and locked that night. She's going back to those days in her mind, as she thinks again about her nephew Stephen taking over again, the house opening up, and the Greenleafs taking their place again, ruling New York."

"Oh dear lord," said Bobby. "We're just trying to renovate a house here. But if that's the way she looks at things, no wonder she seemed so anxious about our work. I told them our schedule for moving them out of their suite so we could renovate it. I said my crew would move their furniture to whatever part of the house they temporarily relocate to. The old lady did not seem happy about that and demanded substantial advanced notice so she could lock up the drawers before any furniture move. Does she think my crew has nothing better to do than go through a ninety-year-old woman's underwear drawer?"

"It is very Victorian. But she wasn't even Victorian. Hoover was president when she was born, not McKinley. All these things together—it's odd. I know she may look back to the library, being there as a teenaged girl, but still—that's her great nostalgic memory after some 70 years?"

Bobby laughed again. "She's stuck in the past—just like your father says you are? The broken library ladder is telling us something."

"It's true," she said, feeling a little defensive. "It's a symbol. She wants it the way it was."

"I'm not laughing at you. I admire you. You know houses."

"I try to. And one more thing. Sergeant Ortiz had already said Heppenstall was cleared—he had a solid alibi. Was it just me, or did he seem oddly insistent he had nothing to do with Karen Lavendell's death?"

Chapter Fifteen

The next morning, Wren got up earlier than usual and began her research over the sourdough bread their housekeeper had baked for them yesterday. She was well into it by the time her father came down.

"Warm bread," she said.

"I don't want to disturb you while you're working," he said.

"Then you have a problem. You can't take the bread into the office. Your rules."

"It's warm enough to eat outside," he said. "And thanks for the update on the plumbing status. Do we really need all that copper and brass?"

"They're the best materials."

"I don't need a lesson in plumbing materials. I do need a reason to explain the bill to Stephen Greenleaf."

"The finest residence in New York deserves the finest materials."

"I've had to remind you before that Stephen is our client, not the house."

"Angry clients are your bailiwick," said Wren. "Anyway, I'll tell him that that house is only around today because they used the best materials. Does he want it still standing in the 22nd century?"

"You're a partner, Wren. He's your client. You're going to handle him, and you're going to make it right." He put his breakfast and marmalade on a plate and headed to the backyard.

Wren had to agree with him. But for now, there was the house—a heavily mortgaged house. Yes, Stephen had made a lot of money on his own, but even for a man in his position, the cost of the house was a stretch. He said he wasn't planning to live in it. Even with his Wall Street wealth, he probably couldn't afford to live in it.

She was also able to find the will made by Stephen's father. It did indeed provide for Agnes to remain in the house until her death, with an established percentage of income from an annuity she owned, paid as rent. The residency rule applied to future owners as well. If she voluntarily decided to leave, she could, and then could stop paying the rent, which Stephen might need to keep the house going. On the other hand, the house may be difficult to sell with a tenant locked in. But she was in her 90's. At her death, the annuity would likely end. Her income, and her residency, might soon become moot. But for years, they needed each other.

On to PH Hospitality. She scrolled through a lot of news stories—and they were having their own problems. If Greenleaf was balanced on a financial knife's edge, so were they. It took a lot of money to buy and rehab properties, even if you cut corners, and you needed to be patient, because the money didn't flow in right away. Even their backers didn't have limitless wealth. And they'd need a lot of cash to pay for Greenleaf House. Who was backing Stephen? There weren't many with that much cash. More interesting was why. What would someone get out of fronting so much money. That took her back to Stephen's secret plans. To a kitchen with professional-level power. But Stephen was not having her chop it up like a hotel. Not like PH Partners was no doubt planning. It came down to her client. She shook her head. The secrets were beyond her.

A text jumped onto her screen, interrupting her thoughts. It was from Stephen. "Coming by to see aunt. Let's talk."

Talking with clients was part of her job—her father was right. And even if he was not giving her the whole story, she might very well get something. Keep it pleasant, she told herself. And avoid calling him a pompous bourgeois vulgarian.

Time to get off to Greenleaf House. She slipped quickly back into her bedroom to pick up the suitcase she had already packed. Could she escape from the house without a conversation with her father?

No such luck. He came in from the yard as she was leaving.

"A suitcase?" he asked.

"The group tonight," she said, sticking her chin out a little. She almost defended her time management, but then decided that was childish coming from a partner in the firm. "I'll be taking the car."

"Enjoy yourself," he said. Did she detect a hint of amusement in his voice, his look? Or was she just being paranoid again?

Wren put the suitcase in the back of their Mercedes wagon. She didn't like driving in Manhattan, but with the suitcase, there was no other option, and she'd be able to offer Lavinia a ride home. And there was room to park the car in the Greenleaf House garage.

Bobby and his crew were already hard at work.

"All well?" she asked.

"Proceeding nicely. No surprises so far."

"A body in the attic was enough," said Wren.

"As long as it doesn't affect my work," Bobby said.

"I'd like to go over the conservatory. Nothing structural there, once it's cleared out. Stephen asked me to recommend a gardener who could get it together. And that copper gazebo looks to be in good shape. The only serious work is the flooring. We'll want poured concrete, but first, take a look at the drainage."

It must've been grand once. At some point, someone stopped caring, Wren imagined. The plants died, the vegetation rotting where it stood.

But it would bloom again. Stephen had approved the cost for its renovation, and Wren was sure he'd hire someone to keep it up. A couple of wrought-iron benches, with matching table and chairs, gave visitors a place for a cooling rest during a ball. Is that where Ambrose and Susan had first made love, as Hadley had said? A back staircase made it easy to get here from the party, and a passage granted quick access from the main hallway. That would've been very risky. What if they had been caught? Back then, men could bounce back from almost any scandal, especially a man as wealthy and connected and charming as Ambrose. But Susan? Her life would've been over. She had seemingly taken a terrible risk. How had that risk led to the dead servant in the attic?

"You like to garden, don't you?" Wren asked.

"Favorite downtime activity," said Bobby. "You have a small yard in Brooklyn. Do you do anything with it?"

"Not much, just keeping it neat and presentable. I never had much of an interest. I guess...." She stopped, but Bobby was looking at her, waiting for an answer. She smiled wryly. "I guess, as an architect, I find it much easier to bend structures to my will than living things."

Bobby didn't laugh. "I can see that," he said, nodding. He made a few notes. "I'm OK here. I'll catch you up after lunch."

Bobby left, and she thought about what she had said. *Easier* to bend structures? Maybe the word had been *safer*. She thought of Hadley again, who told her the conservatory story. She wondered again about those Greenleafs, in such a different world, but with the connection, both tenuous and strong, leading to the present generation.

She was still thinking when Stephen came into the room.

"Wren—they told me I'd find you here. How's it going today? No more bodies?"

"No...everything is fine."

"Good." He sat opposite Wren at the old table.

"Since you're here," she said, "I can let you know that I came across someone who may have insights into the history of this house and who can help with the renovations. I'd like to bring her here but want to make sure it's all right with you." It was his home, after all.

Stephen gave her a look.

"And what is this expert's services going to cost me?"

"No charge," she said.

"Now, that's a phrase I never thought I'd hear from Fontaine Partners. And that brings me to what I wanted to talk to you about. I got the paperwork on the roofing. Isn't there a somewhat more...economical solution?" He smiled at her wryly. "Or is this something that I have to discuss with the senior partner?"

"I'm in charge of this project, not the senior partner. There are many other options. But none as good, or as appropriate."

"What do you mean by 'appropriate'?"

She fought to remain calm and patient. "Every single piece of that house is harmonized with each other. The walls, the paint, the flooring, the windows. Benjamin Greenleaf planned everything to go together. They are integrally connected—including the copper roof. It wouldn't be the same if you did something different—it wouldn't look right."

He looked a little overwhelmed, and Wren wondered if she had gone too far.

"You can't paint, or stain, or dye, or whatever, a less-expensive material to look like copper."

"Stephen—there are medieval houses in England with their original copper roofs, just a little repair work. In fact, most of your roof is still good. It's mostly maintenance and patchwork here and there."

"We don't even get everything new for this price?" he said, his voice rising.

"When your great-grandchildren are your age, that roof will still be protecting your house. Use second-rate material, and you'll be replacing it in 20 years."

"Meanwhile, I'm paying for it."

"Actually, the savings are long-term. Copper needs very little regular care." She was about to punctuate that observation with an uncomplimentary comparison between Stephen and his great-grandfather Benjamin—but no. She could see her father shaking his head. She said nothing more, and just waited.

"Maintenance a decade from now will be someone else's problem." Ah, but whose, Wren wondered. "But if you say the house needs it, I'll respect your recommendation. Just keep in mind that, unlike my ancestors, I'm not a robber baron. As for any outside consultants that I do not have to pay for, you have a free hand—no need to ask. Some art historian?"

"Your cousin, actually. Hadley Vanderwerf, a descendent of Susan Greenleaf's brother."

"Ha! I lost track of them over the years. Aunt Agnes kept up with that side of the family, more or less. I haven't seen them since...anyway, do what you think is necessary. And if there is anything behind the scenes that you can use to save a dollar, I'd appreciate it."

"Of course. I spend only what is necessary."

"Do you think your father would have some ideas on economizing?"

Wren felt a little patronized at that, and her first thought was to lash out—but no. He was baiting her. He was trying to goad her into getting angry and then contradicting herself, which he could exploit.

Oh yes. He didn't live in the family house anymore and wore a modern suit, but he worked on Wall Street. Wren knew that the history of trading stocks on Wall Street was as old as the Greenleaf family itself and was as cutthroat then as it was now. Perhaps she had misjudged him and had been seduced by the bonhomie. But for that matter, perhaps she had been seduced by Benjamin Greenleaf too. The aesthete came from a long line of robber barons.

"Wren?" he asked, looking at her curiously.

"I'm sorry. Professional characteristic, considering answers carefully. After all, we're talking about houses that can last for centuries. But about my partner. I have worked under him for years. You would find him far less flexible than I am."

Stephen just stared for a moment, then laughed. "You know what, Wren? You're probably right. Rank hath its privileges." She tried to read his smile: *you won, for now, Ms. Fontaine, but this isn't over.* "Anyway, thanks. I'm going to see Aunt Agnes now."

Alone again in the room, she steeled herself for a phone call. Feeling her palms sweat a little, she punched in Hadley's number. She felt a little relief when Hadley answered—not sounding crisp or harried, though, just joyful.

"Wren…'little bird'…I was hoping to hear from you! I was going to call you myself. Anyway, you put this whole family history thing back in my mind, and I got a few more stories from my father and a couple of other relatives."

"Thank you. I'd like to hear them. In exchange, would you like to see the house?"

"Wow! Really? I didn't want to push—but yes."

"Okay. If you come tomorrow afternoon, say, after work, I could show you around and then, maybe, dinner?" Was she too tentative?

"Sounds great. I'll leave here at 5:00. See you soon!"

Wren's heart was pounding as she put away her phone. So this may be…OK. People were so…exhausting. With luck, she'd hardly have to talk to any for the rest of the day. Just focus on the house, this lovely secretive house. Even the thought of it relaxed her, and then she remembered the group tonight, which gave her an extra jolt of pleasure.

She was planning to touch base with Bobby, but as she approached the main hall, she heard voices on the stairs. Just out of sight, she saw who it was—Stephen and Conor.

"It's been nice of you to visit Aunt Agnes so frequently," said Stephen, but Wren heard a tone in his voice. Her first instinct was to step forward and say hello—but she stopped herself. She wanted to hear them.

"She treats me like one of the family. But you already know that," said Conor. The same ironic tone.

Stephen stopped at the bottom of the stairs. "All right. What now. Still riding that same horse?"

"Why shouldn't I? I'm supposed to forget what Uncle Ambrose did to Fiona—"

"Yes, thank you, I know the story. We all know the story. Fiona disappeared, and my scapegrace uncle must've raped her and banished her somewhere. So what?"

"So what? We now have Fiona's body. Who else could've put her there except the Greenleafs."

"You've got a great idea there. Write a screenplay."

"This is my family, Stephen."

"And mine. I've never given a damn about the illustrious history of Greenleafs. That's Aunt Agnes' particular obsession. I have zero interest in how Fiona—if that's indeed who that is—ended up in the family attic. It was before we were born, before our parents were born. May I suggest you spend more time looking forward instead of backward."

He started to head out the door, but Conor grabbed him by the arm. Stephen didn't look happy about it. What would have happened if a Murphy had grabbed a Greenleaf 120 years ago?

"There's more than one dead body, don't forget."

Stephen's voice lowered dangerously. "I hope you're not implying I know anything about that."

"Of course not. But it's a problem for you, isn't it? I have no idea what you're doing with this place, but finding yourself in the middle of a murder investigation isn't going to help." Wren could just see his smirk.

"Just what is it about us that you hate? We paid your tuition—"

"And I'm supposed to be eternally grateful, right?"

"Don't let's start that again." Stephen sighed. "This was your home too."

"The Murphys were never more than hired help. It was never our home like it was for the Greenleafs."

Wren thought Stephen would explode after that. But no. He mastered himself and threw an arm around Stephen. "You know, we're more alike than you would like to think. Yes, you were the son of a servant, and I was the son of the owner. The owner of this magnificent wreck, watching it fall apart while my nutjob aunt filled me with stories of balls with men in tailcoats, and ladies in long dresses. It was my past, but not my life. Stop envying my life."

"All right," said Conor, after a long pause. " I have no right to blame you as a Greenleaf descendent, but I need to know what happened to Fiona. We were part of this house, too, and she was family. I know you understand that much. Because if you didn't have a sense of responsibility for this house, you'd be walking away from it, not fixing it. You're right. We're the same about that. What if we find Benjamin Greenleaf's diaries? Can I see them, to see if there's anything there about what happened to Fiona?

"Stephen—one thing we have in common is keeping PH Hospitality away from this house. God knows what they'll end up destroying to pull this place apart. All the nooks and crannies here, old pieces of furniture, papers stuck inside a book cover, stuck behind picture frames and forgotten. Look, let me search this place. I'm a professional, and I won't charge you a dime—"

"No. Thank you, but now is not a good time for surprises. God knows what that detective is thinking. All kinds of connections between the two murders, and I don't want to pour more fuel on the fire, to give him more ideas."

"And you don't trust me to be discreet?"

"No, I don't," snapped Stephen. "You're obsessed."

"Stephen—"

"Just listen. Just hear me out," he was softer now, trying to persuade rather than command. "Try to see the big picture here. Try to take the long view. Aunt Agnes was very close to her grandfather. He would entrust them to her, perhaps for judicious editing and publishing at some later date. But after all this time—I think she wisely burned them all in that ballroom fireplace before it was shut up forever. Or she may have them in her suite, and I'm not going to search her personal items. I promise, I swear, that I will not throw out anything and will show you everything found. But after everything is done." He stuck out his hand, and Conor took it after a pause. "I don't want to fight with you. There are plans in place, and when I can tell you, I will. But I can make you a promise. If things come off as I have planned, you will be part of its future, and it will be a very bright future. But if you screw it up, there won't be anything for either of us."

"All right. But I still need to find out what happened to Fiona."

"She's been in our attic for over a century. She can wait a few more months."

Conor considered that. "You aren't the only one who knows people. What if I made things difficult here? Maybe if PH Hospitality got control, I could cut a deal with them."

There was a long pause as the two men just stared at each other.

"You know, Conor, that should really bother me. But as crazy as my aunt is, she is right when she says you love this house as much as any Greenleaf. You couldn't bear to see PH Hospitality chop it up. No more game playing, OK? Stay focused on the present, and I promise you won't regret it."

Conor looked like he was going to say something more, then stopped and just nodded, and they left together.

Chapter Sixteen

The Sedgwick Hotel had never been fancy, but it had a pleasant old-fashioned air about it, with lots of wood paneling and framed paintings of Hudson River landscapes that were handsome if you didn't look too closely. The staff was attentive to the group, and the members, who skewed to an older demographic, liked such standard fare as stuffed mushrooms and pigs in a blanket. In the lobby, a sign announced: "Meeting of the Gilded Age Society—The Roosevelt Room."

Best of all, they had a series of small rooms that had once been used, according to legend, for students at NYU. They made excellent changing rooms for tonight, the annual period costume evening.

Wren had brought a relatively simple late-Victorian day dress in a dark purple that she thought flattered her. *Susan Greenleaf might've worn something like this,* she realized. She gave herself a final look in the mirror. If her hair were longer, she could've done it up elaborately, like some of the other women did, but she had always found it annoying when working. The group was a fun escape, she reminded herself, and a chance to give back—but not her life.

She said hello to the fellow group members. Word had spread about her job at the Greenleaf Mansion, and so she found herself at the center of attention as fellow members congratulated her. They hung on her every word as she satisfied their curiosity about the marble in the ballroom and the ornate plaster ceiling in the dining room.

"Can you get us inside?" several members asked. She told them she'd speak to Stephen Greenleaf about a reception when the work was done later in the year, and their eyes glowed at the possibility. From their perspective, Wren had the enormous good fortune of actually spending her working day in the Gilded Age, or at least in a home from the era.

How funny I am, thought Wren. Here I am, "playing house." Others in the group did this occasionally, but in Greenleaf House, she did it daily. She knew better than most the dark side of the Gilded Age—was she being childish? Was her father right about the silliness of the group? Yes, the group did raise money for scholarships and sponsored an academic meeting each year. As a member of the group's education committee, she delivered volunteer guest lectures at CUNY's history classes and had her firm offer paid internships. But at the end of the day, was that just an excuse to slip occasionally into another time? She shook her head. It would bear thinking about.

Meanwhile, she found Lavinia, who probably had more outfits than anyone in the Group. Today, she took a military turn, resplendent in blue as an army officer.

"Dear Wren, that color is perfect for you, but if anyone is going to get color right, it would be you. How goes the house, and your mystery?"

"Making progress on both fronts."

"Good. Let's talk after the speaker." Tonight, it was a clothing historian on "Fabric in the 19th century."

More people joined them, and instead of the usual anxiety, Wren felt herself relax talking about the design, clothing, and manners of the Gilded Age, and as always, she found it so refreshing to share her insights into historic home design with people who actually cared.

The presentation was both witty and informative, and afterward the bar opened, and a buffet awaited them. Lavinia led Wren into a corner.

"I can't stop thinking about the Greenleaf mystery," she said. Wren gave her a quick update on the Greenleafs and Vanderwerfs.

"I just can't see how the death in the attic relates to Susan and Ambrose's affair."

"With people like the Greenleafs and the Vanderwerfs it's about position. At the end of the day, that was the single driving force behind their decisions—and actions," said Lavinia.

Erik Leopold, the medical examiner who had accompanied Sergeant Ortiz, slipped in beside them. He appeared today to be a prosperous merchant, with a long coat over a lavish waistcoat that was adorned with a heavy gold chain. "Everything is fake except the Phi Beta Kappa key," he always said.

"The architect and historian in close talk. I can guess what you two are discussing. Have you brought up my small part?"

"I didn't want to break a confidence," said Wren.

"No problem at all. Lavinia—by chance, I was the medical examiner on both the cases I'm sure the pair of you are discussing. I have a few insights, if you're interested."

"Hold nothing back—you're the expert," said Lavinia. A year ago, Erik had given a presentation on nineteenth-century medical practices that had met Lavinia's high standards for historical accuracy.

"Yes, please," said Wren.

"I'm sure Sergeant Ortiz wouldn't be pleased—but remember, we're talking about the attic body, which is not under his jurisdiction, and not the Lavendell murder, which is." *Wink-wink: Never mind that they were tied by the same firearm.* "It was a small caliber bullet, probably coming from a 'pocket pistol,' a small gun a gentleman might carry if he had reason to go to a bad neighborhood. It fits easily in a jacket pocket and can be lethal at close range. It might not go through a body, and although we can't be certain, it seems with our unnamed victim, the bullet was partially deflected by a rib."

"A gentleman's weapon," said Wren.

"Well, judging from the size of the bullet, it's unlikely it's a serious military handgun, which you wouldn't find just lying around in a house like that. That is, this seems to have been an inside job. I can't imagine some thug broke in, killed a maid, and then buried her in the attic," said Erik.

"Uncle Ambrose," said Lavinia. Erik raised an eyebrow.

"There were two gentlemen living in the house—brothers," explained Wren. "Benjamin, who was married and who built and owned the house, and his black sheep brother Ambrose, who lived there. We have hints it was him."

"But it doesn't sound like you believe that," said Erik.

"The party line seems to be that Ambrose was having an affair with her and when she proved difficult, he killed her. But I don't know...."

Erik laughed. "I'm a pathologist, not a psychiatrist. But maybe I have a few more things I could add. Now, I know nothing about architecture, but I imagine it's a very exacting job. However, when dealing with a century-old death, I can only deal with 'maybe' or 'probably.' With that in mind, I spent some of my own time on this case."

"Nineteenth-century bodies—that's a fun hobby," said Lavinia.

"Your job is your hobby," said Wren. "I guess we're the lucky ones. " She smiled. "How everyone here would envy us."

Erik considered that, and Lavinia nodded approvingly.

"My mother said I was born out of time," said Wren. She looked around at the room, at everyone in their period clothes, talking on period topics—back to a more orderly time, a slower time, a time Wren felt she understood.

"I suppose we are the lucky ones," said Erik, and he said it seriously. "So if you want to go back to that poor girl's death, I spent a lot of time looking at the nick on her rib, trying to figure out how that bullet hit her, and where she was. There's a little guesswork here. Maybe a lot of guesswork. But here are my two conclusions: first, that the injury to the rib is consistent with a shot from behind her. And second, whoever killed her was sitting."

"Really? How can you tell that?" asked Wren.

"The angle. Again, as best as I can tell from the bone wound. The bullet traveled up from the middle of her back. "

"Why?" asked Wren. "Why did someone shoot her in the back—she was walking away. I had wondered if someone shot her in a rage, but from behind, while sitting—so cold-blooded."

"Well, as I said, beyond my pay grade."

"Don't apologize," said Wren. "This is so much more than I ever could've expected. I need to figure out what happened in that house, and this moves me forward."

"Ah! But I have one more piece of information. Again, just for us, since this is technically not a police investigation." He posed like a conjurer, ready for the big reveal. "The young lady in the sea chest was a mother."

"Oh! I didn't think it was possible to tell from just a skeleton," said Wren. Lavinia looked surprised too, and she didn't surprise easily.

"When a baby passes through the birth canal, the pressure is so intense that tendons leave scars on the pelvic girdle."

"Yet another reason for me to be glad I missed out on that experience," said Lavinia dryly.

"Yes, that detail does put it in perspective," said Erik. "Anyway, the scarring is a one-time event. I can't tell if she had one child or a half dozen. But she definitely delivered at least one."

Wren did her best curtsey. "You are a genius, sir. Seriously, that gives us a lot to think about. Maids couldn't get married. A pregnancy meant immediate dismissal. So something was going on here, based on when she died."

"Your bailiwick. Glad I could be of help. I may write a piece for the Journal of Forensic Medicine. I'm going to refresh my drink—but, a final bit of advice. Just speaking in general terms, of course, since you're interested in forensics. When someone is shot, there is blood at the scene, in a fairly predictable pattern. If that is absent, it may indicate that the person was shot, and died, in a different place from where the body was found."

"Is that relevant more than a century later?" asked Wren.

Lavinia laughed. "Of course not. But your information is useful *if* we were talking about a modern murder."

"Just talking hypothetically," he said, with another wink. "Wren, good seeing you. Lavinia, a pleasure as always. See if you can convince your wife to come next time—I'm always the only sawbones here."

"So, who fathered her child?" asked Wren when they were alone. "If it was wicked Uncle Ambrose, why was she still there instead of being sent away? And where was Karen Lavendell killed? That's what I meant about being born in the wrong century. I think I have a better idea of that maid's death than Karen's."

"The past is never dead. It's not even past," said Lavinia, quoting Faulkner.

"That's certainly true here," said Wren, and she told Lavinia about the conversation she had overheard between Stephen and Conor. "I think that's what Miss Greenleaf likes about Conor. The obsession with the house. She once said Conor has a sense of history about the house, even though his family weren't owners."

"Yes, my dear, but think about what else that conversation means. Think about people, about the young Conor, a housekeeper's son, looking at this family. He wouldn't have seen it falling apart—little boys don't notice things like that. But he would've absorbed the fact that his mother's place was as a servant. Think of the resentment brewing."

"But he's made a success of himself now."

"Our childhoods never leave us, Wren. You should know that."

Of course, she did. It had been quite a balance between her affectionate mother telling her it had been all right, she would do better next time. And her perfectionist father telling her it should have been right the first time. And then, they were alone with each other. He struggled to give her some semblance of what her mother had. She struggled to realize he was only going to be partially successful. And here they were.

She wondered if her mother had still been alive, could she have helped her become as competent emotionally as she was technically. Perhaps not, but at least her mother would've helped her feel better about it.

Other people joined them, eager to hear more about Greenleaf House, and Wren didn't get a chance to talk more about the girl in the attic until they were driving uptown toward Lavinia's apartment.

"This is very nice of you—I could've just taken a cab."

"It's just a few minutes, and there's no traffic at this hour."

"Then let's use our time wisely. If you can reflect and drive simultaneously, I was wondering if you had something you can add to your comment that you had a better idea of that maid's death than Karen's."

Lavinia let Wren think that over without prompting her for an answer.

"That maid—let's say it was Fiona—had a circumscribed life, about what she did and how she lived day-by-day. Everyone did at that time, but especially servants. I can't know the whys and wheres and hows of Karen Lavendell, a twenty-first-century business executive, but I'm thinking about

Fiona and her employers. She's serving tea on a tray in front of someone, turns her back, and is shot."

"Whom is she serving tea to?" Lavinia asked.

"Just her killer, I guess. It could be more, if there was a conspiracy, but if the whole point was to keep a secret, it may have been just one person. Fiona would be standing. She wouldn't sit in front of her employers. Now, Fiona may have been hired for the nursery, and that was her room, but she'd be working elsewhere because there were no children yet. Why would she serve tea in that room, unless...." She paused. "Unless she wasn't serving tea. It was her room, but she was in bed with someone—with Ambrose, in her room, where it would be less likely they'd be discovered. Let's say they continued their affair even after she delivered their child. She was asking for more money, threatening to make a scene, and Ambrose didn't want another scandal. He had his gun in the nightstand. She got dressed, and as her back was to him, he shot her in the back."

"Reasonable," said Lavinia. "But you don't sound convinced."

"If it were her room, why would she be leaving? Unless she had to go to work, and he was going to lie in? Anyway, it wouldn't be that much of a scandal, that much of an expense. A pregnant maid simply wasn't that big a deal. Even if he lost his temper with her, I could see him hitting her, but coolly shooting her in the back?"

"It's not what a gentleman would do?" asked Lavinia.

"A gentleman would kill—but not like that," said Wren. "I thought maybe another servant killed her, but that would mean stealing the master's gun and getting the body upstairs with no one knowing."

"So it would seem that Fiona's circumscribed life makes it almost impossible she was shot?" There was a teasing tone. "What if he didn't want Susan, his real love, to find out he was also having an affair with a maid, that he had, in fact, fathered her child. Now he could see that as catastrophic."

"That's plausible," said Wren. "Did he really love Susan? Or were women just toys to him? Either way, there is some situation that she was in that makes sense—I need to know more about the family, and I will."

"If you don't mind a little help, you've got me curious, Wren. I'd like to dig deeper into the home's history. Not the architecture—that's your area. But these families had complex financial histories, and I'm wondering if that played a role. If nothing else, it'll be something for my book."

"Mind? That would be wonderful. But don't go to too much work on my account."

"Why are you still so self-effacing with me? Your father told me you called a client a pompous bourgeois vulgarian."

"It wasn't to his face."

"It should've been."

Wren felt a little twinge. "I can't believe my father complains to you about me." Then she wondered if she sounded whiny.

"Oh hell, Wren, he was proud of you." Wren pulled up in front of Lavinia's building.

"And just one more thing." She tried to sound casual. "I have a date tomorrow."

"Good for you," said Lavinia. "Where did you meet?"

"In the course of my research. Hadley Vanderwerf, a descendent of Susan Greenleaf's brother—she's the one we looked up. I'm not...I mean, that's not the only reason...."

Lavinia patted her hand. "Of course." She gave Wren a look. "But there's something else, isn't there?"

"Hadley told me the family—the Greenleaf-Vanderwerfs—weren't very nice, and I knew that, I mean, I knew that *intellectually*. I wrote a paper for you on social conditions in nineteenth-century New York. But *emotionally* I'm having a hard time resolving the man that built that house with such artistic sensitivity with the man who gathered so much wealth—and who may have murdered or at least covered up a murder. I know...that makes me sound very naïve."

"It means you see nuance. It means you see people are complicated. It means *you* are complicated."

Wren laughed. "And I have a feeling Hadley is complicated. She leads a different life, but of course, she is still one of them. She's the one who told me firmly that they aren't nice people, and yet...I think she's quite nice. At least, I'd like to think so."

"So you're trying to figure out the difference between the nice ones in that family and the not-so-nice ones?"

Wren thought that over again. "Maybe I should spend more time thinking about individuals and not lumping people together. Giving people the same attention as houses."

Lavinia smiled wryly. "You two kids have a good time and don't stay out too late." Wren laughed. "Thanks for the ride. And take it from a longtime researcher, just let your ideas marinate for a while, and eventually, they'll coalesce. "

"Personal or business?" said Wren.

"Both, my dear."

Wren watched Lavinia enter her building, her mind bouncing between Susan and her descendant, Hadley.

Chapter Seventeen

Susan, Benjamin, Ambrose, and Hadley ran around her mind until she fell asleep, but working in the house again soothed her. A little after 5:00, Bobby said he and his crew were calling it a day.

"See you tomorrow. I'll be staying a little later. I have a special guest coming." She fought to remain casual. "A descendent of the Vanderwerfs. Benjamin Greenleaf's wife Susan was a Vanderwerf. Time to get an impression from the women's side of the family."

"Good idea." He paused. "Maybe she knows something. Like I said, I'm getting along with Mrs. Ryan, but the pair of them are secretive about something—always looking over our shoulders, and then quietly talking to each other. Anyway, have a good evening."

As Bobby and his crew left, Mrs. Ryan watched them go, as was her custom. Before she left, Wren called up to her from the landing.

"I will be here a little longer. I have a historical specialist coming, with Mr. Greenleaf's permission. I'll get the door when she comes."

Again, the look that she wanted to ask a question, but stopped herself.

"Very good, Miss," she said.

Wren reviewed the guest bedrooms and made some notes about walls that would have to come down to join the smaller ones. Whether it was going to become a hotel or remain a private residence, people wanted big bedrooms now.

She heard the bell around 6:00, and it was Hadley, looking up at the façade and standing by a large wicker hamper.

"Wren! I'm so excited. I've wanted to see the inside for so long." She followed Wren's gaze to the hamper. "Oh, that's dinner, left over from a job and no need to waste it—it's a cold supper, because I figured the kitchen might be torn up. But it's super good, and I want to talk to you, and it'll be so much easier to talk here than in a noisy restaurant."

"Half the time I end up eating dinner in my bedroom with a plate balanced on my knee anyway," said Wren. She grabbed a handle, and the two women brought the hamper inside. Hadley looked around in wonder. "There are no original Vanderwerf residences left, so it's great to see this and think, this was my family's world once. Wow—I'd love to stage an event here. I wonder what Stephen Greenleaf is planning to do with this?"

"He hasn't even told me," said Wren. "If it were mine..." she broke off, but Hadley had cocked her head and was looking at her. "I would live it in myself."

"Cool. I heard Cousin Stephen made a mint on Wall Street. Maybe he wants to live here himself?"

"It's costing him a mint just to fix it up. And even maintaining it would be a stretch on anyone's wallet. But it's not about money. Not just...people just don't live like this anymore." Hadley considered that and nodded in agreement. "I'm not sure that Agnes Greenleaf, the house's last resident, realizes that, either."

"Aunt Agnes. Aunt Myrtle made her sound a little odd, but Aunt Myrtle was a little odd too."

"I told Stephen, but not Aunt Agnes, you were coming this evening. Would you like to meet her?"

"It's fun to surprise people," she said, clapping her hands in delight. "Do you think Stephen gave her a head's up?"

"I think Stephen tries as much as possible not to talk to his aunt. I can introduce you, then I'll give you a tour, and we can have dinner."

"Sounds super," said Hadley.

Hadley almost stumbled on the stairs, she was so involved in looking around the house, as Wren spoke about the significance of the banister and the plaster ceiling.

Wren knocked on the door, and Mrs. Ryan admitted them.

"Hello, I'm meeting with a distant cousin of Miss Greenleaf's, and I thought she might like to meet her." For a moment, Wren thought Mrs. Ryan might refuse them admission, but then opened the door further to let them in.

Miss Greenleaf was reading another weighty tome and looked up. As entrancing as those books were, she must've occasionally craved some variation in her routine.

"Miss Greenleaf? I came across a relation of yours and thought you might want to meet her. I was hoping she had some family story that would help me with the renovation." Looking eager, Hadley stepped forward. "Cousin Agnes, I'm Hadley Vanderwerf. As I calculated it, we're second cousins, twice removed."

Aunt Agnes just stared for a few moments, her lips pursed. Was she angry? Just upset?

"Yes. You're Brent's girl. I was at your christening. I was at your father's christening and his marriage." Seeing the guests were likely to stay for a while, Mrs. Ryan provided chairs, and they sat. "Your parents are well?"

"Yes, thank you."

"You take after your mother. I remember she was very beautiful. We all wondered how your father landed a woman like that."

"We've all wondered that," said Hadley cheerfully. Wren thought Aunt Agnes smiled at that. "You and I haven't met, unless you count my christening, but I feel I know you. I was close with my Aunt Myrtle, and in her later years, she enjoyed telling me stories. Susan Greenleaf was her great-aunt, and I heard lots of stories about this house in its glory days."

"Glory days," repeated Aunt Agnes. She seemed annoyed at that, as if she didn't like the reminder that the glory days were long gone, had disappeared before she was even born. "I knew your Aunt Myrtle well. We were very close when we were young, before she married and moved away. She liked telling stories even when she was young but had a tendency to exaggerate. I imagine it got worse as she got older. It always does."

"I couldn't say," said Hadley. "I only had her accounts. I heard that Susan was a lively girl."

"She was my grandmother," said Aunt Agnes. "She was a pretty girl when she was young." She paused. "Maybe I was wrong about you. There was a mischievous look about my grandmother, about the Vanderwerf girls generally, and I see that in you now."

"Thank you."

"That wasn't a compliment."

That didn't faze Hadley at all. "That was *wonderful*. Wait'll I tell Mom and Dad." Hadley's failure to be cowed did not please Aunt Agnes. "Aunt Myrtle said that Susan was having a fling with Uncle Ambrose, her brother-in-law. You don't think of people doing that back then, but I guess they did."

Again, Wren watched Aunt Agnes' fingers grip the chair as Mrs. Ryan tensed up.

"We do not discuss Ambrose Greenleaf in this house. That has been a longstanding rule. As a Vanderwerf especially, you need to know that."

"Because of what he did with Susan Greenleaf?" Hadley wrinkled her nose. "That was more than a century ago."

"Cousin Hadley. Susan was a Greenleaf by marriage only. She was a Vanderwerf by birth, and her behavior was—I am sorry to have to say—less than ideal. But she was chaste. My grandmother liked telling stories, and Aunt Myrtle liked hearing them—and exaggerating them over the years."

"What was she like, then, my great-great-great Aunt Susan?"

That seemed to take Aunt Agnes aback, and she just stared for a moment. "My grandmother knew the importance of this house. I will tell you that much."

"So, no romance with Uncle Ambrose?" She sounded disappointed.

"For reasons I will not discuss, especially with a Vanderwerf, I will tell you—again—we do not discuss Ambrose Greenleaf. I'm tired, and you must excuse me. Please give my regards to your parents." She seemed to shrink into her chair and turned away from them. Mrs. Ryan briskly ushered them out and firmly closed the door behind them.

"I'm so sorry," said Wren.

"For what? That was so much fun. And this is from someone who works with rock musicians. What's all that about Ambrose? I mean, I thought the whole thing was that he was hot and heavy with Susan. Was she lying? Or was Aunt Myrtle?"

"Let me give you a tour," said Wren. "There is something I want to show you."

Hadley linked her arm with Wren's. "The evening is shaping up well."

Wren first took Hadley to the portrait hallway. "Here is the famous Susan with her husband, Benjamin."

"Ooh, that's better than the one we have. She was so beautiful. And I see what Aunt Agnes says about an impudent look. At least, that's what my grandmother said. Do you think I have that, Wren? I'd like to think so." Fortunately, she didn't seem to expect an answer. "Do we have a portrait of the mysterious Ambrose? I don't think I've ever seen what he looked like."

"They hide it," said Wren and showed her into the little room.

"Oh! So here's Susan's lover—if that was the case. More handsome than his brother and look at that smirk—I bet he was a bad boy, even if he didn't seduce his brother's wife." She stared for a long while.

Wren next took Hadley through the ballroom, dining room, library, going over the details on the chair railings, lighting fixtures, floors, and doors. It took a while for her to realize how boring she was being.

"I'm sorry," she said.

"You keep apologizing for no reason."

"No one cares, except maybe other architects, and even then. You're being polite."

"I'm polite. You're passionate. I like passionate people. I embarrassed you—I'm sorry."

"Now, you're apologizing," said Wren. Hadley laughed. Wren showed her into the twin master rooms. "This was Susan's boudoir."

"I feel like I've been here. From the stories of Aunt Myrtle—if they were even true."

"That's what I want you to see. Have a look at the hardware on the doors. What are they lacking?" Hadley looked and frowned. "A lock. The story was that Susan kept the key around her neck—isn't that what Aunt Myrtle told you? But there are no locks on this door."

"I see. But couldn't they have changed it later?"

"That would be almost impossible. Look how perfectly the hardware fits into the door, a custom job in a walnut door. I bet this hardware was custom too. Every bit of this is original."

"I'm so disappointed. I found that story so exciting. Do you think Myrtle lied to me, or Susan lied to Myrtle?"

"I didn't know Susan or Myrtle, so I couldn't say," said Wren. "But who am I kidding? I wouldn't have known anyway. I don't read people very well." She gave a self-deprecating chuckle and looked at Hadley, curious about her reaction. Nervous about her reaction.

"I don't know if you are as bad as you think you are, but if it isn't your strong suit, I will remember that and be more explicit," she said with great seriousness.

"Thank you," said Wren, not being able to think of a better response. "Anyway, I knew Agnes Greenleaf was very touchy about Ambrose, but that was odd about Susan. Why so defensive about her? As she pointed out, she was really a Vanderwerf, only a Greenleaf by marriage."

"As I said, I have some more family gossip. Let's have some dinner, and I'll share it with you. Where should we serve it? It seems ridiculous to have it in a dining room that could serve 50."

"How about an indoor picnic?" said Wren. "They have a conservatory here I haven't shown you yet, and there's a table and chairs there."

"Super," said Hadley.

They carried the hamper into the room, and Hadley grinned. "This is fantastic. Once it's together, it'll be a great party place."

Wren marveled at Hadley's perfect packing: strapped-in plates, silverware, and glass tumblers. She also produced a cut-up chicken, sesame noodles, and a green salad, all efficiently stored in plastic containers.

"I know," said Hadley. "I've gotten good at this."

"You have. I saw from your office that you seem to handle a lot of musicians."

Hadley sighed. "Yeah. It seemed so cool, getting to go backstage and feel like one of the insiders. But all they want are hamburgers and ribs and beer, and it's hard to get them to pay. I may give up la dolce vita and concentrate on my parents' elderly friends. They have money and appreciate good food." She covered the table with a cheerful checked cloth. "And my homemade lemonade. Don't even ask. It's my secret recipe. Tell me what you think of it all."

Wren suddenly realized she had forgotten lunch during the busy day and was starving. But the food was well worth waiting for.

"My God," she said. "This is divine." The chicken was moist, with some subtle seasonings, and the noodles were spicy without being overwhelming.

"Like the food served here in the glory days?" asked Hadley.

"I doubt they ever had food like this," said Wren. "Your company employs a great chef."

"That would be me," said Hadley, looking uncharacteristically shy. "I've always liked cooking but didn't want to spend my nights in a hot kitchen with men trying to grab me. So I started my own business. I have employees—but I'm the chef. The recipes are mine."

"I live with my father, and both of us are pretty useless in the kitchen. Order out, restaurants, and a housekeeper who cooks occasionally. Could you move in with us?"

Hadley lowered her eyes coyly. "Gee, Wren, I like you and all—but it's just our first date."

"I'm sorry—I was just saying—"

"No, I'm sorry," said Hadley, laughing. "I was teasing. I know what you meant, and that was just messing with you. But I do like you."

"I like you too," said Wren quietly. "But this really is perfect. All that's missing is crisp white wine."

"Oh," said Hadley. She suddenly looked downcast.

"I'm being rude," said Wren. She had just insulted Hadley and wished she could handle people as well as houses. Once again, she kept saying the wrong thing. "I was just joking. I don't drink much anyway."

"No, it's not that. I wanted to wait...but what the hell. I can't drink, you see. I can't because I used to drink a lot. I barely got through college—just held it together enough to get through school. But then things really went off the deep end—and I was out of it for a while. I was way out of it. Anyway,

I haven't had a drink in four years, three months, three weeks, and two days. I was going to wait longer to tell you...but I like to think I know people. I've been a bit of a mess, but I'm okay now. I think that you will be okay with that—okay?"

Wren looked at her for a few moments. "You look unsure of yourself. You struck me as someone who isn't usually unsure of herself."

"That's nice of you to say, Wren. But I am unsure now. If you don't want..." she let the words trail off.

"Thank you for telling me. Believe me, I am unsure of myself a lot."

"Really? You're taking on the job of bringing this mansion into the twenty-first century, and you're not sure of yourself."

"I'm sure of my skills in my job. But I don't work with people very well. I often don't read them or say the right things."

"Oh, but I'm good with people," said Hadley. She laughed again. "It's everything else that's a problem."

"I'm sure that's not true," said Wren, and it came out more solemnly than she expected.

"Thank you," Hadley said. "So...this isn't going to be a problem?"

"No...of course not. But I feel bad now. I think I did something wrong. I told you I wasn't good with people, and now I think I made a mistake. You are being honest with me, and I wasn't completely honest with you."

"Oh...you're seeing someone else? Did I come on too strong? I do that—it goes with my job."

"Oh no. Something different. I'm afraid that I first looked you up because I had an ulterior motive. And it has to do with your family. I mean, your family a long time ago." It wasn't fair to hide this from Hadley, never mind if Ortiz wanted it kept quiet. "And so I have to tell you a secret. The full reason I visited you in your office. As we started work here, my contractor, Bobby, and I broke into a sealed attic in this house. Inside we found an old sea chest. And inside it was a skeleton."

"My God..."

"It was of a young woman, shot to death. We believe she was one of Benjamin and Susan's servants, a maid named Fiona Murphy. And it's

129

connected to another murder…." She told Hadley what she knew about Fiona and Karen Lavendell—two women killed a century apart by the same gun. "It's your family too. And you're being so helpful. I couldn't not tell you. But you might not want to let the Greenleafs know that you know, even if they are your cousins."

"Wow. Just…wow. I knew our families were screwed up…but wow. You think the body is this Fiona Murphy?"

"Perhaps. Maybe Ambrose was having an affair with her but killed her when she became demanding. Still, I don't like that. And why is Karen dead—with the same gun?"

"No," said Hadley, shaking her head. "I'm sure Ambrose was a rogue—that's a word my grandmother would use. But he wasn't a cold-blooded murderer. Although I'd like to think that, while he would have killed a man in a duel as a matter of honor, he wouldn't have shot a woman in the back. But maybe I'm just being a romantic."

"I think you're being practical. The fact is, at that time, for a man to seduce or even rape a servant girl was no big deal. Even if she got pregnant, she could be bought off and sent away. There was no legitimate reason to kill Fiona…unless he really was having an affair with Susan and didn't want it to look like he was cheating on her with a maid."

Hadley poured herself some lemonade. "I have some stories for you. And after what you just told me, they may make a lot more sense."

Chapter Eighteen

"So I made some notes about what I remembered from Aunt Myrtle. She had two sons, but they had little appetite for family gossip and didn't have anything to add. It's a woman thing, I think, so after I wrung my father dry, I went to his sister, my Aunt Emma, and she knew Aunt Myrtle even longer than I did, of course, and remembers a time when the family was more tightly knit. When they could still bully the family girls into going to debutante balls." She pulled an iPad from her bag.

"Okay—according to family lore, Susan was beautiful and lively. But reading between the lines, there was something a little...off about her. A little Scarlett O'Hara, you know?"

"Vague scandals?" asked Wren.

"Yes...well, gossip anyway. Apparently, before her marriage, there was a scene at a ball. What's a dance card? I felt I should know."

"Women would write down the names of the young men they were going to dance with."

"Really? Wow. That must've been something. Anyway, there was some fuss about who was supposed to dance with who, and Susan felt that another debutante was taking away someone she was supposed to dance with, and it got pretty ugly. Or whatever passed for ugly in that set."

"It's more your world than mine," ventured Wren. "But don't people in clubs and so forth get angry when someone is paying too much attention to someone else."

Hadley thought about that for a moment. "You're right, Wren. I've seen it happen. Especially when they're coked up."

"So nothing changes?" asked Wren.

"I don't know. I don't think Aunt Susan ever spent the night in a drunk tank. But the principle is the same. And she also caused jealousy. She was caught with a married man."

"Caught? As in, in bed with him?"

"You know, that wasn't clear. But I don't think it went that far—what did Aunt Agnes say—she was 'chaste.' Another old-fashioned word. The bar for bad behavior wasn't very high at the turn of the century. I think it was just sitting in some room like this at another party, with a married man old enough to be her father and showing some ankle. Apparently, even showing an ankle was a big deal back then. That's how it came down to me—the so-lovely Susan, a quick and gentle touch on a gentleman's arm, and he was so flattered this young woman was hanging on his every word, and then smirking when his irritated wife tracked him down." Hadley was smirking herself. "Anyway, the family pushed her to marry Benjamin. He was wealthy, and very steady. Word has it he was a good businessman, rather dull. Rein her in and make her behave."

"I don't know about dull," said Wren, looking around their room. "Maybe straitlaced, but not dull. I think this house was his dream. Rich men have always used their money to build houses that were an extension of themselves. I've seen it again and again. If it's just money, you get nothing but vulgarity." She looked at Hadley. "Money can't buy you taste. This is Benjamin's house. But after houses like this were built, it was the women who ran it. The houses affected them, but a strong woman could also stamp their personalities on the home, and I'm wondering if Susan did too. I'm guessing she did."

"Funny you should say that. I think it was Susan's too. Benjamin built it, as you said, but Susan furnished it. My Aunt Emma said it was a joke among the Vanderwerfs about how Susan could spend. She chose the furniture, even hired cabinetmakers for custom pieces, imported carpets from Persia, attended auctions for the paintings." She wrinkled her nose. "But do architects care about those things?"

"We do. They're important. They're the clothes of a house. Some architects also doubled as interior decorators. Some still do. I'm glad to hear that about Susan. That makes me like her—that she cared what the house looked like. It was her house too."

"My father showed me an old clipping, 'Mrs. Greenleaf Shows Off Her Mansion,' all about the young bride having a party, with all the best people, of course. It was all about her, well, showing off. So he built it, but she dressed it, like you say. She was the one who did the party thing. That's something I know about—in every couple, there's one who likes a party, and one who just goes along. So maybe, Benjamin wasn't really dull, then, he just didn't deal well with people and was better with houses," said Hadley. She fixed Wren with a look. "Kinda like you."

"So I'll be Benjamin to your Susan?" Wren smiled.

"That's insulting. To both of us." She gave Wren's hand a quick squeeze.

"I got the sense that Aunt Agnes was close with her grandfather Benjamin. She spoke of him with affection," said Wren.

"She could have known him well; he died in 1947."

"Really? That's when Aunt Agnes made her debut. It was apparently the last event they ever had in this ballroom. Ambrose had died a year or two before, still in Buenos Aires, but I didn't check on Benjamin." It took them only a few minutes to find Benjamin's obituary, fairly substantial as a leading member of a leading family. Wren scooted around and looked over Hadley's shoulder.

"Okay—an endless list of the clubs he belonged to, the committees he chaired," said Hadley while scrolling. "Here we go: 'He died at home after a long illness, just a week after the debut of his granddaughter, Agnes Greenleaf, at the family home.' I guess he hung on to see her make her debut. Maybe knowing those days were gone."

"That's interesting. Aunt Agnes told me about her debut but didn't mention her grandfather was dying. Did she just forget, or was she trying to hide that?"

"I don't think you'd forget that—in the same house. Another oddness. And I also got a few tidbits on Ambrose. I'm still disappointed if they didn't have a fling. I mean, it's so great to have such a scandal in one's family background. But now you showed me that the doors didn't lock—and we have only Aunt Myrtle's word. I mean, the other Susan stories come from a variety of places, but the affair—that was an Aunt Myrtle exclusive. But I got a bit on Ambrose, too. His reputation had spread.'

"He really was a bad boy?"

"For sure. And if what I heard is true, which it may not be, Susan must've known. Maybe she did have an affair with him—we don't know. But she couldn't have been that ignorant. Apparently, he didn't discriminate. Women in his class, other men's wives, actresses, servants—"

"Like Fiona," said Wren.

"Could be. No one had any names. Or no one wants to admit it. The families are still around, and people are still touchy. And no one would care about who did what with a servant. Anyway, regardless of who he did or did not sleep with, it was becoming increasingly embarrassing having him in New York, and as my Aunt Emma said, you had to be very bad to the point where they couldn't cover it up anymore, so they sent him to Buenos Aires, far away. And it was a real lively town then, my father said. And Aunt Emma said everyone knew he went through his money on 'riotous living.' That's how they put it. Had relatively little left when he died."

"But what he had, he left to his niece, Laura, who was married and living in London. I doubted she needed the small amount of money he left. How odd. What was he really like, I wonder? His character is just one of so many things we don't know about the family. The two murders must be connected beyond the murder weapon. The old one may be ancient history, but I don't want the new one to shut down my work here. So there we are."

"There we are," repeated Hadley. "I hope you find out what happened. I'll help as much as I can."

"Because you want to find out about your family? I was hoping you could tell me something. I am trying to make sense of Aunt Agnes and Mrs. Ryan. There is something odd there. I mean, we have a housekeeper. She cleans and shops and cooks us some dinners, and we like her. But we're not involved in each others' lives, and she has her own place. It's not like with that pair. There's something else going on with them. Is this an old money thing?"

Hadley laughed. "Come on, Wren, you know what it was like back then, we were completely dependent on our servants, and they were completely dependent on us."

"Yes—at the turn of the century. But we're not at the turn of the century. This was not their world. It's like they're living their ancestors' lives."

"It's about family. It's about tradition, which families hang onto when the reasons are long gone. Aunt Agnes wants to pretend the Greenleafs are still important. How many options do you think Mrs. Ryan had? It's better to tell herself she's a loyal family retainer, not an aging widow with no skills hanging on until the old lady dies. Look at me, Wren, and see where I come from. The world has moved on, but not everyone can move with it. Aunt Agnes wasn't forced to move on, and so she hasn't. It's so much easier for some people to live in a past they understood than face a present that they don't. I don't know Stephen at all, but I bet some part of him still sees this house as essential to who he is. His name is still Greenleaf. "

Wren just stared at her for a moment.

"I was way over the top, wasn't I?" asked Hadley. "Christ, I'm really sorry."

"No, that's not it at all. I just never thought…you're right, of course. I didn't think about that. Thank you."

"I don't understand people, but I understand this house," Wren continued. "Aunt Agnes and Mrs. Ryan may have a folie à deux, but they wouldn't without this house."

"You're saying it's haunted?" asked Hadley with a grin.

"I'm saying their pretense couldn't hold up anywhere else. If Stephen Greenleaf packed the pair of them off to a nice modern garden apartment in Scarsdale where the condo board restricts the colors you can paint your front door, they couldn't keep this up. At some level, they know that. "

"I think you're right, Little Bird."

"I'm not really a little bird," said Wren.

"I'm sorry—I give people nicknames, but if you don't want—"

"No, it's not that. My name actually comes from Sir Christopher Wren, a famous English architect, who lived about 300 years ago, and who my father admires."

135

"Wow," said Hadley. "So your family is odd too. But it's okay. I have a cousin, Frances. We call her 'Frankie' and I don't much like that nickname, so just as well you weren't named for Frank Lloyd Wright."

Wren laughed. "I never looked at it that way."

"I won't call you 'Little Bird,' again," said Hadley.

"It's OK...if it's just the two of us."

"I think we're getting on okay," said Hadley.

"Yes, I think so."

"How about if I kiss you?"

Wren blinked. "Why did you ask?"

"Because you strike me as someone who isn't big on spontaneity."

"That's not entirely fair," said Wren, feeling a little nettled. "I can be spontaneous. At times."

"We're having a five-minute discussion on whether we can kiss."

And Wren leaned over and kissed her.

Chapter Nineteen

"You're cheerful this morning, Wren," said Bobby.

"Every day we don't find another body in this house is a cause for rejoicing," said Wren. "Also, I sent an email to Stephen late yesterday suggesting we don't knock two of those guest bedrooms together but leave them as two rooms, just adding a connecting door. It spoils the proportions."

"I bet he liked that!" said Bobby. "How do you explain 'proportions'?"

"I didn't need to; I just told him it would save money. All we need to do is add a concrete lintel."

"Sounds good."

"Also, I asked if Stephen would like to come by for a look. It gives me an excuse to talk with him. I need to get a sense of what's happening, after Heppenstall and all that. I want to see what the angle is on PH Hospitality, so we can look out for our interests."

"Yeah, I don't want to work for that bunch. And Stephen can look over our work—he's the client. It's his privilege." Then he grinned. "But my music."

Wren had a productive morning. She thought again of what she had told Hadley, that Greenleaf House was haunted. Of course, it was—how could it not be? The spirits of the seductive and possibly unbalanced Susan, her bright but clueless husband, and his amoral brother Ambrose. Susan Vanderwerf, ancestress of her equally seductive niece, Hadley, in the same room Susan had reportedly first made love with Ambrose...

Thinking about the previous night's dinner, she was absently eating a tuna sandwich when Stephen Greenleaf showed up. He looked a little harried.

Wren wondered if it was the stress of his usual job or the twin murders hanging over him. Over the house.

"Wren—good to see you. Glad to see you're progressing well. You want to give me a quick tour?"

"I'll grab Bobby and show you what we've done and go over the next steps. No unpleasant surprises—"

"You mean no *additional* unpleasant surprises," he said with a grimace. Wren could've kicked herself, but quickly rallied.

"I'm an architect. We've had no unpleasant surprises in the structure of this house, and that is what Bobby and I are concerned with."

They picked up Bobby in the kitchen and discussed that room and then went over a few other rooms where significant work was happening. He said little, asked few questions, but listened and watched closely.

"Good, good," he said. "I asked you to renovate and restore, and that's what you're doing. And I agree about just adding a door to those rooms we discussed. I hadn't realized what you had said about proportions, but seeing them, I know what you mean."

"Your great-grandfather knew. I know he hired a distinguished architect to design this house, but Benjamin Greenleaf knew what he wanted, or at the very least had the wit to listen to his architects. He must've been remarkable."

"Aunt Agnes thought so," he said. "Anyway, very nice. You want a few words with me, Wren? Because I have a few things to discuss with you."

Bobby gave a quick salute and left to rejoin his crew, and Wren and Stephen headed back down to the Rose Parlor. He closed the door behind him, and they took their seats.

"So—Hadley Vanderwerf. I figured it out—3rd cousin once removed. Was she useful? Because she upset Aunt Agnes to the point where she called me. You have to know how rare that is." Wren was going to apologize—but Stephen seemed amused, not upset, so she held her tongue.

"She had stories about the house. If your Aunt Agnes was close with her grandfather, Aunt Myrtle was close with your great-grandmother Susan. The more I know about the house, the more I can make it look like the day

Benjamin and Susan walked in after their honeymoon."

He nodded at that. "Really? OK then. That is the goal, after all."

Wren took a deep breath. *Remember, you're the boss. You're in charge.* "The thing is, I was wondering if you had any stories? I've heard from Miss Greenleaf, from a collection of Vanderwerfs, but not from you."

"Yes. A fair question. My father knew our days in this house were numbered. He was forward-looking. He knew I wouldn't want to live here, shouldn't even think about it. He didn't talk about family history. He was raised to manage family concerns that had been sold or merged, leaving nothing to build on, just a portfolio of stocks that could no longer keep up this house. He knew that. He regretted it. But not Aunt Agnes, who just refused to accept it."

"But she didn't talk to you about the family history?"

"My father discouraged her. And seeing that I didn't care, she wasn't going to trust me with her memories. Neither of them told me the Uncle Ambrose story. I always thought it would come down to me eventually, but my father died suddenly, and Aunt Agnes is too angry with me to share anything. She still hopes my wife and I will move here, take 'my rightful place.' Maybe if I did that, she'd give me the full story. But I'll tell you this. My father and Agnes were much closer to their grandfather Benjamin than to their grandmother Susan. I never knew her, of course, but she could be—the word they always used was *mercurial*. She was a Vanderwerf in spirit, and we were Greenleafs. Susan, her great-niece Myrtle—they were a little livelier. Hadley's grandmother had been a Broadway dancer. You can imagine the fuss Aunt Agnes made about that." He raised an eyebrow. "What is Hadley like? I'm not sure I've seen her since I was dragged to her christening."

Wren smiled. "I'm thinking that she's a Vanderwerf."

"Of course."

"Can I ask—what do you really think Uncle Ambrose did? If you don't want to tell me, I'll understand. But there was a body in the attic."

"Wren, I don't care about a century-old family scandal. Hell, it might even be fun after all these years, and I'd be open to discussing anything that would let us give that poor girl a name to be buried under. All I got was one cryptic comment from Aunt Agnes. I came home from college for Thanksgiving with a girl I was seeing at the time who lived too far away to go home. Well, my Victorian aunt said, 'I hope you two aren't getting married so young. A hasty marriage can be a disaster. Just think about Uncle Ambrose.'"

"How awful! How did your girlfriend react?"

"She was an English major who liked Edith Wharton, so found the whole thing amusing. But I was so embarrassed, I didn't really think about it until much later, and she wouldn't talk about it."

"But Uncle Ambrose never married, right?"

"Wren, you now know as much as I do."

Do I? she thought. Perhaps about the history of the house. But not what was happening today, battling with PH Hospitality over the future of the house. She steeled herself. Her father kept reminding her she was a partner, and she had to do a partner's work. It was time to prove herself. She went over the script she had rehearsed in her mind.

"Stephen. I know that you aren't ready to reveal the ultimate plans for this house, and I respect that. But you do understand that the more I know, the better we can adapt this house for the future." She forced her voice to be steady and hoped Stephen could not see her beating heart.

He didn't answer right away and looked at her speculatively.

"I've told you what I could. If there are any shortcomings between your work and any future plans for this house, I will, of course, not hold you responsible."

"Our plans are to give you what you want. We took this job because we felt the firm's needs and your needs aligned."

He raised an eyebrow at that. She wondered if she had gone too far. Her father would be handling this better.

"Really? I thought it was because I was paying you a lot of money."

She shook her head. "It's not about money. We have plenty of people wanting to pay us lots of money. We took the job because it was a challenge worthy of us. But it won't be if we're stuck working with PH Hospitality. There isn't enough money in the world for that."

"That…is quite a little speech," said Stephen, but he looked more amused than angry. "Working with you is quite an education. All I can tell you now is to trust me, as you have asked me to trust you. The situation with Karen Lavendell threw me a curve, I'll admit that, but as long as we stay focused, this will work out."

She didn't think she could push further, although it was on the tip of her tongue to ask why he wasn't giving Sgt. Ortiz an alibi.

Then the front doorbell rang, and Wren stood to get it. "I think Bobby was expecting a delivery today, and he may not have heard it."

"Let Mrs. Ryan get it. We pay her enough. Listen, I appreciate your position. There are some things I can't explain, but I've been running an asset management firm for years without a single complaint—you can look it up. I'm on the level—Ha! Now that's a good metaphor for an architect. Seriously, Wren, I am trusting you with my childhood home. It was my father's home, my grandfather's home, my great-grandfather's home. I know you will not do anything to abuse that trust. And I want you to know I won't do anything to impede you. There may be business secrets I can't share with you. But they're just business secrets. Nothing to do with the house. I am trusting you. I expect you to trust me."

"Thank you," said Wren softly. "I know we want the same thing—to keep this job running as smoothly as possible."

"Then we're in full agreement. Just one more thing I should have mentioned earlier. Benjamin kept meticulous daily diaries. He filled one volume after another. At some point, they all disappeared. I'm wondering if they're gone forever—he may have arranged for their destruction. But if you find anything stuck away somewhere, call me right away."

Ah. The conversation he had with Conor! "We'll keep an eye open. In other jobs, we've found odd things stuck behind furniture, underneath mattresses. But we'll eventually be working over every square foot of this house, so nothing will get past us," said Wren. "I've seen how people can become attached to histories, especially family histories, and put things down on paper and save them, even when it would've been more prudent to keep some things quiet."

"Really? Why?"

"An obsession with their place in the world. A justification for what they did—to the world at large. To themselves."

"'Place in the world.' Well, that's the Greenleaf family. Anyway, Thanks for your reassurance. I have a friend in publishing who thought there might be some opportunities."

"We're very careful about anything we find during our work, of course."

"I'm sure," he said. "And I wouldn't want to needlessly disturb my aunt. Again, just come straight to me." *Not to Aunt Agnes. And not to Conor.* He stood. "Thank you so much. I can't tell you how pleased I am with the progress you've made."

They heard a knock, and Mrs. Ryan opened the door. "Mr. Greenleaf. The police for you." Her expression was half irritation, half satisfaction at Stephen's obvious discomfort. Sergeant Ortiz entered.

"They told me at your office you were here, and I thought I needed to speak with you, so why miss a chance to see you again in your lovely home." He took a seat, and Mrs. Ryan left—a little reluctantly, Wren thought—closing the door behind her.

He turned to Wren. "I may want to talk with you later, but for now, I need to speak with Mr. Greenleaf alone." Wren started to get up.

"I don't mind if Wren stays. I have no secrets in this matter."

"That does you credit," said Ortiz. "Nevertheless, this needs to be tete-a-tete. Not a police phrase, but so appropriate for this house." Stephen didn't reward him with a smile. "Will you be around, Ms. Fontaine? I'll want to speak with you afterward."

"I'll be in the house," she said and left, closing the door behind her.

* * *

Ortiz found her half an hour later on the floor of the dining room.

"What are you looking at?" asked Ortiz.

"The floor. Dining room floors are important—the room gets heavy use and needs cleaning. They used hickory here, which was both difficult to obtain and very expensive. It's exceptionally hard and resilient, but there's been a lack of care, so we're ripping it up, adding new planks, but first leveling it to make it even."

"Will it continue to get heavy use?"

"It depends on what Mr. Greenleaf plans to do with it. You can see how many people can fit here. It's for large dinner parties, and it's not even as large as the ballroom."

"Maybe it'll be a restaurant?" said Ortiz.

"I don't know. But I can tell you as an architect that it wouldn't be easy. This house, with its kitchen, was well set up for huge dinner parties. But delivering the same course to 50 people at once is very different from serving different foods at different times."

She looked closely at the sergeant. He wasn't humoring her or teasing her. He was genuinely interested and listening closely.

"You understand these things, this house and the people who lived here, don't you?"

"I know something about them. But I don't think we can really understand what it was like, to have a small army of servants catering to your every whim. There was only one social pyramid in the city, and the Greenleafs were at the top. Even today's rich don't live like this. We say it's a different world, but that's not just an expression. It was not the world we live in."

He nodded.

"I'm sorry. I'm passionate about these homes and their times. I become a lecturer."

"Don't apologize. I asked, and you gave me a very helpful answer. But of course, my main interest is the current murder. What about today? What are they like today?"

Wren got off the floor and took a seat at the table. Ortiz sat at the head, and she sat to his right.

"I told you, I don't know Stephen socially. Just as a client."

"You seem to know the house well. Even intimately, one might say? But not the owners. Interesting."

Wren couldn't place what he was after. Police detectives in movies were usually after one piece of knowledge and tried to sweat it out, bully it out, of a witness or suspect. But Ortiz seemed almost aimless to her. She could talk to him about the house all day, but about the people—she was on shaky ground.

"I was going to arrest Stephen Greenleaf. But that name still carries enough weight in this town that I was told by the brass that I couldn't arrest him without more evidence. Does that surprise you?"

Wren mulled over that. "Even faded, the Greenleaf name is still worth something, in certain corners. It's an old city, sergeant, and it has old memories."

"A fair observation. It's interesting how the house's history, the family's history, is wrapped so tightly with its present. No one was arrested for killing that poor woman in the attic, and now I can't arrest anyone for killing Lavendell. You know, Mr. Greenleaf got quite annoyed when I told him that I suspected him, even though he still won't give me an alibi. He told me in his world, people settled problems with money, negotiations, and if worse came to worse, with lawyers—not murder. But over a century ago, someone in his family decided that even with all the money and influence in the world, a bullet was the only solution." He stood. "Thank you for your time, Ms. Fontaine."

Chapter Twenty

"It's a woman," said Lavinia. She and Wren were sitting in Lavinia's apartment, sharing Chinese food.

"I have a journal paper to write, so I'll leave you to it," said Angela. "Wren, keep an eye on Lavinia's sodium intake."

"Why is that my job?" asked Wren.

"You were sole witness at our wedding—that made us your responsibility."

"Just ignore her," said Lavinia. "I only do Chinese once a month, and my God, this pork is good. Dear girl, you are very nimble with those chopsticks."

"My father insisted. He said no one could be trusted to build a house if they couldn't manage chopsticks."

"Your father is a wise man. A pain in the ass, but a wise man."

"You sound like my mother," said Wren. "But you were saying 'a woman.' Do you mean Stephen is having an affair? That's why he doesn't want to give out a name?"

"I've been poring over these great families for years. Over the decades, the centuries, not much has changed. The way men in these families operate. I'm guessing that Stephen Greenleaf is having an affair. That's why he doesn't want to reveal her name."

"So he'd rather get arrested for murder than admit to an affair?" asked Wren. "He's counting on the police arresting the real killer before the situation becomes desperate and he has to reveal her name to save himself?"

"And meanwhile, he's still protected by his highly placed friends," said Lavinia. "The Greenleafs certainly aren't who they were. But their name still carries some weight in this town."

145

"I wouldn't have thought it of Stephen," said Wren.

"Your naivete is still very sweet. But these things happen."

"I'm sure. But...OK, I'm not married. I could see this destroying a marriage, however. I don't want to be working on this house while the Greenleafs squabble over marital assets. Or while Stephen is on trial."

"So...you think he may have actually killed her?" The professor raised an eyebrow. *She's challenging me.*

Wren paused to find her words. "No. I'm just thinking out loud. But deep down, I don't think Stephen committed murder. And yes, I know I'm often naïve, but I don't think he's having an affair."

"Indeed, Ms. Fontaine. Do explain." And Wren was suddenly back in her classroom, on the spot.

"Stephen has always been honest. He may be hiding things from me, but I think he's honest about what he's said. We spoke about the house, and I think...I think I was wrong. I first thought it was all about money. But I think he may really love his childhood home after all."

"What changed your mind?"

"He has a bond with this house. I can see it, no, I can hear it, when he talks to me about it, when he listens to what I say. Yes, he complains about the cost, but he agrees. He cares. He's truly his great-grandfather's descendent."

Wren felt a little embarrassed at her speech. Had she sounded silly? Lavinia rolled a mu-shu pork pancake with absolute perfection.

"Ms. Fontaine," she said, heavily, like her father. "That's really very arrogant of you to think you know that." She grinned. "I'm so pleased. Now let's think a little more about Stephen. If he wasn't hiding an affair—and I'll trust your instincts here—why isn't he open about what he was doing? You say it's all connected to the history of the Greenleafs."

"Yes. I have to remind him that even if he seems he's looking forward, Stephen is still a Greenleaf—his ties go back to the nineteenth century, whether he admits it or not. Now, he has no doubt turned to private sources of funding for the restoration—silent partners. The Lavendell murder could lead to a scandal. Stephen's partners might then pull out and leave him with no choice but to sell to PH Partners."

"So maybe he was meeting with one or more partners the night Lavendell was killed and wants to keep their name out of it, even if it's necessary to give him an alibi?"

"Perhaps. There may be more to it than that. I may be naïve, but I also know something of history. The Greenleafs made some business dealings that were a little shady. Maybe Stephen is keeping his sources private for reasons other than embarrassment. We do have to ask what's in it for this private party?"

"You're right, my dear. He'd be acting in a family tradition. You ask a good question, though, about why someone would underwrite Stephen. It may be more than cash. You keep going back to the house, to the Greenleafs. Does someone want to connect themselves with that? This may be a big deal, if Stephen is keeping so quiet about them. The question is, who was Stephen meeting with."

"But how do we find out?" asked Wren. "The police can't seem to."

"Your father has an assistant who keeps track of every client meeting for him, even his class schedule, when papers are due. I'm sure Stephen has someone like that."

"He does. Especially during the proposal phase, we dealt with her a lot."

"How are you on a little lie?"

"Lavinia—"

"Oh, for God's sake, just a little one. You know what it's like navigating academic politics at an Ivy League school? I know it's after hours, but if you work for a major Wall Street player, you're used to it. So, here's what you're going to say...."

They went over the script. Wren felt her heart pounding, and her phone was slippery in her hand.

"This is remarkable, Wren," said Lavinia. "You approach the renovation of one of the finest private houses in the country with perfect sangfroid, but this...anyway, you'll be fine."

She took a breath and called Stephen's assistant. She picked up on the third ring.

"Nora! It's Wren Fontaine. So sorry to call you this late...well, thank you.

No problems, just one rather silly question…last week, Stephen was out late with a client, and I ran into them…anyway, it turns out that Stephen's client also was looking for an architect and gave me a card, but it seems I mislaid it." That was the worst lie—Wren never mislaid anything. "Anyway, if you can tell me who he was dining with that night, it would save me the embarrassment of asking Stephen again…oh, thank you so much." She hung up.

"What if she tells Stephen?" asked Wren.

"She won't. She'd have to admit she shared his private calendar. You got the name?"

"Maureen Nyberg."

Lavinia extracted her laptop from under back issues of the Journal of Urban History. "Let's see if we can find her. It's an unusual enough name, and we'll assume this is someone in the greater New York area."

Wren looked over her shoulder, and they got one relevant result, on Facebook: Maureen Nyberg, client management specialist, Severen Mutual Funds.

"So just a Wall Street business contact," said Lavinia. "Are they working on something that secret? I'm not a Wall Street expert, but 'client relationship manager' doesn't sound like a mover and shaker."

"I agree. Could you make the image larger? She looks familiar."

"Of course, that artistic eye of yours doesn't forget a face."

"Yes! Remember some months back my father was invited to give a three-part lecture series, themes and trends in American architecture?"

"I attended. And I remember your guest turn on the 19th century. You were very good."

"Thank you," she said, turning a little red. "Anyway, this woman came up to me afterward. She had some good questions about Gilded Age homes. This is some coincidence—Stephen having a secret meeting with a woman who asked me questions about great houses just a few months before at one of my father's lectures. Let's keep searching on her name…maybe we'll find the connection."

There were a few mentions of her in connection with her job at the fund company—nothing especially revealing. And then a photo popped up: "Leading real estate developer Oren Perry celebrates 40th wedding anniversary with extended family," read Wren. "And look who he's with—his *niece*, Maureen Nyberg. Now that is interesting."

"I know Perry's name—he's some sort of builder, right? He's given a lot of money to Columbia."

"Oh yes," said Wren. "Incredibly wealthy. One of the leading developers of office buildings in Manhattan and a major philanthropist. But what would be his interest in Greenleaf House? He could actually afford to buy it and live there. Still, that would be odd. He has a stupendous penthouse in the city and an estate in the Hamptons. I keep coming back to the details of what Stephen wants—a kitchen suitable for running a substantial restaurant, for example. A hotel with a gourmet restaurant, far classier than what PH Hospitality has in mind? That would be very unlike anything Perry has developed before."

"Wren, I need you to focus more on people than buildings right now. Why did Benjamin Greenleaf, who had devoted his life to making money, spend so much time and energy building that extraordinary monument?"

"He...just did," said Wren. "I never stopped to think why."

"And Oren Perry. Why would he want to connect with this house?"

Wren was silent.

"When they've reached a pinnacle, certain men aren't content to rest. They look for another achievement."

"And you are saying that Perry may have some sort of connection to the house? What?"

Now, Lavinia was silent.

"Oren Perry was born poor. He never went to college. But he's given huge sums to schools in the city, including Columbia, as you pointed out," said Wren. "There's a connection...somewhere." She was quiet again, and Lavinia didn't interrupt her student's thoughts.

"There's no helping it. I need to speak with Agnes Greenleaf."

"About the house's past?"

"About its present."

Chapter Twenty-One

Wren found Bobby supervising the early morning delivery of supplies.

"What's that in the background today?" she asked.

"Verdi's Traviata. You can't beat it for a good soprano voice. And it helps me concentrate." She watched him look over lumber and pipes, his hands running along the surfaces. Any sign or feeling of imperfection, and it would go back to the supplier no matter how much they protested, she well knew. He seemed even fussier than usual, she noted. He had fallen in love with the house too.

"Why does that opera help you concentrate?" she asked. And he looked oddly embarrassed.

"All right. It's not that in particular. I was looking over the performance history the other night. In the early twentieth century, its production at the Old Metropolitan opera house was underwritten by the Greenleaf Family. It sounds silly, but it was a connection to the house. And I liked that."

"No," said Wren. "That's not silly at all. I wish I could keep listening to it with you, but I have to talk with Miss Greenleaf this morning. I want to pick her brain on this place. She knows a lot more than she's saying."

"I'm sure," said Bobby. "I got that sense from Mrs. Ryan. She's kinda lonely. We talk every now and then. She seems a little tense, actually."

"I would've thought that she'd be beyond any tension considering all her years with Agnes Greenleaf. But after the disruption here, two dead bodies...something may have really upset Aunt Agnes, and that's making it felt on Mrs. Ryan. I think Aunt Agnes knows whose body was in the attic,

150

and there's a good chance Mrs. Ryan does too. More than that, they know how it connects to Karen Lavendell's death."

"You're probably right. I haven't heard anything direct, but apparently, the old girl does three things: listen to the radio; read; and keep up an old-fashioned correspondence with a dwindling number of family and friends. She talks a lot about the past. Mrs. Ryan is too loyal to pass along details, but that friend you brought along—Hadley Vanderwerf. Well, apparently, she really upset Miss Greenleaf. Mrs. Ryan hasn't stopped talking about how much that upset Miss Greenleaf—she said she's been unlivable since that day."

"Miss Greenleaf's grandmother was a Vanderwerf, and there was something there. I thought it was just about Uncle Ambrose, but there was something more. After all, Ambrose was a Greenleaf, but it's the Vanderwerfs who are upsetting her." She sighed. "Although she legally has the right to live here until she dies, maybe she's worried Stephen is going to force her out once the renovation is complete. Anyway, thanks for the info, Bobby. I'm going to have to apply some pressure," said Wren.

"You're going to get tough with an old lady!" he laughed.

"Not *get tough*. It's really not that different from a building, I'm beginning to realize. I'm going upstairs and will simply apply a cantilever—Miss Greenleaf is the supporting end. We'll see how much pressure I can put on her."

The metaphor made her feel better, like she knew what she was doing. But her heart sank a little when she remembered that people were not as reliable as concrete, steel and wood. Still, she'd do what needed to be done.

As usual, Mrs. Ryan opened the door to her with an air of "what are you doing here?"

"Good morning! I was hoping that if Miss Greenleaf was free, I could speak with her for a few minutes." And again, the slight hesitation as she admitted Wren.

"It's the architect, Miss Fontaine," said Mrs. Ryan. Aunt Agnes put down her book and looked up.

"Miss Vanderwerf isn't with you today?" she asked.

151

"No. Actually, that's one of the reasons I am here. I thought it would be a pleasant surprise, a distant relation with a connection to this house, but I'm afraid I upset you. I wanted to apologize."

Aunt Agnes looked at her doubtfully, trying to figure out if she was serious.

"Your intentions were good. You had no way of knowing it would be difficult. There are both strong ties and strong feelings when it comes to the Greenleafs and the Vanderwerfs. There was no way someone in your position in life could possibly know that."

A reassurance wrapped in an insult.

"By the way, have they arrested my nephew yet?" she had a malicious gleam in her eye. "I know they're still investigating the death of that developer lady and think that Stephen did it, don't they? There were few details in the papers—Stephen no doubt keeping it quiet as much as possible—but that's what's happening, isn't it?" The old lady had her newspapers and her radio, and she could put two and two together.

Wren took a seat. "That's actually what I wanted to talk to you about."

Aunt Agnes raised an eyebrow, started to say something, and stopped. She looked up at Mrs. Ryan.

"This might be a good time to go shopping," she said.

"I was going to go tomorrow," said Mrs. Ryan.

"But we're almost out of the coffee I like. Why not go today?"

Mrs. Ryan looked back and forth between Wren and her employer.

"As you wish," she said, with just a hint of sarcasm, and departed, closing the suite door behind her with a little more force than necessary.

It was something of an act, Wren realized, the servant with unquestioning loyalty to the mistress of the house. Mrs. Ryan wasn't crazy. By the time she was working here, the house had been mostly closed up, the world it had inhabited long gone. But she did what she had to do. Her need for the job made the charade necessary. The still imposing house made it possible.

Aunt Agnes waited until she was gone.

"All right. What do you know? There's been nothing more in the papers, but maybe you've been speaking with that sergeant?"

"No. They haven't found anyone. I'll be open and honest with you, Miss

152

Greenleaf. They do indeed suspect your nephew, Stephen. It seems he was competing with Karen Lavendell's company for control of the future of this house. My goal is the same as yours—a renovation of this home to make it the way it was. I want to show you something. But first, tell me what kind of wood was used in the dining room?"

"Don't be ridiculous. I have no idea."

"I think you do. I bet Benjamin Greenleaf supervised every aspect of this house, and I think you spoke with him a lot." Wren was feeling unusually confident and sure of herself—and she liked the feeling.

Aunt Agnes looked away for a few moments. "He was especially close to his daughter, my Aunt Laura, who married into the English nobility and moved to London. He missed her, and so liked having another girl around—we became close. And the floor was hickory. He told me oak was also strong, and less expensive, but hickory was best."

"The floor is still mostly good, but water damage has destroyed some planks. I want you to see how I'm repairing them. " She opened her folder and gave Aunt Agnes a piece of paper. "It's a receipt for hickory beams. Oak was almost as good, but almost wasn't good enough for your grandfather, and it isn't good enough for me." Aunt Agnes didn't take her word, but put on her reading glasses, worn on a cord around her neck, and read it before handing it back.

"Thank you. My grandfather would've been pleased. He would take me by the hand and go over every room in the house. He told me every room was his idea. And he liked showing it to me, because he always told me that no one loved this house as much as he did, except me."

"Not Susan, your grandmother? I thought this house was basically a wedding present to her."

"She was a good hostess—I'll give her that. She liked buying the furniture and rugs and paintings, and she did a good job of planning events. She was a lively woman. But for her, the house was just a setting. She didn't love it for itself. Do you understand that? I think you do."

"Thank you. But what about Uncle Ambrose? Did he love it, as his brother did?"

Wren expected another outburst, but Aunt Agnes just looked sad. "Ambrose, Ambrose. Everyone wants to know about Ambrose. Why do you need to know about him? Young Hadley—well, that was just vulgar curiosity. But you have a reason. It's about our history, isn't it?"

"Yes. And your Great Uncle Ambrose. It isn't a regular, garden-variety scandal. I thought it over—chorus girls, other men's wives, even his brother's wife, I hear." She paused, but Aunt Agnes had gotten herself under control—no reaction. "All those were easy to cover up, and no one cares. But you care about the house. So whatever Uncle Ambrose did, it had to do with the house. I'm sure."

"You still haven't told me why you need to know."

"Two connected murders. I think if I knew about the old one, I'd know about the new one. Our goals are the same. We want to make this house the way it was. If the police can't figure out who killed Karen Lavendell, they will sooner or later settle on Stephen. And that could derail my work here. It could even leave it in the hands of PH Hospitality. Neither of us wants that." *Yes, a cantilever. Miss Greenleaf had strong feelings, but you could use them to pry the details from her. She didn't like her nephew. She tolerated Wren. But she really hated PH Hospitality. She'd trust Wren, too, as an ally, if she was up against the wall.*

"Arrest Stephen—ha!" she laughed without humor. "He was a sly child who became a sly adult. I know he's always having meetings about this place. He's trying to find a way to get me out of here with all his friends in this town. I used to have friends..." Her voice drifted off, and she looked away. Wren began to panic—what do you say to something like that?

"I...I thought that you had the right to remain here."

"Yes. That's what my brother—Stephen's father—promised me. He made it legal. But Stephen has friends in high places, including lawyers. He says he's just going to keep this as a house, but I think he's lying. Do you know?"

"No, and that's the truth. All I can tell you is that I'm keeping this as a mansion." *But for what use?* Wren took a deep breath. "Miss Greenleaf. What did Uncle Ambrose do? And who killed that woman in the attic?"

She smiled faintly. "You understand the importance of history, and of symbols. You realize the significance of what it meant for a Greenleaf to preside here."

"And a Vanderwerf, too. Surely you don't dispute the importance of the lady of such a house?"

She fixed a look at Wren. " I'm more Greenleaf than Vanderwerf, but like in Romeo & Juliet, the Greenleafs and Vanderwerfs were 'two households, both alike in dignity.' They were people suited to a house like this. My father married well, too—my mother was a leader in the Colonial Dames of America. My brother's wife was descended from a New York mayor when this was still New Amsterdam. Even Stephen found a suitable wife—her father was a partner in one of the oldest law firms in New York, and her grandfather was a bishop in the Episcopal church. I'd expect no less from anyone sitting at the wife's position at the dining room table."

"But it's been a long time since anyone sat there, hasn't it?"

"Don't play games with me. You know I speak metaphorically. This house was a center of the city. It was. It still can be."

"Of course." Wren paused. She had no idea how to fence further. Nothing to do but be straightforward. "So are you going to tell me what Uncle Ambrose did? Did he kill that woman in the attic? No one can be punished after all this time. But for the sake of the house, I need to know, and I won't tell anyone, including Stephen."

"'For the sake of the house,'" repeated Aunt Agnes. "How well put. Stephen's father was supposed to tell him, but I kept telling him Stephen wasn't ready. I didn't trust what he would do with that knowledge. I still don't. For the sake of the house, as you say, I cannot tell anyone. Stephen is going to...do something with it. I want him to live here, but I'm afraid he'll sell it to those PH Hospitality people. All I can hope is that I won't be forced from here. I won't go quietly, I can tell you that." Wren didn't see a New York City sheriff's officer foolhardy enough to try to drag Agnes Greenleaf out of Greenleaf House.

Wren leaned back in her chair. "This isn't about Benjamin's reputation, or Susan's, or Ambrose's. It's about the house's reputation."

Aunt Agnes gave her a benevolent smile. "Ah. You are listening to me.

You're the first person outside of this family who realizes that a home has a reputation. My brother and I knew Stephen wouldn't understand that, but you do. But that's all I can tell you. All I can do is pray that nothing will happen to destroy that reputation."

Wren sighed; she saw the old lady wouldn't be moved. Still, there were some clues there, if she had the wit to figure them out. The scandal was about control of the house—the romantic dalliances were just window dressing covering what really went on.

She stood. "Thank you for your time. I might've learned enough to save this house."

Aunt Agnes raised an eyebrow. "Save it from what?"

"From people who don't love it as much as you and I do."

Aunt Agnes laughed. "I like that. Well, I won't tell you everything I know, and you won't tell me everything you know, fair enough, but we both love the house, that much is true."

"Just one more thing before I go. I read Benjamin Greenleaf's obituary. He died shortly after your debut. You were close to him, as you said. It must've pleased you that he lived long enough to see you come out."

"Yes, we both were pleased. He had been sick for some time, slipped into a coma a few days later, and then died." Wren watched Aunt Agnes' eyes lose their focus. She was a girl, barely a woman, in a city and country exhausted by years of war. "The house died with him. I told you we closed up after that. I miss those rooms—especially the ballroom. It wasn't like the earlier years, white tie and tails and ballgowns." Wren remembered what Stephen had said, that Aunt Agnes seemed to recall what happened before she was born. "Anyway, he couldn't come to the party, of course, but I visited him in his room before and after. We spoke one last time."

"What did you speak about?"

Aunt Agnes chuckled. "That was a long, long time ago," she said. Her look said, *nice try, but no dice.*

"I believe your grandmother, Susan, lived for some years after, though?"

"Yes. But as I said, she was a Vanderwerf. Her daughter was in England, and she wasn't especially close with her son or daughter-in-law. My cousin

Myrtle—the one who was so close with Hadley—came over and talked with her, and then Myrtle and I would have an afternoon together."

"You mentioned your father and mother, but not your grandmother, Susan. I know you were closer to your grandfather—Benjamin—but after he died, you didn't grow closer to her?"

"No. It just...no. Surely you have relatives you're close to, and others you just aren't?"

"Of course."

Aunt Agnes was looking a little grey, Wren saw. The old lady was still sharp in her mind, but Wren remembered she was over 90 and probably tired easily. She felt a little guilty, grilling her for family secrets.

The door opened, and Mrs. Ryan walked in.

"You're still here, Ms. Fontaine?" she asked. She glared at Wren. "Miss Greenleaf, you don't look well. Let me get you a tonic." She turned to Wren. "I would've thought you would not bother Ms. Greenleaf with business items better handled by Mr. Greenleaf."

"For heaven's sake, stop fussing and just get me the tonic," said Aunt Agnes. Mrs. Ryan rolled her eyes and disappeared into the bathroom. She came back a few moments later with a cloudy drink—an old-fashioned "restorative." Wren's own grandmother had put great faith in them. Aunt Agnes drank it, and the color came back to her cheeks.

"I'm sorry if I overtaxed you," said Wren as she stood. "Thank you for your time, Miss Greenleaf."

"It was rather fun," said Aunt Agnes. "This one here—" she pointed to Mrs. Ryan "has heard everything already. Right?"

"Yes, Miss Greenleaf. I am going to get you your pill now." She went back to the bathroom.

"You know, I could tell you more if you were family. Stephen has two sons, about your age, I'm guessing. Both as dull as he is, but well-mannered, and if you married one, you'd be a Greenleaf. You'd be family."

"I'll keep that in mind," said Wren, inching toward the door.

"But maybe..." and she saw again that malevolent gleam in the old lady's eye. "Maybe they're not your type. After seeing you with Hadley the other day, I'm thinking you'd be more likely to become a Vanderwerf." She laughed. "Almost as good, my dear, almost as good."

My God, nothing wrong with the old lady's mind.

Wren closed the door behind her and collapsed on a chair in the hallway, with her face buried in her hands. She had no idea how long she stayed there and might never have left if she hadn't heard Bobby coming up the stairs.

"Everything OK?" he asked.

"Just another round with Aunt Agnes." She sighed.

"Now you know what your father has to go through, trying to manage insane clients."

"I suppose."

"Learn anything?"

"She's not as crazy as we may think. Aunt Agnes knows how important this house is. As a practical home—its day is long gone. But as a symbol. She knows that very well."

"And that makes her sane?"

"Stephen Greenleaf doesn't like his aunt. But more than that, he's a little afraid of her. I think I'm learning why."

Chapter Twenty-Two

Lavinia was right. She needed to think like a historian, continue where her professor's research had left off. Aunt Agnes had taken her only so far, but now it was time to look at the legal history of the house, the underpinnings of vague rumors and insinuations.

Wren made herself comfortable in the Rose Parlor and called Knight & Knight, the title company they usually worked with.

"Dana? It's Wren Fontaine. If you have a few moments, I have some questions about the Greenleaf title."

"Oh! I hope there are no problems. It was a bit of a task, a house that old, but it was very clear."

"No problems at all. It's just me doing some research on the house's history. If you say Stephen has clear title, mortgages aside, I'm sure you're right, but I'm curious about the history. Could I come around and see what's in your file, and make a few copies?"

"I don't blame you. It was like taking a step back in time for this—an interesting bit of legal history. I didn't send you more than the conclusions, but as usual, we made some notes for our records. And you don't have to come by. We scan everything that comes through the door. Give me a few minutes, and I'll email the whole thing. As I said, it was interesting—you'll see when we send it over. All of it kosher, but even Knight Senior said he had never seen anything like it."

Wren felt a little thrill at that thought of complexities, that Greenleaf House had a complicated legal history—the body wasn't the home's only oddity. It wouldn't do to forget the body, most likely, if not definitely, Fiona, the maid who went missing. The maid who was seemingly memorialized with a portrait of Ambrose, the family black sheep.

It would be hard to find anything about her, an unimportant girl with a common name who died or disappeared more than a century ago. But not so Lady Laura—Benjamin and Susan's daughter, who married an English nobleman. She was the sole beneficiary of Ambrose's will. Why? She couldn't have known what happened. But if she was told later, when her brother Caleb was also told, the secret never made it down to Stephen. An old family secret, and Ambrose trusted Laura with whatever money Ambrose had left, to make something right....

Dana's email with attachments popped up, and Wren smiled as she read the brief introductory memo and the attachments. It made sense, and she told herself she should've realized this would've been the case. Everything kept leading back to who had control of the house.

When it was built, Benjamin Greenleaf was a very wealthy man, but it was a family concern back then. The money wasn't his to do with as he wanted, not entirely. This was more than a home, it was an HQ, a place where the extended family could gather. A symbol of their importance in this city.

The house had cost $6 million, more than $185 million in current dollars. Knight & Knight had found that although Benjamin had paid for much of it from his own pocket, a lot came from money borrowed from the family business, a private concern owned by multiple Greenleafs.

Even if this was Stephen's home, the entire family had a stake in it. Wren imagined them all gathering at luncheons, dinners, and balls to meet other wealthy and powerful people. It wasn't just a house. It was a symbol of Greenleaf power. And they wanted it to be a symbol forever. That's what Aunt Agnes knew.

Dana had also forwarded the home's trust document that governed the family ownership: Benjamin couldn't sell the house or move it out of the family. It had to remain a Greenleaf property, passed down the Greenleaf line. Benjamin and his direct descendants held the majority, but it had to remain with the closest Greenleaf descendant.

But times had changed. By the time Aunt Agnes had been born, those days were gone, and the Gilded Age splendor existed only in the movies that people flocked to in an attempt to forget the Great Depression. The symbol of Greenleaf power became a white elephant.

In 1934, Caleb Greenleaf, Benjamin's son, paid off those still listed in the trust to dissolve it, so he and his direct descendants could have a free hand. The various Greenleaf cousins were probably grateful for hard cash in the 1930s, and all too eager to give up any share in a mansion that had outlived its purpose, when there was no one left to buy it from them anyway.

Caleb Greenleaf—Benjamin Greenleaf's only son, Stephen Greenleaf's grandfather. Before the trust was dissolved, he was the heir. But what if he hadn't been around? The nearest relative was Ambrose, but he had had no children. What cousin was next in line?

Had Fiona done something to interfere, to get herself killed and forgotten, stuffed into the chest?

She kept going back to motive. Fiona had a brother, Kevin, who was the Greenleaf coachman—and Conor Ryan's ancestor. He must've had some idea of what was happening—of what had happened.

But he had been powerless to do anything.

*** ***

Ezra Fontaine asked Wren about the house while eating more sourdough bread at breakfast. "You're happy with the progress?"

"Absolutely. As we thought, we're going to need some new joists in the dining room. TJIs, of course."

"What do you mean, 'of course'? The house didn't use TJIs in 1895. I thought the goal was period restoration."

"You're testing me to see if I've gone crazy. No one can see the joists. And the bathroom fixtures will be the latest modern appliances."

"Speaking of plumbing, since no one can see the pipes, as you say—"

"We'll still be using copper."

Ezra frowned. "CPVC is just as good in most applications and is less expensive."

"But it's not copper. Don't stint, you taught me that."

"But there's something called profligacy. Anyway, anything about the deaths in the house? I assume you haven't forgotten."

"The nineteenth-century death is fascinating but really doesn't affect the project at hand. Still, it's clear there's a connection to the Lavendell death."

"Yes, the Lavendell death. Are they going to drag our client to prison?"

"He says he has an alibi, but he doesn't want to use it unless he has to."

"How do you know this?" he was unusually sharp. *Serves me right for trying to pull a fast one on the old man.*

"You told me I needed to stay close with our clients. I've stayed close and learned things." Ezra raised an eyebrow. "Anyway, if you spoke with Stephen, he'd think *you* didn't trust me, and then *he* wouldn't trust me."

"I won't call him," he said, a little nettled.

"How are the Rivington plans coming?" she asked, to change the subject.

"My *daughter* is checking up on *me*?" he asked.

"Not your daughter. Your partner."

"Junior partner."

Wren finished her coffee. "I'll see you tonight."

Bobby's van was already in the driveway when she arrived, and when she entered, she heard the workmen and the opera strains throughout the house. She wondered if Miss Greenleaf and Mrs. Ryan heard the music in their apartment and if they minded—or even enjoyed it. Even if Miss Greenleaf didn't like it, mused Wren, she probably wouldn't want to risk looking vulgar by complaining.

And then Sgt. Ortiz stepped out of the Rose Parlor.

"Good morning, Ms. Fontaine." His smile was brittle.

"Sergeant?" She blinked. "How can I help you?"

"Could I have a minute of your time?" he asked with exaggerated politeness. "Your client is already here."

She stepped into the parlor.

"Good morning, Wren," said Stephen. He smiled sardonically. Bobby was also there, not looking happy.

Ortiz took a seat. "I'm sorry to tell you that Andrew Heppenstall, a preservation activist—that seems to be what he called himself—was found dead last night. You all have a connection to him."

"He wasn't shot, was he?" asked Wren.

"Now that would be something, a third death with the same gun. But this was different. In fact, it may have been accidental, or even suicide, but considering Karen Lavendall's recent death, I'm inclined to be more than a little suspicious. He was found in his apartment with an overdose of various narcotics, according to an initial report. They're still working on the details. The thing is, he had no pills in his house, no history of prescriptions for any narcotic, so that leaves us with a lot of questions. Mr. Greenleaf, you knew him?"

"We never met face-to-face. We exchanged phone calls and emails. He was very concerned about what I was doing with my house." Wren heard the emphasis on "my."

"Were your exchanges acrimonious?"

"You could say that. I normally welcome interest in my house, but he was challenging and threatening, as if he had a right. I understand that's his usual M.O. Anyway, it's been some weeks since we last had any contact."

"Did you save those emails? I'd want to see them."

"Probably."

"Good. If you could forward them."

Ortiz turned to Wren. "Mr. Heppenstall kept a journal. We found that he had met with you and Mr. Fiore. What did he give as the reason for getting in touch with you?"

"He snuck up on Ms. Fontaine," said Bobby. "He was a nut. Scared the hell out of her one evening, near the house. It was a good thing I was meeting some friends nearby and saw him."

"Yes," said Wren. "He seemed upset and anxious. But after he calmed down, we agreed to talk. He was worried about what was going to happen to the house, especially if it got into the hands of PH Hospitality."

"Did he sound afraid of anyone?"

"No," said Wren. "He was just...upset."

"I can't imagine anyone wanting to kill him," said Stephen. "He was annoying, even abrasive, but I can't imagine he was ever in a position to really threaten anyone."

The mention of pills sparked something in the back of Wren's mind. She remembered all the medicines in Aunt Agnes' medicine cabinet. She met Bobby's eyes—he remembered too. She shook her head—later, not in front of Stephen. Or Ortiz.

"Can you tell me where the three of you were last night?"

"I was home, with my wife."

"Likewise," said Bobby. "We had a couple of the kids around, and I spoke with my neighbor around 10:00 before going to bed."

Ortiz turned to Wren.

"Out late with a friend," said Wren. "I didn't get home until after midnight."

"Could I have this friend's name and contact information."

"Hadley Vanderwerf. I have her number."

Her eyes slid to Stephen. Did he wonder why his architect was out late with his cousin? Did he even care? She thought of that old phrase—Stephen Greenleaf was a "man of the world." She thought she saw his eyebrow go up a few millimeters.

Anyway, Wren knew Hadley wouldn't mind. In fact, she'd be amused.

Ortiz stood. "Thank you. I expect to follow up in the near future. For now, Mr. Heppenstall's death is being treated as suspicious. Mr. Greenleaf. Have you given any further thought to your alibi for the Lavendell killing?" His eyes flashed to Wren and Bobby. *He wants us to know our client is still a suspect.*

"Because of sensitive business arrangements, I can't just yet, but I will be able to in the coming weeks, I'm sure," he said with a smile.

"Of course," Ortiz responded, not looking convinced.

"May I leave now? I have some meetings downtown." Ortiz nodded.

"Wren, Bobby, so sorry you've been dragged into this. But none of this should affect our schedule. I'm just going to say a quick hello to my aunt." He left.

Wren was thinking about how to introduce the pill information, but Ortiz was ready for her.

"So. I'm wondering if you have anything to tell me now that your client is no longer present."

Bobby nodded. "I want you to know that my boys and I don't snoop. We're in a lot of houses, and that's a strict rule with us. But Mrs. Ryan asked me if I could take a look at the medicine cabinet in her suite's bathroom. And I couldn't help but see it was full of various sleeping pills."

"You know about medicine, Mr. Fiore?"

"I had an aunt with a problem. We were always on the lookout with one thing or another, and the names became pretty familiar to all of us."

"Ah. Of course." His eyes glanced upstairs. "Lots of people have those medicines today. Although I appreciate your frankness."

"If that's it, I'll be getting back to work," he said. He nodded at Wren and left.

"Do you see Mr. Greenleaf borrowing his aunt's medicine to poison Mr. Heppenstall?" he asked.

"I'm not a detective. But I am an architect. Everything being done here is strictly within the bounds of the Landmarks Commission. Mr. Heppenstall offered no threat to Stephen Greenleaf that I'm aware of."

"I'm sure," said Ortiz absently. "I still can't get over this house. The crime goes back to it, doesn't it? It's all connected."

"Again, I'm not a detective. But there never was a house like this in New York. And there never will be one again. This house, any house really, even a little cottage, sets a tone for the people who live in it. It just becomes more noticeable when it's something like this."

"It sounds like architects also have to be psychologists."

"I never looked at it that way, but I suppose you're right."

"Police officers too. Thank you for your time." He thought a moment. "Vanderwerf. Why is that name familiar?"

"She's a relation of Stephen's. The Vanderwerfs are also connected to this house, so maybe that's how you came across it."

"A relation? Would this Hadley inherit this under certain circumstances?"

"No. It's a very distant relationship—third cousins, once removed, we calculated. Stephen Greenleaf's great-grandfather, Benjamin, built this house. His wife was a Vanderwerf. Hadley is descended from her brother."

"Ah. But wasn't that the plot of *Pride and Prejudice,* that sometimes estates go to distant relatives?"

That surprised her. A police detective who knew Jane Austen. She could also see he was amused at her surprise. "Exactly—an entailment. Actually, that's a good question. We did a title search on this house before starting work. Stephen has a clear title, although there are mortgages. But when the house was built, it was a part of a family trust and had to go to the nearest relative. That trust was dissolved decades ago, however, and since the Vanderwerfs were not related to the Greenleafs, except by marriage, there was no situation that could've given it to them. And even if there were an entailment, Mr. Greenleaf has children."

Ortiz smiled. Wren suddenly wondered if he had been playing with her. "You are a fount of knowledge. Thank you."

And before she could say more, he left.

Wren felt frustrated. She wondered about the pills and why Ortiz didn't seem interested in them. He hadn't thought that Heppenstall could possibly have been in the house. But Wren remembered how well he seemed to know it. She hadn't told Ortiz that.

But that was just a supposition, she told herself. Ortiz was entitled to her knowledge, but not her conclusions. And as for Stephen spending an evening with the niece of a powerful politico? If she and Lavinia had found that out, Ortiz could as well.

Wren was still musing when Stephen came back down, and she met him in the foyer.

"There was no need to pass off Hadley as an unpaid consultant," he said. "As the architect in charge of this project, you have carte blanche to bring in anyone you want."

"I wasn't lying about Hadley as a consultant. I did need her insights into the family history of this house. That she has become a friend is immaterial." It came out more brittle than she expected. Stephen didn't seem to care. Wall Street players were not easily rattled, she knew.

"I didn't mean to give offense," he said. "And there's no need to be embarrassed."

"I am not embarrassed," she said. "I am just very private. And now, if you'll excuse me, this meeting has put me behind schedule." She headed to the kitchen. She didn't hear Stephen say anything but imagined what he was thinking: "Architects. Jesus Christ."

Chapter Twenty-Three

Wren spent the next two days waiting for the other shoe to drop, for Sgt. Ortiz to come back—more about what happened to Heppenstall or another attempt to find out about Stephen's alibi for Lavendell. But it was quiet, and she and Bobby got a lot accomplished as his crew worked room by room.

They went over plans in a corner of the kitchen while the workers took their lunch break. Bobby's wife packed him an impressive spread, while Wren made do with a tuna sandwich and carrot sticks from a nearby deli. More Italian opera filled the room.

"Which one is this?" asked Wren.

"See if you can figure it out," he said. Wren closed her eyes and focused on the sound.

"Cosi fan Tutte?" she said.

"Very good."

"Does it qualify as Italian? Mozart wrote the music, and it debuted in Austria."

"The libretto is in Italian and written by an Italian. Also, it's Italian in style."

"A comic opera about fickle women who can't decide whom to marry. I wonder about the women who lived here—their loves. If they saw themselves in that opera."

"I don't know about the women, but they didn't see that opera, not back then. It wasn't staged in America until 1922. Too risqué for respectable theatergoers," said Bobby.

"Really?"

"It was easy to shock people back then. Can you imagine being shocked by a Mozart opera?"

"How is your budding friendship with Mrs. Ryan? Any additional gossip?"

He shook his head. "Something spooked that lady. Came around to see how the kitchen was going—I guess sent by Miss Greenleaf to make sure we weren't goofing off. Couldn't even get her going on church gossip and the advantages of an education with the Good Sisters. She was one tense lady. But I guess working under Miss Greenleaf has its problems."

"You'd think she'd be used to them. I think she's tough, but we have three murders now. It's hard on her, and she's being hard on Mrs. Ryan. Harder than usual. I hope she relaxes a bit. We're going to need to talk to Mrs. Ryan."

"It'll be hard to get her to turn on the Greenleafs," said Bobby, shaking his head. "Ladies like Mrs. Ryan are old school. They're a type."

"They're a type that goes back a long way, to the Murphys who worked here when this house opened. They were part of it too—this house. If they weren't in this house, things might be different. But for now, although she works for Miss Greenleaf, Stephen Greenleaf rules here."

Bobby laughed. "He *rules* here? This isn't a castle."

"It was to them," said Wren. "We don't even think of the words anymore, but even in a little cottage, we call the main bedroom the *master* bedroom. It was the *master's* room. He had servants and employees and people who sought his favor. Loyalty was a currency. Mrs. Ryan works for Miss Greenleaf, but they live in Mr. Greenleaf's house. The house affects people, changes them. "

"You're making it sound like they're possessed," said Bobby.

"In a way, yes. You start thinking about the decades of owners and servants, and the mutual loyalty they had for each other. The house reminds them of that. And maybe Mrs. Ryan needs a reminder about who she owes her loyalty to. "

"You're going to figure out how that girl ended up in the attic? And Mrs. Ryan is going to help you?" He shook his head. "It beats me, and I've seen a lot of funny things going in and out of people's houses. Anyway, if I can keep things going with Mrs. Ryan, I'll do what I can."

* * *

Wren let Hadley in a little after 6:00, and Hadley gave her a quick kiss.

"Thanks for the head's up—that detective did come around and asked me to give you an alibi. So cool—it was like being in Law & Order. Can you give me the details?" Wren told her about Heppenstall.

"Dear God, Little Bird. What the hell is going on here?"

"I was hoping you could tell me. When we got this job, my father said families like the Greenleafs—and, I assume, the Vanderwerfs—were not like other families. You had a different way of looking at the world."

"Well, yeah, but we don't keep killing people. Three dead bodies. Jesus. I guess they're looking at Stephen too?"

"He said he was home with his wife."

"Yeah, they never believe that on TV. Did Stephen have a motive?" She grinned. "Do you?"

"Ha! They must think so if I had to get an alibi. But no, the man was a fanatic, annoying, but no threat to anyone that I'm aware of. However, Stephen is still on the hook for something else. He does have an alibi for when Lavendell was killed. He won't tell the police, but I found out anyway." She heard the pride in her voice at what she had done with Lavinia's help. Hadley's eyes lit up, and that made Wren smile.

"You're not such a good girl after all. So did he have a mistress?"

"I don't think so. He was having dinner with the niece of a very prominent developer and philanthropist. And this niece is someone I knew slightly—we met when she was attending a lecture my father gave at Columbia."

"So it has to do with the developer?"

"Perhaps. But why not tell the police? We can run some ideas by Lavinia tonight."

"That's great. Speaking of Lavinia, am I dressed OK?" Wren blinked. Hadley was wearing a simple spring dress that fell below the knee.

"Of course. Why? Are there special dresses for meeting professors? And you know more about clothes than I do. At least, twenty-first-century clothes."

"It's so hard. I've forgotten how adults dress. Oh, I have something for going to a wedding and something for meeting with a banker, but everything else is for dealing with musicians and club owners. You know about appearance, Wren."

"Do I?" She smiled. "Perhaps too much. You look lovely. And anyway, Lavinia and Angela couldn't care less."

She still looked uncertain. "They're important to you. And I don't want to make too big a deal of this, but it means something to me that you're bringing me to dinner at their home."

"You come right out and say these things. You say what you feel."

"And that bothers you. Even frightens you."

Wren took a while to answer, and Hadley knew she would, so she didn't mind.

"It makes me admire you, actually. Because I distrust my feelings, so I'm nervous about saying what I am feeling. But you trust and then say them, and so I look up to you."

Hadley nodded, with a grave look on her usually cheerful face. "Thank you, Little Bird. That is the finest thing anyone has ever said to me." Then her face broke into a smile. "But houses. You trust your feeling on houses. That's good. We can work on people."

They caught a cab to Lavinia and Angela's, and from down the hall, they could smell Angela's cooking. It would be right on time—Angela approached cooking a chicken with the same meticulous devotion she gave to her surgeries.

"Wren—wonderful as always."

"Lavinia—this is Hadley Vanderwerf."

"A pleasure, my dear. Come in. Can I get you a drink?"

"It's so nice to meet you. Wren told me all about you. Just a tonic over ice."

"And Wren hardly drinks either. You young people are so healthy. Now, if she told you all about me, you know my magnum opus in the works, a history of the city's great families. I know about the Vanderwerfs, of course, but never met one. Did you know that you had an ancestor who served in the Hayes administration?"

"No, I did not. Do you know if he was as exquisitely boring as everyone else in my family?"

Lavinia laughed. "Wren, I think she's a keeper."

Wren watched the two older women, especially Angela, ask Hadley about her life and background, but noted that Hadley took it all in good cheer. Eventually, Lavinia said, "I think we should let up on grilling the poor girl."

"I don't mind," said Hadley. "I know Wren is important to you. And she's becoming important to me." She squeezed Wren's hand.

"We're a bit overprotective," said Angela. "Wren is special to us. You do know she was our flower girl—"

"Bridesmaid, actually," added Wren.

"Ooh—I must see a picture," said Hadley.

"Right above the mantle," said Angela. Hadley looked at college student Wren, the couple's witness, for a City Hall wedding, smiling self-consciously in front of a beaming Lavinia and Angela.

"Very sweet," said Hadley. "Blue suits you well."

"Have you met the parents yet?" asked Lavinia.

"My parents will just be so grateful that Wren isn't covered in piercings or tattoos," said Hadley. She looked at Wren. "What about your father? You don't talk about him much."

"Ezra is fine," said Lavinia. " As long as you don't bring coffee into his office. He's fanatical about that."

"My father will just be so grateful that Hadley isn't imaginary," said Wren.

After dinner, they talked a while more, then Angela excused herself. "Early morning surgery. I imagine you'll be following up on Wren's mysteries—we're up to three right now, if I have it right?"

"So far," said Lavinia. "Wren sent me a succinct update. Now, I'll pour a little cognac for myself, and for anyone else who is interested."

"Wren—and Hadley too—I'm holding you responsible if Lavinia is hungover tomorrow," said Angela. "It's been a pleasure, everyone. Enjoy the rest of the evening."

They settled into the comfortable living room.

"So, where are you, Wren? What is this about? That's how I told you to start looking at an issue. You've had more time to think, and now we've had a third death—which might be a murder."

"Yes, another person connected to the house," said Wren. "Who loves it, and who wants to control it. Fiona Murphy died because she was a threat to that. And so did Karen Lavendell and Andrew Heppenstall, but I don't know why."

"Then why do you think that? Be specific, Ms. Fontaine." The strict tone of the professor.

"Because there is nothing else that ties it all together. I start working on a house, and someone interested in it is killed. Just a businesswoman whose company settled problems with money and lawyers, but she shows interest in Greenleaf House and is killed. And there was no reason to kill a serving girl unless she threatened the house. If she had been seduced, raped, impregnated—money and influence would cover anything. But if Fiona threatened the house, she'd have to die. We find a body dead in the house, killed with the same gun. And finally, Heppenstall. He's been an irritant all his life, but not a threat—until he came up against Greenleaf House."

"Very cogent. But unless you're writing the screenplay for a horror movie—and I warn you, I detest horror movies—we're no further forward. Did Stephen Greenleaf commit either of the two modern murders? You say he has an alibi for Lavendell even if he doesn't want to discuss it. He's in control of the house."

"I know," said Wren. "That's where I'm stuck. I can't draw the lines from one to another. It keeps going back to the house, but with all my information, I can't draw a conclusion. We have Oren Perry, who is trying to be connected to this house, while others who are connected are being killed. I can feel it's all connected, over a century, but it's like a puzzle that won't fit."

Lavinia fixed her look on Hadley. "Ms. Vanderwerf—you look skeptical."

"Not about what you or Wren said, but about...I don't know about history or architecture. I was a film major at Sarah Lawrence. But I know about people. And I know my family, and families like ours, running this town for three centuries until we became irrelevant. To me, it's about people. A certain kind of people. We need to look at more than the victims." She looked a little embarrassed about her speech. "Anyway, my two cents."

Wren looked at Hadley. "You're right," she finally said. "It centers on the house—I'm sure of that. But I forget people are involved, and I don't always...I'm not always sure about motives, about why people do things."

"Then you have to get back to people. See if you can draw out Mrs. Ryan."

"She won't talk about the Greenleafs."

"But she'll talk about the Murphys. If you approach her right."

"I was thinking of reminding her that although she works for Agnes Greenleaf, the owner of the house is Stephen Greenleaf. And as architect, I represent him."

"That's very manipulative, Wren," said Lavinia. "You're coming along nicely."

Hadley giggled.

"And speaking of the Ryans, don't forget Conor," said Lavinia.

"I can't figure him out. And I don't trust him. He seems to have a vendetta about the alleged mistreatment of Fiona. He has no reason to protect the Greenleafs, no obvious motive for any of the killings. But his feelings of resentment are strong. And he has some sort of very dark job. I hate to say it, but I think if he had a motive, he'd stop at nothing if it would embarrass the Greenleafs and bring justice for the Murphys. But no, not justice. Revenge."

Lavinia nodded. "Good. But if that's all you have on Conor, you'll have to go further. He has a connection to the house, and in many ways, it's as strong as the Greenleaf or Vanderwerf connection. You just don't want to face him. Not out of cowardice—you just don't like being up against people, especially people like Conor. And Wren—I don't know this Conor, but you don't always have to go back to the 19th century for a motive."

Wren sighed. "You're right. But wrong about cowardice. I am a coward about people, and someone like that. I mean, he must be CIA or something, and it's not that I'm afraid I'll be hustled into a windowless van and carried off, but trying to get the better of someone like that."

"We'll do it together," said Hadley. "I deal with horrific music world agents every day. We'll double-team him."

"Okay!" said Wren, suddenly feeling better about it. "And we're still holding onto the information about Stephen's alibi. Stephen is playing another game, and I think it would be very dangerous to underestimate him. I'm going to have to confront him about that, about his connection to Oren Perry and why it has to remain secret."

"Now we're talking," said Lavinia. She poured herself another cognac.

"Lavinia—Angela isn't going to be happy. And she'll blame me."

"Christ, Wren, you're such a good girl."

"I know," said Hadley. "I spent most of college in a pot haze."

"That's good to know," said Lavinia. "Yes, Wren, definitely a keeper."

* * *

It was late when they left the apartment, but because the city spring had reached the evening, they started walking downtown without talking about it. Hadley slipped her arm into Wren's. Wren knew Hadley wanted to talk but was keeping quiet because she knew Wren wanted to gather her thoughts. Wren found her thoughtfulness endearing.

"Our contractor, Bobby, plays opera when he works. Usually Italian. Today it was Cosi Fan Tutte. It's a comic opera about two women promising to be faithful, but their lovers secretly test them by pretending to go off to war, and when they come back disguised as other men, they find how easy it is to seduce them. The opera doesn't make the women look very good. The title is usually translated as 'women are like that.'"

"Not all of us," said Hadley, smiling.

"No, not at all," Wren patted her arm. "I wasn't referring to us. I was thinking about Susan Greenleaf, nee Vanderwerf, and Fiona Murphy. Two women in such different circumstances but very much the same as prisoners of their class and of their time, and I wonder what they did, or what they had to accept, to live their lives."

"What choices do you think they made?"

"Fiona was hired as a nursery maid, but never actually worked as one, gone before Susan had any children. Did she know or suspect Benjamin was incapable of getting his wife pregnant and that Susan is attempting to have a child with his brother, Ambrose? Fiona knows the plan. Maybe she even has proof, a letter, or something. They kill her to shut her up." She shivered.

"That's horrible," said Hadley. "But I can see that. Susan and Ambrose having an affair not being a problem, but Fiona making it public a disaster. So the Greenleafs and Vanderwerfs walk away from it all, and Fiona doesn't even get a Christian burial. We were terrible people."

"They built that house. That's something."

"I'm glad you showed it to me, but nothing could convince me to live there." Then, afraid she had hurt Wren's feelings, said, "I'm sorry."

"Don't be. It's just my silly fantasy. I'd probably find the reality a lot less entertaining."

"You're right. When I was 15, my fantasy was to spend the rest of my life in clubs and backstage with rock stars, and I actually got to live it. But now it's just a job, with people I don't like very much and being with you makes me think I need to be a grown-up."

"That makes me sound old."

"Mature, not old. My 30th birthday isn't so far away, and setting up weddings on Long Island is suddenly more appealing than the tour launch of a death metal group. Don't tell anyone."

Wren laughed. "Whatever you do, you'll be good at it, because you're good with people."

"You're hard on yourself. You're good with people. You just don't like them very much. I think it's confidence. You're confident about houses, but not confident with people, because you know you understand houses, but you're very worried you don't understand people. But I think you do."

"See—you are good with people. You understand me. Anyway, I am going to make more of an effort, and you're going to help me."

They shared a kiss, and continued walking.

Chapter Twenty-Four

"I'm not used to working with architects," said Stephen, looking a little amused. "Is this typical?"

"It is with me," said Wren. "We've done some major work, and I thought lunch, on the firm, alongside a project report, would be appropriate." They stood in the entranceway of Greenleaf House, and Wren watched him look at the house. He was the last child to grow up here, the last person who would be able to say this was a home. "What was it like growing up here?" she asked.

"As a child, you don't question things. You don't wonder why other children live in apartments or townhouses, and you live in a huge, empty place that was more museum than residence. My school friends liked coming here. Can you imagine playing hide and seek in this place? Little boys didn't see the problems." Wren thought about Conor—he hadn't noticed either. He was just a boy growing up in what was practically a castle, but not his.

"Do you miss it?"

He smiled. "Are you asking whether, if I had enough money, I'd move my family here and live here?" He didn't go further.

"I'm being specific," said Wren. "I know everyone is supposed to be impressed with the ballroom, but as an architect, I prefer your formal dining room. Its shape, its proportion, is perfection. The table in that room—I imagine Benjamin had it custom-built to his specifications. It fits in that room so neatly. Benjamin at the head. Susan at the foot. And from that room, they ruled New York's social world."

"I take it you're making a point?" he asked, still looking amused, but Wren thought, a little off-balance, not quite sure where she was going with this.

"A point about sitting at the table. Who were more powerful than the Greenleafs? But I promised you lunch." She headed for the staircase.

"Where are you going? Aren't we going out?"

"We're having it catered in."

He started to talk, then changed his mind and followed her.

"Did you ever dine in the formal dining room as a boy?"

"What? No. That would be ridiculous, a family of three at a table that size. And the age of huge parties like that was long gone by the time I was born. The family had turned what was a sort of salon into a family dining room."

"But you know the room?"

"It wasn't locked, like the ballroom, so although I wasn't allowed to play on the table, which was covered anyway, I could race my toy cars around."

Wren frowned. "That would explain the damage on the lower walls. You do know we'll have to replaster."

Stephen laughed. "Serves me right. Half a century later, I'm paying for childhood indiscretions." He sighed. "Once, I would've had a nanny to make sure I didn't do that. Once. But again, those days had long passed."

"Very well, but today you can sit at the head of the table while we dine. I think it will help us, help me, get a sense of what this house was like."

"So this is some sort of architect thing?" he asked. "Well, why not. We have our ways in the financial world too."

Wren opened the wide, double doors to the dining room. Hadley and another young woman were putting the finishing touches on three table settings.

"Stephen—I'd like to introduce you to your cousin Hadley."

Stephen looked surprised for a moment, then grinned. "I don't think we've seen each other since you were screaming over a font in church. Although I did hear how you upset Aunt Agnes." He gave her a quick kiss.

"I'm sorry," she said.

"Don't be. She may have been a friend of your Aunt Myrtle, but she's been looking down on Vanderwerfs her whole life, and the sense of continuity pleases me."

Hadley laughed.

"Today, I'm doing double-duty as a caterer and your cousin. I already served Wren one dinner here in the ruins of what must've been a fantastic conservatory, so she's letting me do it again. I'm a super cook, and since your kitchen is out of service for the moment, I've had it all brought in. And I'm joining you in today's meeting."

"I see," said Stephen, even though he clearly didn't.

Hadley thanked her assistant, who then left, and the three took their places.

"Stephen, you're at the head, of course. I think every other member of your family got a turn sitting here, and why shouldn't you."

"How thoughtful," he said. Hadley had done them well, with beef fillets, new potatoes, and green beans. They took their seats and started to eat. Wren gave them a quick rundown of her work.

"Good, good," he said. "Now, you already gave me a defense for a copper roof. Can you explain to me again why I'm being billed for miles and miles of copper piping as well? I thought there were cheaper alternatives, if not for roofing, than at least for plumbing."

"For some situations, yes. But for what I want the copper for, copper is best."

"Why?"

"Copper withstands 1,000 pounds per square inch. Nothing else combines strength and flexibility, and weight. It bends to fit, and despite its strength, it's lightweight, so needs very little support. I use copper because this house deserves copper."

"It *deserves* copper. That's fascinating. But I'm your client, not the house. What do I deserve?"

Wren steeled herself. "I bet in summer you wear linen suits, right? I bet your sheets are real linen too. It's much stronger than cotton and also breathable, but the flax plant is very difficult to harvest and process, so it's much more expensive than other options. And yet you spend the money."

"You're right. But I'm a living person, Wren. I have to be comfortable and look good during the day, and my wife and I want to be comfortable at night."

Wren felt strong feelings rise, a sure sign she was going to say something she probably shouldn't. "A house is a living being, too. Your great-grandfather Benjamin knew that. This house is what it is because he gave it perfection every step of the way. It deserves copper like you deserve linen."

Stephen just stared at her like she was going out of her mind, and she felt herself turning red.

"Wow," said Hadley. "Didn't you know, Wren, no one is allowed to put Greenleafs in their place. Except Vanderwerfs."

Stephen looked back and forth between the two of them. "I have a feeling that hiring you is going to turn out to be the best decision I ever made. Or the worst. There won't be an in-between."

"Stephen. You should be thanking God that the family home is in the hands of someone who loves it as much as Benjamin. Now eat your lunch."

Wren felt grateful for the support and decided it was a good time to change the subject. Of course, this could be even worse.

"There's another topic," she said. "Something that can affect future plans. I admit I'm being selfish, but to be blunt, if you're arrested, that could put this project into jeopardy, and I don't want that. I've rarely wanted anything as much as I want to restore this house."

She was afraid that would irritate Stephen again, but it didn't seem to hit him very hard. Again, Wren realized that he hadn't made it on Wall Street by buckling easily, and at least they were off the topic of money. He didn't respond to Wren but turned to Hadley.

"You really cooked this yourself?"

"Absolutely."

"I'm impressed. It took 120 years for someone in this family to learn their way around a kitchen. I'm not sure my great-grandmother knew where the kitchen was in this place. Although you are always welcome as family, I had wondered why you were here. I'm guessing now it has to do with what Wren wants to discuss next. Not just the house, but the family who has lived here."

"Yes, it's because she is family," said Wren. She took a breath. "Stephen—I found out where you were when Karen Lavendell was killed. You don't want

180

to tell the police. We want to know why."

That did get his attention.

"You were spying on me?" He looked more surprised than annoyed.

"No. But you're not the only one with contacts in this town." Wren fought to keep the smugness out of her voice, but Hadley couldn't resist a little smirk. "The niece of the prominent developer, Oren Perry. It seems innocent enough, which made me wonder why you're hiding it."

"I see." He still sounded a little stunned. "What if I told you it didn't concern you?"

"Anything in this house concerns me," she said.

Hadley took over before it got heated and put her hand gently on Stephen's arm. "Cousin Stephen, this is a family matter. If I don't have a financial stake in this house, I have an emotional one. My family built this too. We don't want to see it go down."

"It will go down if this gets out," he said.

"I believe the past and present are connected," said Wren. "The body in the attic, Karen Lavendell, and Andrew Heppenstall. It's one thing. I doubt if the police even realize that. You need to trust me that I can bring this to a successful conclusion without anyone being arrested. They won't hold off forever."

"So you're a historian, architect, and now detective."

"Putting a century-old house back together is detective work, I'm finding."

He sighed. "Hadley, I barely knew who you were until a few days ago. Wren, not much longer. Can I trust you not to go to the police?"

"I'm going to assume you're not covering up a crime," said Wren.

"Thank you," he said drily.

"If that's the case, I'll keep your secret, unless the police ask me outright, and that doesn't seem likely. Hadley and I agree on that."

He sighed again. "I'm trusting you. Not only to keep my secret but to wrap this up before even my influence can't save me from being arrested. All right. I was dining out with Perry's niece. How do you think I found you and your father, Wren?"

"Maureen Nyberg was auditing my father's lecture series. I remembered meeting her briefly. It was odd to have someone like that in a lecture like that, and who made a point of seeking me out as the nineteenth-century expert."

"You're right. And you were no doubt worried about my ability to pay for this, to find myself with no choice but selling to PH Partners if my backers pull out. You know better than anyone how much money I'm pouring into this house. I have plans for it…which I can't discuss now. But it's not like there are lots of options for a place like this. If I can't go forward, partnering with PH Hospitality would be my only option, and we don't want that."

"So what are you doing?" asked Wren. "What can you tell me?"

"Look. I knew Oren Perry. I knew he was restless—looking for the next chapter of his life. I also knew he liked a low profile. He made it clear he didn't want to involve himself in a project that would blow up in his face, that would damage his reputation. We arranged to have his niece Maureen, who was in his confidence, to sound out your father and serve as a go-between. We didn't want anyone to see Oren and me in communication—that would tip our hand. Neither of us wanted PH Partners to hear what we were up to so they could try to stop us. He was planning to put up a lot of money himself and bring in some associates who also would write checks. Anyway, Maureen went to your father's class and was impressed with both of you. Perry, of course, knew your firm by reputation, but he trusted Maureen to evaluate both of you in person. We had serious money behind us. I could be confident that even if costs exceeded our estimates—like needing several tons of copper—" He gave Wren a wry look. She coolly smiled back. "Anyway, I was confident. This is a Greenleaf town. PH Hospitality is new here and might find financing was not going to be easy for an outsider."

That made sense. But Wren still wondered what was in it for the Perrys—more than friendship, no doubt, and realized it may be just as well she didn't know anymore. But she had to make sure she was treading on solid ground.

"All right," said Wren slowly. "So we're a favorite firm of Oren Perry." She wondered if her father knew about this. "But why so secretive with Perry? "

"As I said, he likes a low profile, and with the murders—I can't have the police poking their noses into this. If they start wondering if Perry and I have a connection, he may feel things are getting too hot for him. He doesn't want to be even peripherally connected with the murder of someone who might be seen as his rival. But the way we work it, in a few weeks, Perry will be completely committed, and it will be too late for him and the syndicate to back off. That's just how long I need to hold off on giving the police a solid alibi."

"You hired me to fix up this house to look like it was the day your great-grandparents moved in, with relatively few changes—but enough power for a professional kitchen. And the specs for the ballroom can make it a conference room. We're not getting the whole story here."

Stephen spread his hands out. "I gave you some information because you forced me to. Because I needed you to know that my connection with Maureen and Perry was maybe underhanded but not illegal. But my plans for this must remain private for now."

"You may not have a few more weeks," said Wren. "I'm sensing that Sergeant Ortiz is going to be very persistent."

"Well then, you better find out what happened in that attic and why it's affecting what's happening today and the current murders, if that is indeed the case."

"Wren says it's all about the house, and I think she's right," said Hadley. "But it's about people, too. So your father never passed you down the secret of Uncle Ambrose? It didn't seem to make it down the Vanderwerf line either."

"No, I really don't know. You think he killed that girl in the attic—supposedly Fiona?"

"Our research shows that Fiona had the room where you say it happened. And she was gone from the house by 1900. We wonder why. Even if he had seduced her, raped her, there was no need to kill her."

"If you say so," he said. "As I said, I have little interest in family history. By the time I was in high school, I realized just how ridiculous it was, living in this drafty mausoleum, stuck in a Masterpiece Theatre costume drama." He smiled. "My father knew my feelings. Maybe that's why I was left out of the secret."

"But you know about the present. This was also Conor's home."

"Yes. Mrs. Ryan was a Murphy before her marriage. There have been Murphys here since Benjamin and Susan moved in. The last full-time housekeeper was a Murphy—some great-aunt of Mrs. Ryan's, I think."

"How well do you know him?" asked Wren. Would he share their arguments?

"Not very well. We both grew up here, but we're a generation apart. And he was—"

"—just the son of a servant, after all," said Hadley, with a wicked smile.

Stephen eyed her speculatively. "Yes, he was a servant's son. At one time or another, I had met all the Ryan children—he has two sisters, if I recall, considerably older. Mrs. Ryan had worked here before her marriage and then on and off over the years. Conor had come with her and then made his home here with his mother."

"You must've gotten a sense of him as a boy," said Wren. "He seems to have done well for himself—he must've been bright." She wanted to see if Stephen knew what Conor did for a living.

"Yes—I suppose he has. Does high-level research for some defense contractor, I think. You know...." His voice trailed off, and he looked lost, she thought. Hadley was about to prompt him, but Wren shook her head. She recognized a fellow thinker and wanted to give him time to work it through. "He was interested in this house, in the family, more than I was, who took it for granted. He was young when he came here, but old enough to realize he was moving from the outer boroughs to...this." He waved his arm. The dining room probably had more square footage than the boy's entire apartment. "He asked a lot of questions about the family—he was an intense boy, terribly curious about it all. He spoke a lot with Aunt Agnes, who found him amusing and told him about our family. I think she liked the idea of having a child around who, unlike me, had an interest in this place."

"Why not? This house was as much Murphy history as it was Greenleaf," said Hadley.

Stephen just grinned. "One thing Aunt Agnes always said about the

Vanderwerfs, they had a good sense of humor. But yes, they were here through the years. Anyway, I'm not bragging, but my father, Aunt Agnes, and I all helped Conor over the years, with college and as an undergraduate, and there was always a room for him here."

"Even as your money was disappearing?" asked Wren.

Hadley shook her head. "Economics was never my strong suit, Wren, but like I said, among families like us, we were often broke, but never poor."

Wren caught a look between them, between people with a shared family, a shared history, and knew her father was right. She could never understand...

"Why all this curiosity about Conor? I can't imagine Aunt Agnes telling him any secret about Uncle Ambrose. But do you think he knows something about the history of this house, something he learned from his mother? He struck me as secretive and is awfully close to my aunt. I always thought it was just a quirk...but is there something else?" He looked at Wren deeply. She knew he was concerned about what Conor knew, and about what he might do, and would hope if Conor had confided in her, she would share.

"In fact," said Wren. "Conor has some rather dark views of the Greenleafs. When the body was found, he told me from the start, he thought it was Fiona Murphy, a sister of his ancestor. And that Ambrose had raped her and killed her to cover it up. And every dime you gave him is blood money."

She expected a hot denial, even for him to stomp out of the room. But he just scratched his chin and looked thoughtful. When he spoke, he addressed Hadley.

"Your parents, or your Aunt Myrtle—did they give you a sense of family, of what it meant to be from a family like this one, with a connection to this house?"

"Oh God, yes. But I always thought it was ridiculous," said Hadley.

"So did I. But Aunt Agnes takes the tradition very seriously. Conor was a lesson to me. It never occurred to me that a descendent of the servants here would be as attached to the history of the house as those who built and owned it. That says something about me, and not to my credit, I'm sorry to say. But this house has inspired a great deal of fanaticism." He gave Wren a wry look. "Even to you, Madam Architect."

"I'm not a fanatic about this house," Wren said. "I'm professional."

"Really? The copper, the hickory, the master plasterer—whatever the hell you call him—to fix the ceilings. Isn't that obsessive?"

"Oh, come on, Stephen!" said Hadley. "You hired the best firm in the business, and when they do exactly what you tell them to do, you start complaining. You're the one who's the fanatic."

Wren felt herself warmed again by that spirited defense. Spirited and well-timed—she was about to lose her temper. Better it came from Hadley than from her.

"For me, this is about business," he said heavily. "Just business. While I admit it's somewhat intriguing, I don't give a damn about that body in the attic. And the two recent deaths, while tragic, are not statements about the history of this house, about which, again, I couldn't care less. Wren—you seem to think that Conor is obsessed with the house's past. Two people with connections to this house have been killed in recent weeks. In my line of work, we settle disagreements with lawyers. My secrets are business secrets. If the pair of you want to play detective, have you considered Conor?"

"What would be the motive?" asked Wren.

"I can't imagine. But I admit I can't figure him out. You don't think…." He let his voice trail off and frowned.

Wren thought again about the overheard conversation. Stephen was a businessman. No, not just a businessman, a Greenleaf, and they hadn't reached their heights without being ruthless. "I'm not a robber baron," he had joked with Wren. But here he was, throwing Conor under the bus.

"I think we're wandering from the topic," he finally said. "You wanted more about this house to protect your interest. I have told you what I could, and I can give you reasonable assurance that nothing will happen to stop the work on this house. I am not without resources." He gave them a reassuring smile. "That was very good, Hadley. Thank you for cooking it, and thank you, Wren, for sponsoring it—and for giving me my first opportunity to preside over a meal in this room. Very nice. I trust I was helpful—and that you will as much as possible keep the information confidential." He stood. "I have to get back to the office. You know where to reach me if anything comes up." He paused. "You work for me, Wren. I trust if Conor pushes for...any information, you'll let me know."

He didn't wait for a response, just walked the length of the dining room without looking back, and closed the door on his way out.

"Well," said Hadley. "That was some performance, making it clear without saying in so many words that it was the housekeeper's boy."

"It goes deeper." She told Hadley about the overheard conversation between Conor and Stephen."

"Wow. Do you see what I mean, Little Bird? We're terrible people."

Wren smiled. "Did it occur to you that maybe Conor is the terrible person here?"

"You mean, is he a murderer? I don't want to think that. I'm romantic, and I want to think that he's motivated by justice for poor Fiona, his relation."

"She was somebody's mother. You can tell from a skeleton, apparently. She had a baby."

"Oh! But that's so sad. She never got to watch her child grow up."

"I know," said Wren. She thought of Fiona, locked in that attic, forgotten, unmourned, and the child she would never know. And all of a sudden, she started to cry.

"Oh God, I'm so sorry."

"No—I lost my mother when I was 19. You couldn't have known what that meant to me. It's silly, but thinking about mothers...."

Hadley got up and gave her a hug. She didn't say anything for a while, and Wren was grateful for that, just enjoying being held.

"But you see," Hadley eventually said. "You understand now. You understand what Conor feels, what the Murphys felt, what that lost child felt. You know, you're a bit of a fake." Wren looked up from her tissues in astonishment. "You want everyone to think it's always about the house, but it's really about people."

She forced a smile. "Maybe."

Hadley looked around. "One way or another, there were a lot of problems here. Do you think there was love? Were the other marriages just partnerships between distinguished families? Was there love here at an point?"

Chapter Twenty-Five

H er father was in his study, going over one of his projects, when Wren got home. He looked up from his desk with a look she had long recognized. She remembered it from middle school when she had come home from school with a note saying "Wren has done 'A' work in history but does not seem to be able to work effectively with her fellow students in a group setting."

"Ah, doesn't play well with others," he had said. "I guess you're going to have to become an architect like me."

He put down his reading glasses. "I got a call from Stephen Greenleaf today. I was surprised. We hadn't spoken since signing the contract."

"Indeed?" said Wren, trying not to look too curious.

"Do you know what he told me? He said you were a 'piece of work.'"

"Sounds like a compliment. He certainly seemed to be pleased with our progress."

"Even all the copper fittings?"

"We've ironed out his concerns."

"Yes. But we're off-topic. Why did he call you a piece of work? That's not the usual sobriquet for an architect."

"Let me ask you something, *Ezra*. Did Stephen tell you why he chose you? Was there a competitive bidding process?"

"That's simple—I'm the best."

"I'm your partner. *We're* the best."

"Ooh. Nicely played."

"Anyway, I know we're the best. But Stephen is an investment advisor.

How did he know about us? It never occurred to me to ask. Until now."

"I assume you found out about Stephen's long-term friendship with Oren Perry? He told me that Perry was backing him. Do you think I'd devote so much of the firm's resources if I didn't think it would all work out, even with a bank guarantee?"

"Dammit, why didn't you tell me?" She slammed her hand on the desk, then crossed her arms across her chest, and he saw just how angry she was. He could offer no glib explanations.

Ezra sighed. "I should've. I know I've been telling you that you have to be a partner, but then I decide that I'll take on the back-office work by myself. I feared you lacked the...experience to navigate those complexities. But I was wrong. Anyway, I told Stephen that I wouldn't take on the job unless we could be certain he'd be able to see it through."

"Perry's niece, Maureen Nyberg. She was auditing your lecture series and talked to me about nineteenth-century homes. That's not a coincidence."

"Is that a question?"

"No. It's a statement." She looked hard at her father. She felt her heart pounding, was almost dizzy, but she wasn't going to back down.

"Wren, I am not known for my work in historical renovation. That's your specialty. I won't lie to you. There are other architects with more experience than you, and Stephen might've gone with them. But he went with us. He went with you. This is a New York situation. Perry had to be made to feel comfortable enough to back Stephen, and to that end, he wanted it kept local and go with a well-known New York name, and Fontaine fit the bill."

"So it was just because we're local?"

"Of course not. Stephen wouldn't have engaged us if he didn't have confidence in you. And if I hadn't thought you qualified, I wouldn't have risked the firm's name and reputation. But you want more details. Stephen needed a lever, and Maureen, Perry's niece, and confidant, slipped into my class not to check me out, but to check *you* out. She's always helped out her uncle when he needed to stay in the background. You impressed her. The word went to Stephen that if you were on the job, Perry would write the checks and get his friends to do so as well."

190

"When Karen Lavendell was killed, Stephen was having dinner with Maureen. I guess Perry and Stephen used Maureen to keep in touch. It would look bad if they were too close. They didn't want PH Hospitality to know about their plans. They might use whatever influence they had to block the syndicate." Wren folded her arms and shook her head. "I thought I was operating in a *Downton Abbey* world. And it's beginning to resemble *The Godfather.*"

"You can't possibly be that naïve," said her father. "What did you think the Greenleafs and all the other families were up to all those years? Didn't you learn anything from Lavinia?"

"Of course. I know there's a good chance that the Greenleafs were complicit in Fiona's death. My heart breaks for that woman in the attic, and for the two current deaths no doubt related to the house. But it's not the house's fault. The house is a legacy, a gift, to the city. That's how I see my work." She looked at her father, proud of what she had said.

"You're right. That was well said. Our work on houses is subject to our judgment and the rules of our profession. Nothing can alter our commitment not only to the safety of our projects but our artistic vision. But there are economic and even psychological considerations too. We must live in the real world."

"Meaning I don't?"

"Meaning you don't always want to. I know your mind is on your work, but you're still thinking about the women in hoop skirts waltzing across the ballroom floor."

"Hoop skirts went out of fashion a half-century before that house was built. I'm so glad for Mr. Greenleaf that the house is under the supervision of the Fontaine partner who knows a little something about the relevant history."

"Touché," said Ezra.

"And you owe me an apology."

He sighed. "You're right. Stephen gave me the backstory early in the process and swore me to secrecy. But I should've told you—I'm truly sorry. However, I am impressed that you uncovered it on your own."

"You're not going to flatter your way out of this. Don't keep things like this from me again."

She watched her father closely. "Humble" didn't wear well on him. He gave her a wry smile.

"You're right, daughter."

"It's not your daughter talking to you. It's a partner in this firm. And are you sure you don't know what he has planned? Heppenstall seemed to have a lot of details. I wish I had pressed him more."

"Wren. I needed to ensure that we would get to properly handle the house, which means that it would remain under Stephen's control. That was it. None of this should've been as big a deal as it has become. It's these murders that have put the focus on everything, on the fact that our client is a suspect, that his financing is endangered."

"That's true. But that still doesn't excuse your hiding the details from me."

"Again. You're right. But Wren, for now, we can't ignore the two murders—"

"Three."

"Excuse me?"

"Three. Fiona Murphy stuck in the trunk."

"That's hardly relevant. Wren—"

"But it is. It's all together. The house is the motive, over 100 years. I can feel it. Plus, the same gun was used to shoot whoever was in the attic and Karen Lavendell."

Ezra shook his head. "I wish your mother were here. She understood you." He sighed. "In any event, the worksite is dangerous. Don't be there unless Bobby and his crew are there, and always leave with someone. People are more important than houses. You are more important than Greenleaf House."

Wren smiled. "Be careful. I'll report you to the AIA for heresy like that." She stood and kissed him on his head. "Goodnight."

Chapter Twenty-Six

"I'm sure I'm the first in my family to sit at the drinking side of this bar," said Conor. He turned to Hadley. "I assume you're the member?"

"I'm allowed to come twice a year on my father's membership. Although this is only the second time I've been here—my father took me here for my 21st birthday. It's not really my scene. But it's a bit of family history. A Vanderwerf helped found this club and served on the first board. Cin-cin." She sipped her tonic water and smiled. The tables were spaced far apart, and white-jacketed waiters walked easily between them. Everything was old wood and brass and crystal. "I know," said Hadley, following her guests' eyes. "This place doesn't look real, does it?"

"That's the thing about the past," said Wren. "It's copied, and then mocked, and so eventually everyone forgets it was real. But these were real people. Greenleaf House wasn't a museum, it was a home. And this is where the men came to talk about politics and money and mistresses. Sláinte, Mr. Ryan."

He smiled and raised his glass.

"So where did the Murphys go when they got thirsty?" asked Wren.

"Hannigan's. It's been here as long as the Murphy's, still with the same family. They made it more upscale over the years, but it's still welcoming. This place doesn't seem welcoming.

"Anyway, I'm here because you asked me, Wren. I misjudged you. I should've listened to my mother. One of her favorite sayings is 'still waters run deep.' So you wanted to talk to me, but there's a reason you wanted to do it in one of the oldest, most exclusive WASP clubs in New York and bring along a Greenleaf in-law." He pointed his thumb at Hadley without looking at her. "This is your doing. Why?"

"You're the keeper of secrets," said Wren. "The man in the secret office with the secret quest on Greenleaf family history. You may bring marzipan to Aunt Agnes. But you don't really like them. And you only came today because you're hoping I know something that you don't. I want to know how Fiona Murphy ended up in that attic."

"Just curiosity?" he asked.

"No. But I care about the house. And this has something to do with who sits at the head of the family table. Hadley has insights into the family. So do you. We all win."

"Win what? I know what happened. Ambrose raped her and killed her. The family hid her body to save them the embarrassment of accusations."

"Oh, Conor, give us some credit. Our set hardly won awards for political correctness but killing maids and sealing them in an attic?" said Hadley.

"Then can you tell me how she ended up there?" he asked with exaggerated patience.

"Conor, we're still working through that," said Wren. "We can agree that it seems likely the Greenleafs had some knowledge of it, but this may be a more complicated scenario. I'm sure you found that Ambrose left his money to his niece, Laura, in England."

"Very nice, Wren. I told you there were things I couldn't discuss. But it seems you go there anyway, so I might as well be frank. So yes. The family traded a substantial piece of Greenleaf net worth for a title and a chance to mingle with royalty."

"But why did Ambrose give what little he had to her? He was exiled to Buenos Aires before she was born. He never even knew her."

"You speak in the tone of someone who already has the answer to that question," said Conor.

"In part," said Wren. "I have a dear friend who's a leading expert in the history of this city's old families. I spoke to her last night. Ambrose's money made its way to London. But at that time, a minority owner of record was still the Greenleaf Family Trust, which wouldn't be dissolved for some years. And New York is very good at keeping trust records. Almost as soon as the money came to Laura it came back to the Greenleaf Family Trust, under the auspices of the former Laura Greenleaf, and then it was paid out, under Laura's instructions. But that was the end of our paper trail. I'm wondering if you can pick it up."

Conor raised an eyebrow. "Your friend is very good. I'm impressed. But you're right. Laura was an outsider. She left the Greenleaf fold, so to speak, and was now more part of the English family. Because of that, my belief is that Ambrose felt he could trust his niece, in a way, he couldn't trust his brother or sister-in-law, or his nephew for that matter. He wanted to make some amends—blood money—and left what money he hadn't frittered away in Buenos Aires in trust for the Murphy family. He was afraid that Benjamin and Susan wouldn't honor his wishes, because they knew the story of what he had done and wouldn't approve of wasting family money because he felt bad. But no one would've told Laura the story. So he could trust her. The money probably came with a letter telling her what to do. If he had left the money directly to the Murphys in his will, everyone would want to know why a Greenleaf was leaving everything to the Irish help."

"That's about par for the course," said Hadley. "And people say the Vanderwerfs were the flighty ones."

"It's my family, not a joke," said Conor. "The money went to the family of Kevin Murphy. Kevin was Fiona's closest relative, her older brother. He was my great-great-grandfather. Kevin was able to start a business on the side and eventually leave service. God knows what they told Kevin to accept this."

"That was more than a century ago. A long time to be bitter," said Wren. "You wouldn't have gotten this far without some tales told by your mother. But she probably wasn't clear or consistent, just snatches of stories at family events when everyone had a little wine."

Wren took a deep breath. She didn't want to go there, but she knew she had to give something to get something. She had to do the work of a partner. And partners had to deal with people.

"My mother died when I was a teenager," she said.

Conor blinked. "I'm sorry to hear that. As you know, I lost my father when I was young."

"I heard. I wanted to bring that up to show you I understand what you went through. Where you come from. Anyway, that's when you moved into Greenleaf House. It must've been difficult."

He shrugged. "I still had my friends, my school. My older sisters visited."

"And now you had Aunt Agnes. She must've been bored, day after day, and with you and your mother living here, she had a new audience for her stories, about how things were. About how the Greenleafs lived. About how the Murphys served them."

"Children don't have much interest in history. That came later," he said, and Wren heard a hint of sullenness.

"Of course. But children can be very sensitive to the present. I...I, of course, was pretty much grown when my mother died, but I was still young, and an only child. I was at Columbia, and so many times I reached for the telephone to talk to her about my day...only to remember again she wasn't there. My father was not someone you made small talk with."

She looked at Hadley—were her eyes getting moist? *Please don't fall apart, or I will too!*

Conor. What was in his eyes? Did she see some sympathy there? Perhaps. And confusion. He didn't know where this was going.

"I suppose I was luckier than you. I lost the parent who was emotionally remote. And I had my sisters. Wren, I don't quite see—"

"Yes. But your mother was working, and your sisters were out of the house. I'm thinking of Stephen Greenleaf. He probably visited fairly often. Aunt Agnes was probably not as—well, let's say she was more tethered to the present back then." Conor laughed at that and nodded. "The whole family came, I guess. Stephen is twenty-five or so years older than you. He probably had sons your age, or a little younger. Those boys didn't go to the same school as you, did they? They probably went to a school with uniforms. And summers? Some fancy sleepaway camp. And you? A YMCA day camp, or a family trip to Jones Beach."

Stephen didn't look confused anymore. He looked upset, and Wren felt a little thrill—and relief. *I've gotten to him.*

"Stephen told me that he used to race his toy cars in the dining room. Children probably weren't even permitted in the dining room when it was built. How about you, Conor? Were you allowed to race your cars there?"

"No," he said after a pause. "Not the servant's son. I had a room in the nursery suite, next to my mother's. If I was a good boy, I was allowed to 'perform' for Aunt Agnes."

"Perform?"

"Parade anything I learned in school for the delight of the lady of the manor. If I did well, I got a cookie. So I bring her marzipan now, as a thank you."

"Did Stephen's sons get cookies?" asked Wren.

"What the hell do you think?" he shot back. "You know damn well they did. I was sent to the kitchen to get them."

"You were no doubt older."

"Nothing to do with age. I was the servant's son. I waited on the master's children."

"We're horrible. You probably figured that out pretty quickly," said Hadley.

"You got that right."

Wren almost winced at the disgust in his voice. But Conor, a keeper of secrets, had probably learned to keep his own counsel from his youngest years. The child wanted the cookie. The adult wanted to know the Greenleaf secrets locked inside Aunt Agnes' head, in the hope she'd reveal them to the man she believed loved the house more than her nephew did.

"That must've hurt very much. Little boys can be very sensitive to slights like that," she said.

"Did you invite me here just to review my childhood hurts? Share and share alike, okay? Did it hurt a lot when other girls had their mothers visit, and you didn't?"

"Yes," said Wren softly. "It hurt a lot. I suppose the difference is that I didn't let my hurt turn into a crusade to bring down a family decades later, based on a century-old murder. This is not about family justice. It's about you, humiliating them as payback, fetching cookies for the children who owned a house where your presence was merely tolerated."

He eyed her but didn't say something for a long time. Eventually, he turned to Hadley. "Thank you for the drink, and for the opportunity to stand on this side of the bar. Have a good afternoon."

He got up and left. Wren stared into her glass. Conor was wounded, and there was no telling what he might've done in that state. Could she figure out what he'd get out of killing Lavendell or Heppenstall?

"I'm sorry," said Hadley, breaking into her thoughts.

"For what?" asked Wren, genuinely confused.

Hadley smiled. "I'm sorry you were hurt so badly when you were 19. I'm sorry my family hurt Conor so badly. And I'm sorry someone as private as you got stuck in the middle."

Wren put her hand on Hadley's.

"That's very kind of you to say," she said.

"For God's sake, Wren, it's not kindness. I like you…very much." She leaned over and kissed her.

"Do you think that was the first same-sex kiss in this establishment?" asked Wren.

"Look around you. I think it was probably the first kiss, period." They both laughed. "So where do we go from here?"

Chapter Twenty-Seven

Wren had given some thought to how best to tackle Mrs. Ryan, whose roots with the family and the house ran as deep as Aunt Agnes'. She could've done it in the house, where Mrs. Ryan was comfortable, to give her a reminder of those roots, but the connections with Aunt Agnes might be too strong. Wren knew she may not be able to work with people very well, but she knew about interior atmospheres and how they could affect people.

Hadley's presence was essential, of course, as a reminder to Mrs. Ryan about where her loyalties lay.

Getting Aunt Agnes to sign off on the plan had been tricky too. After returning to the house after drinks with Conor, Wren had kept an ear open for when Mrs. Ryan went on an errand and then found an excuse to have to visit the suite.

"It's going well?" asked Aunt Agnes.

"Proceeding nicely, thank you. It'll be some months yet, but I'm looking forward to giving you a tour when it's done. It'll look like the day Benjamin Greenleaf walked across the threshold with his bride."

"But without the servants," said Aunt Agnes, unwilling to show any pleasure. "The maids in their aprons. The butler in his suit with shiny buttons."

Could she have even remembered that? Was there even a proper butler in this house by the 1930s?

"Yes, of course. But that brings me to my next question. You and Stephen have been helpful with your knowledge of the house. I was hoping one more person could help—Mrs. Ryan."

"Ha! How could she help?"

"She has lived in this house for years. Her family's history is this house's history, as much as the Greenleaf's."

That earned Wren a sly smile. "But they were in the kitchen, not in the dining room or ballroom or library."

"Oh, but who cleaned the library? Who served at dinner?"

"That's not what I meant. Don't play games."

"I'm not. I'm an architect. Rooms must be beautiful and useful. The Greenleafs knew how beautiful this house was. The servants knew how they were used. How to set up the chairs in the dining room, how the furniture was cleaned and cared for in the bedrooms. I would like your permission to talk to Mrs. Ryan about this house and family memories."

She fixed a suspicious eye on her. "Just what do you expect to get out of talking with her? Gossip?"

"I'm not interested in gossip. I'm reviving this house, not writing a book. And surely you don't expect Mrs. Ryan to share gossip? No, let's call it a servant's eye view of the house. It will help me finalize some details, the home from a different perspective."

"Ask her yourself. She doesn't need my permission to talk to you." Aggrieved and wistful for a day when the mistress's permission would've been necessary. But not today, when Miss Greenleaf needed Mrs. Ryan more than Mrs. Ryan needed her.

"I know. But I think she'd balk unless you told her it was OK with you. We'll take her out to lunch."

"Oh, all right," she had sounded reluctant, but more afraid of the message she might send if she said no. "I suppose she deserves a nice lunch. But don't try to get her drunk. Although she's Irish, believe it or not, she's not used to drink."

Mrs. Ryan cautiously agreed, after confirming Miss Greenleaf approved, but the next day, she looked guarded when she met Wren and Hadley at the bottom of the stairs at the appointed hour. She wore a fancier dress than usual, and higher heels.

"If I understood you correctly, Miss, you wish to discuss my memories of the house and stories I heard from older members of my family, who used to work here."

"Exactly," said Wren. "The more we know about the house, the better we are able to recreate it exactly as it used to be."

"Very well. But I will not discuss the family," said Mrs. Ryan.

"It's my family, too," said Hadley. "Miss Greenleaf has as much Vanderwerf blood as Greenleaf. I shouldn't expect anything but discretion from a member of the Murphy family."

Mrs. Ryan stared at Hadley for a moment, perhaps wondering if she was being mocked, but decided a relation of Miss Greenleaf's dear friend Aunt Myrtle was legitimate.

"Thank you, miss," she said.

"I thought we'd go to Hannigan's, on the east side," said Wren.

"I beg your pardon, miss. Hannigan's?"

"Yes, you know of it?" asked Wren.

"It has been around for many years." She paused. "The Murphys, my father's people, have long patronized it."

"Have you ever been?" asked Hadley.

Again, a sharp look. "Yes, miss, but not since I was younger, a long time ago."

Outside, Wren hailed a cab, and soon they were settled in what may have been Manhattan's most old-fashioned restaurant. She had remembered Conor bringing it up, and if it had long been a Murphy haunt, she was confident Mrs. Ryan knew about it. As she had told Hadley, she had wanted Conor a little rattled, bringing him to that WASP headquarters.

But she wanted Mrs. Ryan relaxed—back in her element. She had wondered how to get Mrs. Ryan away from Greenleaf House, from the reminders of her background, her duty. Conor had inadvertently given her the solution.

Wren caught a brief smile on Mrs. Ryan's face as she took in the restaurant. Although Wren had never been inside, she had no trouble believing what Conor had said—the place was no doubt fancier than when it was founded in the 19th century. The Irish had prospered, and Hannigan's had prospered too. Linen tablecloths and arugula salads existed next to a well-populated bar decorated with signed pictures of sports stars, actors, and singers. Some of them Wren knew, and others had no doubt been famous before films, before even radio, and their fans were long gone.

A server in a white blouse with black apron and slacks handed out menus. "Can I get anyone something to drink?"

"A glass of your house white," asked Wren. Mrs. Ryan hesitated. "I'll have one as well," she said, a little self-consciously. Hadley caught Wren's eye and winked, then ordered a plain tonic.

Chapter Twenty-Eight

Mrs. Ryan seemed very pleased with her wine, and roast chicken with mashed potatoes and broccoli.

"Is the food here as you remember?" asked Wren.

"It is good," said Mrs. Ryan. "The menu, of course, has fewer of the old specialties. Times change." She wasn't happy about it. Yes, it was the house, Wren saw again. If the two women were living somewhere else, the modern world would've sneaked up on them. But in that old house, the memories of old customs, old traditions—and old cuisine—stayed with them.

"You must've seen many changes in the way food was served at Greenleaf House. It's something I'm interested in, to make sure the plan of the house continues to allow the free flow from the kitchen to the dining room. I can't think of anyone who would be more knowledgeable about that than a Murphy."

Mrs. Ryan sighed. "It's been a long time since there were meals served in the dining room."

"My Aunt Myrtle told me about the old days, although like Miss Greenleaf, she was born after the house's greatest years, before the first world war," said Hadley. "But her memories and stories were all one-sided. Who sat at the table. But who cooked it, and served it, and how it got from the kitchen...."

"Exactly," said Wren. "We were hoping you could fill in the blanks. And please understand this is all in confidence among the three of us."

"Thank you. And you're right about how things worked here. The family didn't bother with those details in the old days. We took care of it—that is, the Murphys who came before me." Wren thought she heard pride in her voice—and perhaps a hint of criticism as well. "It was beautifully organized, you see. My Murphy grandfather, Brian, explained it to me." Mrs. Ryan launched into details, the table in the kitchen where the cook put the platters, the large sink where the dirty plates ended up, the dumbwaiter where the kitchen maids pulled the platters into the waiting hands of footmen upstairs. "They sealed that up in the 1950s. Some man from the city said it wasn't safe anymore. They didn't want to repair it. Mr. Greenleaf, Mr. Stephen's father, said he doubted they could even find someone who could fix it."

"Actually, Bobby—Mr. Fiore—said he could fix it, and was going to. I don't know if they will use it again, but I promised the Greenleafs a full restoration, and I'm keeping my word," said Wren.

"He's a good man, your Mr. Fiore," Mrs. Ryan said. She seemed genuinely grateful. She had a little color in her cheeks. Wren realized it had been a long time, if ever, that someone had ever asked Mrs. Ryan for a story, for an opinion. Conversations with Miss Greenleaf were probably one-way.

A shout came from the bar, where an enthusiastic group of men was watching a ballgame on TV. Mrs. Ryan was momentarily distracted. Hadley used the moment to give a discreet wave to the server. All that talking had made Mrs. Ryan thirsty, and her empty wine glass was slipped away and replaced with a fresh one without her noticing.

"My grandfather remembered when they first installed a TV here," she said. "He, and his friends and his brothers—they spent a lot of time thinking about how things were. I know a lot of this seems very old, even silly, to young women like you. It's not that we're unaware of how things are today, but you get used to a certain way things are done, and it's hard to change. We spend a lot of time in the past. Not just with Miss Greenleaf. Even the Murphys look back at the past."

"But I see your son—and probably your other relatives. Doing better than they were generations ago."

"That's true," said Mrs. Ryan. "But the family still looks back. It doesn't make sense, I know, but there's an attachment..." she shook her head. "I don't suppose you understand."

"I do," said Wren, and Mrs. Ryan thought about that. *Oh yes. Still connected to that house. Even if it wasn't yours, the family is still connected to it.*

"Perhaps you do," she said.

Wren looked at the TVs. "So, were they annoyed at the change in tradition?" asked Wren.

"That was one change they liked. My grandfather thought TV was a gift from God," said Mrs. Ryan. "He had another reason to spend as much time here as possible. In fact, it was in this room that he told me all about the old days. My grandfather was a regular, you see, and my brothers and I could come here on special occasions. He was born in 1897 and started working at the house as a boy. Then came the war. Most of the men joined up, and after the war...." She gave a little shrug. "Things had changed."

"In the house or for your grandfather?" asked Wren.

Mrs. Ryan blinked. "Both, I imagine. He continued to work at the house, but only for special occasions now—and there was a small family business. But he liked talking about the old days. He told me how Greenleaf House was really two houses, the house the family lived in, and the house of the Murphys and other servants, who kept it going 'behind the scenes,' as he said."

"Brian Murphy—I'm just trying to understand the family relationships. Brian was Fiona's nephew?"

At that name, Mrs. Ryan gave Wren a sharp look. Had she brought up the name too quickly?

"Yes," said Mrs. Ryan after a moment. "Brian Murphy's father, my great-grandfather, was Kevin, and as a young man, he was the family coachman. Fiona was his younger sister."

"Did she marry and have children?" asked Wren.

"No," she said sadly. "But I could be wrong. She ran off, you see." She drank more wine and looked down at the remnants of her lunch.

"That's what you were told, right? That was the family story," said Wren. "Until the day we opened the attic."

"I can't talk about the family," said Mrs. Ryan, barely above a whisper.

"I'm not talking about the Greenleafs," said Wren. "I'm talking about the Murphys."

"It was the Greenleaf's House," she said.

"But your grandfather said it was two houses. I'm talking about the Murphy's part. I'm talking about the Murphys, who lived in the servant quarters, until one of them apparently ended up in the attic."

She wouldn't meet Wren's eye. "I can't," she said. "We promised. Kevin, and Brian too, after he joined the family."

"I'm sorry—you said, after he *joined* the family?"

"Yes, joined the family. After he was born," she said. "Fiona had shamed us, shamed the Greenleafs, and promises were made."

Hadley reached over and put her hand on Mrs. Ryan's arm.

"Promises, Mrs. Ryan. Promises to Susan Greenleaf, nee Vanderwerf, mistress of the house. That is my family, my inheritance as much as Miss Greenleaf's. This is about Susan, isn't it?"

"I can't talk about the family," said Mrs. Ryan, but more in sadness than in anger.

"My family," said Hadley. "Not Greenleafs, but Vanderwerfs. Susan was born and raised a Vanderwerf." Mrs. Ryan looked at Hadley, and then back at Wren. *She's wavering.*

"Tell me about Susan Vanderwerf," asked Wren. "Two people are dead—three if you count Fiona—and there is no more time for secrets." After a moment, Mrs. Ryan nodded slowly, and turned to Hadley.

"I will tell you what I can, miss, about my family, and about Susan Greenleaf, who, as you say, was a Vanderwerf, and about the Murphys." She reached into her leather bag, the one no doubt saved for "good" occasions, and fished out some tissues. She wiped her eyes.

"Will you be telling us what you told Conor?" asked Wren. Mrs. Ryan's lip curled.

"For all he lived here as a boy, he never really understood what it was all about. Miss Greenleaf always said Conor appreciated the house, but he didn't understand the way it worked. My other children are the same, I'm afraid. Times are different. I suppose everyone always says that, and now I'm the last of the Murphys with any ties to the house and the family. But you are a Vanderwerf, miss, and you, Miss Fontaine—Miss Greenleaf says you understand the house, even more than Mr. Stephen does, and I believe that. And so, you will get the real story, as far as I know it. Fiona, as I said, was my grandfather Brian's aunt, but he never knew her and didn't speak about her. You ladies don't have children, but you are not so old that you've forgotten being one, and how you get a sense that there's something going on that the grown-ups don't want you to know, and it makes you want to know all the more."

Wren thought about Conor, the little boy growing up in a ruined manor that wasn't his.

Mrs. Ryan smiled briefly. "At least, that's the way it always was among us. We'd know about an uncle who was a little too fond of the bottle, a cousin who had to get married with unseemly haste. But about Fiona—nothing. She had just disappeared. We imagined she ran off with an unsuitable man. Of course, I don't have to tell you about the rumors about her and Ambrose. He was handsome and very much a ladies' man. She was young, and everyone said she was very pretty. There were romantic stories about their running off together, and I passed them on to Conor when he pushed me for details. I just gave him the same stories we all heard. But we knew they were lies. Ambrose was sent away—a big deal was made of it, on the ship to South America, and Fiona certainly wasn't with him."

"But Susan," pressed Wren.

"Yes, what about my Aunt Susan? What was her role?"

"I would've thought your Aunt Myrtle told you, miss," said Mrs. Ryan.

"She told me a story that may be as much a fairytale as the ones you were told," said Hadley. "Ambrose and Susan had a passionate affair."

Mrs. Ryan's eyes lost their focus. She was looking into the past.

"My eldest brother asked our grandfather Brian that once," said Mrs. Ryan. She forced a sad smile. "For his curiosity, he got a smack in the head. My grandfather said any man who accused Ambrose of seducing his brother's wife was damned, and no one would criticize Ambrose in his presence. He was furious."

"You believed him?" asked Wren.

"You didn't see him, Miss. He wasn't above criticizing the family, especially after a drink or two. But it was never about something important, just about how someone ate too much or made a fool of himself courting a girl, that kind of thing. But he exploded over Ambrose. No one brought him up again."

Just like Miss Greenleaf. But she wasn't defending Ambrose. She was disgusted with him.

"Were you close with your grandfather?"

"Oh yes," she said. "He had only sons, and all his grandchildren were boys, except for me, so I stood out. My grandmother had died some years earlier, and I was the one he wanted with him on his deathbed. The priest had given him last rites, and he asked to see me alone. 'Eileen,' he said, 'It will be all right. God has forgiven my father'—that is, Kevin—'and Susan Greenleaf as well, even though a Protestant, and I will be reunited with my family in Heaven." She buried her face in her hands. "And that is all I can tell you, Miss." She dabbed more at her tears. "And all that time, she was right over our heads."

"Did you get any sense that your grandfather, that any of the Murphys, knew what really happened to her?"

"If it were just a Murphy secret, I would tell you," she said. Wren considered that. *Just* a Murphy secret. That meant it was a Greenleaf secret too. Brian Murphy respected Ambrose. Aunt Agnes...did not.

"You said that Fiona was known to be beautiful. Was her brother, your great-grandfather Kevin, also good-looking?"

"Oh, yes, my grandfather said Kevin was quite a man for the ladies. The great families liked that, you know, parlor maids and footmen and coachmen who looked handsome, and Kevin would've had a sharp uniform—a handsome man on top of their fine coach. It was said Brian was the same—although a boy, he had Fiona's features, and that's why his father favored him."

"But about Susan. I'm just a little curious about the deathbed comments about her. It seems normal to bring up his family at his death, but why Susan Greenleaf? What did she do that your grandfather thought she'd be forgiven?"

"I couldn't say, Miss."

Can't or won't, thought Wren. But Mrs. Ryan was done. She had pulled herself together.

"Thank you for your insights," said Wren. "I assure you again, this is all confidential. We won't reveal our conversations to Miss Greenleaf or Stephen."

"Thank you. I don't want them to think I was disloyal."

"You haven't been disloyal," said Hadley. Mrs. Ryan seemed grateful for that.

"Just one more thing," said Wren. "Something much later. Miss Greenleaf talked about her coming out party. It was right after the second world war, the last great party the house has seen. Before your time, of course, but maybe your parents had spoken about it? Again, it will help us get a feel for the space."

"Oh yes, a bit of family legend." She perked up at that, perhaps feeling they were on safer ground. "Things were very different by then, of course. The Depression, and then the War. My father—Sean—left service to the Greenleafs and joined up right after Pearl Harbor. He saw some action but made it through. My eldest brother has his medals. Anyway, he came back, got married, and worked part-time at Greenleaf House. There was very little full-time staff by then. Much of the house was closed off. But there was going to be this one last party for Miss Greenleaf's debut."

"A *last* party?"

"No one said anything, but as my father told me later, they could see...the house was no longer being run as it had been." She forced that last bit out, as close as she would come to criticizing the Greenleafs. "But it was going to be a grand evening. My father talked about it for years after." She perked up now, smiled at better memories. "A band, fine foods...."

"So soon after the War, there must've still been rationing. I suppose the family could get around that," said Hadley.

A knowing smile. "I suppose so, indeed, miss. I do know that my father never stopped talking about that evening. All the young gentlemen were in uniform. The ballroom was cleaned up and used after so many years."

"It must've been very exciting for Miss Greenleaf," said Wren.

"I'm sure it was," said Mrs. Ryan. "She likes to talk about it. Her escort was a naval lieutenant, Charles Barrington, and everyone said he was so handsome." She smiled, as if it had been her own memory. But if the story had been told over and over again, the line may have been indelibly blurred.

"He must be a Barrington of Barrington & Askew," said Hadley. "They're a big and distinguished firm. Do you think he wanted to marry Miss Greenleaf? It would've been an excellent match."

"But no," said Wren. "To marry would mean leaving the house."

Mrs. Ryan looked surprised, but only for a moment. Then she smiled slowly. "You understand, miss. Miss Greenleaf has said it often, that you loved the house. She has said, 'my grandfather Benjamin who built this house loved it most of all. I loved it second best,' and she said that you, Miss Fontaine, and my son Conor, are tied for three." Wren looked at her closely. *Do you understand, miss, just how great a compliment that is?*

It gave Wren an entrée to her next topic.

"Yes—Benjamin Greenleaf. I heard he and Susan Greenleaf were still alive then, but it was Benjamin's final days. He died just a few weeks later. But it must've been a comfort for Miss Greenleaf to have her grandfather still with her on that important day."

"Oh yes. He was bedridden by then. But Miss Greenleaf said how she visited him in her pretty dress before the start of the evening."

"Did she visit him at the end of the evening?" asked Wren.

Mrs. Ryan looked at her. "Yes, miss. Yes, she did. He didn't know how much time he had left, Miss Greenleaf always said. He had some presents to give her, family heirlooms."

"Do you know what they were?"

Mrs. Ryan started to talk...then remembered herself. "I don't know. As I said, miss, I can talk about the house, but not about Miss Greenleaf."

"Of course. Anyway, I heard both the library and ballroom were used, but both were shut up after that party, and remained shut up."

"Yes, that's true. My father was the one who closed them, in fact. Mr. Greenleaf, that is, Miss Greenleaf's father, Mr. Benjamin's son, had the keys.

The staff cleaned up that night. And the next morning, my father and Mr. Greenleaf locked up both the ballroom and the library. And that was it."

"The library—its ladder is broken. Was it broken then?"

"It broke during the war. There were no supplies to fix it, and no men around to take care of it anyway. "

"Was Miss Greenleaf sad about that the rooms being closed off?"

"The next morning, when she found out, I heard she was furious. She liked those rooms. But her father said he wasn't going to keep them open for her to sulk in."

Once again, she realized she was talking about Miss Greenleaf. She looked at her watch. "Thank you for lunch, but I need to get back."

"Of course. You've been very helpful, and I appreciate your time and memories."

Wren paid, and as Mrs. Ryan put on her jacket, Hadley caught her eye: *Oh, you know something, Little Bird.*

"By the way," said Wren as they were walking out the door. "Stephen Greenleaf asked me to look out for some diaries that belonged to Benjamin. Mr. Fiore and I will look out for them as we work. Do you think that Miss Greenleaf has an idea of where they are? The elderly are sometimes forgetful, and maybe she mentioned something to you."

Again, the long look. "I don't involve myself in Greenleaf business matters," she said.

"But the diaries were not business. They may have been the heirlooms that Mr. Benjamin gave Miss Greenleaf."

"I couldn't say, miss," said Mrs. Ryan.

Yes, you can. You just did. He gave Agnes the diaries. But why? Did they contain the secret of Fiona?

211

Chapter Twenty-Nine

"So what do you know? You learned something," said Hadley. Mrs. Ryan had gone back to the suite, and Wren and Hadley were sitting in the Rose Parlor.

Wren leaned back on the worn couch and closed her eyes, and Hadley said nothing, and they just sat in the quiet of that faded room.

"Families," said Wren. "Mrs. Ryan and Miss Greenleaf have that in common, those tight connections with previous generations that bring that story into the present. I wonder…." Wren was quiet for a while. "I have to put Lavinia on a trail. She'll love this, and it'll be something for her book." She dashed off an email, then leaned back and smiled slowly, triumphantly. "And the families have this house in common: The power of those who sat at the table, who was the master at one end and who was the mistress at the other. For over a century. And it isn't over." She sighed. "But I can't prove it. Benjamin wrote it all down. He was dying, and he knew it. I think he saw them as a legacy, as perhaps as a defense, for the decisions he made, and entrusted them to his granddaughter—the only one who loved the house like he did. Did he expect her to treasure them? But she knew what was in those diaries and that no one else would understand. That ballroom has the most beautiful fireplace. That night, she took the diaries her grandfather gave her. And that was the last night that ballroom would be used. Everyone knew that. It would have a fire for the last time. She took the diaries and burned them. So unless she wants to talk, there is no way of proving anything."

"You mean, proving Ambrose killed Fiona? Benjamin kept a record and told his brother he'd be silent as long as he left the country and never came back?"

"Poor Fiona," said Wren. "It wasn't really about her. She just got in the way."

Hadley eyed Wren closely. "You sound very sure of yourself. How can you be so sure?"

"The same way I know what's behind the walls in this room. There's only one way it can be. And there's only one way Fiona could've died."

Hadley leaned over and put her hand on Wren's knee. "Little Bird, you're brilliant. But people aren't houses."

"You're right. I'm being arrogant. And people were passionate here, I'm sure. But it was a passion for the house. It still is. It's just not about Fiona. That's of historical interest, but today I know what's really important are Karen Lavendell and Andrew Heppenstall. It's all of a part. Everyone died for the same reason. For control of the house. For the right to sit at the head of the table."

"What about the gun?"

"Probably at the bottom of the Hudson," said Wren. "I'll tell Sergeant Ortiz. Maybe he can do something. Maybe he can find evidence I don't know about. I don't want to forget that the murders we have to worry about are the modern ones. The gun is the same, and so is the motive."

"But you said you had to tell Ortiz something. Tell him what?" asked an exasperated Hadley. "I still don't know what you're talking about."

Wren laughed. "I'm sorry. Too much of my life spent by myself, talking without having anyone else in the room. I'm being awful, and I'm sorry." She stood and held out her hand. "Come. I want to look again at the portraits upstairs. And while we're looking at them, I'll tell you a story."

* * *

They sat on the couch in Hadley's Manhattan apartment, the remnants of dinner still on the table.

"Thank you for the nice dinner," said Wren. "I'm sorry I'm not better company."

"What is it? The Greenleafs? The Vanderwerfs? But no, it's your father, isn't it?"

"Yes. I mean, it's all those things, and the thought of three deaths and no one punished. I'm glad I figured it out, but it's all academic, unless Sergeant Ortiz can pull a rabbit out his hat. But why did my father lie to me?"

"You told me he was a man of—I remember your exact words—great personal honor."

"That's what's so disappointing about this."

"But he might've made a promise to someone else. If he had done that, someone who told him he had to keep it to himself, then he wouldn't violate it for family's sake, would he?"

"I suppose," said Wren. "Still...we're partners in the firm. What about your father?"

Hadley laughed. "Oh, Little Bird, you've seen what we're like. Nothing changes, really, in what we think is important. From time to time, we build lovely houses—" Now, Wren laughed. "But beneath the façade...anyway, we can be very sentimental. One of our saving graces. It's not all about money and power. We genuinely like grandmother's pendant and grandfather's pocket watch. But you're not sentimental about things, are you?"

"No, I suppose not," said Wren. "Not about things. I have my mother's jewelry box, but I never wear any of her pieces, never even look at them. I treasure my memories of her, but things are just that...things. I like the jewelry only as artwork."

"But you love Greenleaf House?"

"Again, as a work of art. It's about the perfection of the building, for me, not the family connection."

"Wren—you love this house like a person."

"Perhaps," said Wren. "Maybe because houses are easier to understand and more reliable than people."

"Maybe you will find that isn't always true," said Hadley quietly.

"Maybe," said Wren. She smiled. "At least, I very much hope so." They were quiet for a while. She looked at Hadley. "Was your Aunt Myrtle sentimental?"

"Absolutely! She had several pair of kid gloves that had belonged to Susan

214

Greenleaf. My God, do you know how long it's been since anyone wore kid gloves? They were so soft and beautiful. When I was a little girl, she sent me to wash my hands, and when they passed inspection, she allowed me to try them on."

"She left them to you, didn't she?"

"Yes. I have them. I know...they were originally Susan's. But I will always associate them with Aunt Myrtle. I'll never wear them for real, but sometimes I try them on—Wren, are you OK?"

Wren had closed her eyes.

"Your secret inheritance from Aunt Myrtle. But Agnes Greenleaf also had a secret inheritance. One she has been waiting to collect for more than half a century. I was wrong about her."

"What?"

"The keys to all the locked rooms are hanging on a hook in the kitchen, except for the front door keys, which I keep with me. Aunt Agnes is going to collect her inheritance. She can't wait anymore—she'll have a pretty good idea of what we got out of Mrs. Ryan. There have already been too many deaths to see who gets to sit at the head of the table." She stood. "I have to go back to the house."

"Should we call Sergeant Ortiz?"

"And tell him what? I'll leave him a message, but I have to go—"

"*We* have to go," said Hadley. "It's your job. But it's my family. We'll get a cab on the avenue. And I have a can of pepper spray in my bag."

"Why?"

"Oh, Wren, you lead such a more wholesome life than I do."

Wren had second thoughts when the driver dropped them off. New York cabbies tend to be blasé, but even he asked, "Are you sure? Here?" The house was dark and seemed much larger by night, less Edith Wharton and more Bram Stoker. She had felt guilty allowing Hadley to come but was now glad she did.

Wren let them in through the front door, glad they had worn soft-soled shoes. Even their breathing seemed to echo in the foyer. She didn't dare turn on the lights, but enough light came in from the street to show them up the stairs. Wren took Hadley's hand as they walked along the carpeted hallway, and around the corner, they saw the library door open and a light on inside. It would've been better if they had come earlier, but they were not too late.

Wren and Hadley slipped in quietly. Aunt Agnes was dressed in a robe and had climbed the ladder. She was slowly removing books from a high shelf. Of course. There was no better place to hide books than among other books. Sentimental indeed, she had saved her grandfather's diaries. A slight girl, perhaps dizzy from champagne, she had hidden these books away, knowing that Caleb Greenleaf and Sean Murphy would be locking up those rooms. But she probably hadn't realized it would be forever. And those keys had been in possession of her father, then her brother, then her nephew, for over 70 years, and she never had a chance to get them—to hide them better, edit them, or finally destroy them before Stephen or PH Hospitality came across them. Even if she had persuaded someone to let her view it, she'd never be left alone inside long enough to retrieve the diaries from the top shelf.

Until the architect left them in the kitchen. One of those sleeping pills, no doubt, slipped into Mrs. Ryan's evening tea, and the path was clear.

Wren just looked, not knowing what to say, even how to get Miss Greenleaf's attention in that large room, as the old lady balanced on that damaged ladder. Wren just stared, imagining her going step by step to reach those books, a decades-old memory of where she left them, a film playing in her mind before she went to sleep, night after night, year after year.

And then she had it. A large leather-bound diary. No wonder it was hidden in the library—there was no way she could hide that in her suite, and there were likely several volumes hidden in the shelves as well, many with incriminating notes, slid carefully behind never-read volumes for decades.

"Miss Greenleaf," said Wren. It felt like she was shouting in that room. The old woman stopped but didn't turn. Just rested against the ladder. She had been defeated. She had waited seventy years, covered up a murder, committed two more, and had been caught maybe half an hour before completing her task.

"That ladder isn't safe," said Wren. "Let me help you down before you fall."

CHAPTER TWENTY-NINE

"Aunt Myrtle wouldn't have wanted you to end up like this," added Hadley.

"Both of you," said Aunt Agnes grimly. "You're both here." But she still didn't look at them.

Wren knew she couldn't go up the ladder herself; it was barely supporting Aunt Agnes.

"Climb down. Hadley and I will stand at the bottom to ease you down. Leave the books there. We can get them after Mr. Fiore fixes the ladder."

At first, it looked like Aunt Agnes would comply. She put down the leather book. But then, instead of climbing down, she half turned to face Wren and Hadley. She smiled.

She held on with her left hand and reached into her robe pocket. Out came the tiny handgun that had killed Fiona and Karen—and was about to kill both of them.

I don't understand people, and now my ignorance is getting both of us killed. Of course, she would take the gun with her tonight, so easy to hide all these years in the bottom of a jewelry box where no one would dream of looking, a gun that unlike the diaries had been long forgotten.

What to do next? Scream? Run? Plead? But no. That final shift of weight was all it took. The cracked railing broke away from its support and the ladder came swinging down in a long arc. When wood and iron hit the floor Wren could swear it was heard the length of Riverside Drive. It drowned out the sound of that tiny body breaking on the parquet, the little gun skidding into the dark end of the room.

They just stared for a while, then Hadley slowly walked to the body and placed two fingers on Aunt Agnes' neck. She shook her head.

Wren reached into her pocket for her phone and realized her hands were shaking. She called Sgt. Ortiz again, and this time, got him.

"Wren—I got your message. I was going to call you in the morning."

"I guess…I guess I didn't make it sound urgent. I think you should come to Greenleaf House. It's all over." She hung up and looked at the diaries on the floor. "She didn't burn them after all. Benjamin saved them until the last minute, but Miss Greenleaf couldn't bear to get rid of them."

"We're awful," said Hadley. "But as I said, we can be sentimental."

Chapter Thirty

O f everything that happened that night and into the morning, the reaction that surprised Wren the most was Mrs. Ryan's. As Wren suspected, she had been drugged and was sleeping heavily. Hadley had offered to wake her and break the news, as a member of her employer's family, however distant.

She seemed surprised to see Hadley in her room, and Wren stood in the background.

"Mrs. Ryan, I'm sorry to tell you, but Miss Greenleaf left her room in the night and had an accident in the library—a fatal accident. The police are here now."

"I see, miss. Thank you for telling me." Nothing more. She knew. If she wasn't aware of the details, she knew it would end like this, knew from the day that body was found in the attic. There had indeed been a secret that the Greenleafs failed to pass down to Stephen. But the Murphys knew it too—and it also had been withheld from Conor. Mrs. Ryan was sad, but not surprised.

"Do you want me to call Conor?"

"Oh…ah, yes. He should be here too. Thank you. Also, Miss Greenleaf attended services every Sunday at St. Thomas. I know she would want a priest."

"Of course."

"And Mr. Stephen?"

"He's already here."

"I will get dressed. If Mr. Stephen or the police want to talk with me,

I will be in the suite. Also, the Greenleafs are always buried out of Frank Campbell."

"Can I get you anything?" asked Hadley.

"That is kind of you. But after a shower and quick breakfast, I will be fine."

"OK. Also…if you're worried, I'm sure Stephen Greenleaf won't be rushing you out of your room here."

Mrs. Ryan blinked and looked at Hadley in confusion.

"Of course, miss. Mr. Stephen would never do that. The Greenleafs and the Murphys always take care of each other. They have been doing so for a very long time."

Yes, they had. Greenleafs and Murphys had been living—and dying—here for a long time. Even if the last member of each family in residence was about to leave, it was just life as usual in the Greenleaf House, and Mrs. Ryan wasn't going to fall apart.

In the library, Sergeant Ortiz was continuing to oversee the accident scene. They had taken away Agnes Greenleaf, and Stephen was wandering around looking a little dazed. Wren looked out the tall window and saw it was beginning to get light.

"Let's go over this again, ladies," said Ortiz. "If I understand you and Ms. Vanderwerf correctly, this was merely an accident. An old lady becomes obsessed with some lost documents and tries to retrieve them in the middle of the night. Why?"

"She was going to wait until the ladder was repaired. Once the workmen had started there, she assumed it would be left unlocked after the workday was done, and she could sneak in and get the diaries. But she became afraid that with my poking around and asking questions, I'd find the diaries before she had a chance to do that. She'd have to risk the broken ladder—and take the keys, which I left in the house each evening."

"And you just happen to think of this and race here to save her. And she thanks you by pulling a gun on you. Is that right?"

"It's a little late in the day—or maybe too early—for sarcasm," said Wren. "I know nothing about guns, but I'm sure you'll find the one you found here was used to kill both Fiona Murphy and Karen Lavendell."

"I'm sure. We have to do some formal tests, of course, but it's the kind of gun of that period that would go with that kind of bullet."

"A pocket pistol," said Stephen. He was looking out the window and turned back. "We had heard stories. Benjamin and Susan honeymooned in what were considered rough areas in Eastern Europe, so he had bought a small handgun, something to keep in his jacket. I doubt if he ever used it after that, and we all assumed he had lent it to some friend in his club or a cousin, and it was forgotten. Apparently, he gave it to Aunt Agnes—a keepsake along with the diaries."

"I know what this is about," said Wren.

"She really does," said Hadley.

"Yes. And if you can give me an hour or two with those diaries, I can prove how Fiona was killed."

"That's really not my interest," said Ortiz. "I'm here about the Lavendell and Heppenstall murders."

"They were killed for the same reason as Fiona Murphy."

Ortiz raised an eyebrow. "But how did Agnes Greenleaf end up with the gun? My understanding was that she would barely be able to get down the hall to the library. She didn't get out of the house and kill Lavendell in the middle of the night. So, who shot Lavendell and then gave the gun back to her?"

"Two hours with the diaries," said Wren.

"I've indulged you, but this is not about family secrets anymore. This is about two homicides, two modern-day murders."

"And I have the solution. Or I will have it if I can just have a little time with these diaries."

"Are those diaries evidence? If so—"

"They're evidence of the murder of Fiona Murphy."

"I don't care about her murder."

"We can't solve the modern murders until we've solved hers." She felt herself get angry, then softened her tone. "I'm sorry. I can tell you something now—the motive. Three people were murdered for the right to sit at the head of the table in that dining room."

220

"That's insane," he said.

"I know," said Wren. Ortiz sighed. "All three murders—120 years worth of secrets and death. One solution." She knew she sounded histrionic. But it might work. He looked like he was going to argue, then turned to Stephen. "This isn't a crime scene, Mr. Greenleaf. These diaries are your property. It's your decision." Stephen looked back and forth between Wren and Ortiz.

"Oh, come on, cousin," said Hadley. "I think 120 years of family secrets is enough."

"Very well," he said. "But I have my own interests to protect. Go ahead, Wren. But I'm calling my lawyers."

"Thank you," said Wren. "I'm taking these down to the Rose Parlor for some quiet, and we'll meet in the dining room in two hours. Meanwhile, sergeant, I think you'll want—I don't know the exact name, the people who check crime scenes?"

"For this? It was just an accident."

"Not here. You'll want to look for bloodstains in Fiona's old room—Stephen can show you there. You can find old bloodstains, right? I looked it up—bloodstains can last a long time, can't they?"

"Umm, OK. Our crime scene people are practically magicians. But—"

"Do you want to solve this, or don't you?" asked Wren. "Now, I need to call my father. He should be here too. Also, Bobby has a ladder here. It will help me reach those volumes...."

* * *

Wren quickly settled herself in the Rose Parlor. As she expected, a well-educated Victorian gentleman like Benjamin Greenleaf wrote in a perfect copperplate. Wren had read such manuscripts before, so she didn't stumble over it. There were fascinating pieces about the house—the layout of the rooms, how the morning light came in, the way he had designed it for the flow of residents, guests, and servants. He was almost poetic about it —but she quickly skipped through those parts. She'd have plenty of time later. For now, she had to focus on Ambrose, Susan, and Fiona.

She almost missed the essential part, not because of the script, but because there was no lead up. It was all here: his wife, his brother, and Fiona. He described exactly what happened, exactly what Wren had known in her heart had happened, because, like the house, the people were structured like that. His prose was efficient and unadorned, with no clue into his thoughts: His final word on the matter: "It was a very unfortunate accident, and I do feel bad for Ambrose, but it was of his own making. I was forced into the distasteful task of handling it myself. Ambrose is making arrangements for Susan to visit with her cousins in Philadelphia. This whole event has been so hard for her, and she needs to rest. Perhaps the servants have some knowledge of what happened, but none of them should be so foolish as to cause problems. Fortunately, it was in a quiet part of the house. They will be told Fiona has run off. The child has been with his Murphy relations anyway, and of course, I will distribute a few dollars as necessary...." Her eyes blinked, and she just read the sentence again and again.

Hadley came in with takeout coffee and a croissant.

"Quick break, Little Bird, just a little sustenance, and I'll leave you alone."

Wren put her face in her hands and started to cry.

"I'm sorry. I thought you liked croissants," said Hadley, and that got a smile through the tears.

"No. This is sweet and thoughtful. Thank you. It's not that."

"Didn't you find what you liked?"

"I found exactly what I expected, only worse."

"Wow. Some family, aren't we?"

"Benjamin cared only for this house. He wrote pages about it. But his own wife and brother—and that poor girl. Just in passing. Something that might've interrupted his obsession with this house. No one spent a minute about her. She was stuck in that room, forgotten and unmourned by everyone. Even her family...."

"We'll see her properly buried now. Mrs. Ryan and Conor will have a grave they can visit."

"Oh, it's not that, not just that. I was seeing this only as a house, not a home, and my father warned me not to do that, and now it's like a slap in the face. It was a home for people, even if some of them desecrated it, but mostly it was a home for Fiona Murphy, who was probably stupid and greedy, but she didn't deserve this. She didn't deserve what happened to her. And all I could see was the beauty in this place, and not until reading this diary, did I see the people." She wiped her face with some tissues. "She was a mother and missed years she should've been with her only child. Just like...just like me and my mother."

"You never fooled me, Little Bird. I never thought you did this for the house. I think it was about Fiona since the day you found her in the attic. It wasn't about the house as much you think." She stood and gave Wren a kiss on top of her head. "See you in a bit, and don't worry, I won't tell your father that it took you a while to realize you knew all along it was about people, about your mother, and not about the house. By the way, he's here. And Conor."

Wren smiled. "I'm looking forward to having them at the table. We'll gather at 11:00."

* * *

Wren stripped in the bathroom and washed up as best she could, then leafed through the notes about the diaries, about an obsession that had lasted more than a century and the murders that tied them together. She looked at her watch—she was running late. Good. Her father told her to keep clients waiting. Show them you were busier than they were. An architect of his stature could get away with that. She'd have to learn how to get away with it too.

Her phone buzzed—it was from Lavinia. Perfect timing. "Got it. When can we meet?"

"Greenleaf House—Now."

"On my way."

They were all sitting there when Wren entered. Sergeant Ortiz, looking a little bemused, as if he knew he had lost control of the situation and was wondering how it had happened. Mrs. Ryan—she was prim, as always, but there was more. A little worry—sadness? Conor sat next to her. He wasn't worried, just curious.

Stephen Greenleaf wasn't entirely happy with what was happening but was resigned to the whole thing. *It's your fault. If you had trusted me, we could've avoided this. You're concerned that this will wreck the deal with your backers. But no. When they see, the magnificent work I'm doing on your ancestral home...*

Finally, her father, looking faintly amused, maybe a bit...proud?

Hadley caught her eye and winked at her.

Then she saw that they had left the seat at the head of the table empty. Of course, it was her meeting. One chance to sit at the head in the finest room in the finest house...the center of New York City. She would be the mistress of Greenleaf House.

"Thank you for coming. I wanted to talk about this house and the three families who lived in it—the Greenleafs, the Vanderwerfs, and the Murphys—and about an obsession to sit where I am right now."

Lots of raised eyebrows at that.

"In 1895, Benjamin Greenleaf moved into this house, this absolute dream of his, with his bride, the former Susan Vanderwerf. They were wealthy, good-looking, socially prominent, and had the finest house in New York. Only one problem. Susan apparently was unable to easily conceive. Or maybe she had miscarriages. Or the problem may have been with Benjamin. We don't know—maybe we'll find more in her husband's diaries. We only know she didn't have her first child until seven years into her marriage. Aside from any family sadness, there was a dynastic problem. The family trust required that the house be passed to the closest Greenleaf heir. So it was a problem if Susan didn't have a child."

"But she did, eventually, my grandfather Caleb and great-aunt Laura," said Stephen.

"Yes, but something happened meanwhile. Benjamin's brother Ambrose."

At that, the door opened, and Lavinia walked in. She gave Wren a thumb's up and took a seat at the table next to her father.

"Ambrose had an eye for the ladies. And one of them was a maid—hired in anticipation of a baby. Fiona Murphy, sister of their coachman. It seems Ambrose and Fiona—"

"We know the story," said Conor impatiently "Ambrose raped her and then killed her."

"No, that's not what happened," said Wren. "And please don't interrupt me again." The next bit just slipped out. "Or I'll ask you to leave."

She could hardly believe she said that. But it was the house. She knew people put their stamp on houses, but a residence like Greenleaf House could also stamp its personality on the people who lived there. It had done so with her, and for that moment, she wasn't just running a meeting—she had indeed become the mistress of the house, with all the power that entailed.

Conor looked a little stunned, and his mother glared at him. Hadley snickered. Even Stephen relaxed enough for a smile. *Oh, I don't think you'll be smiling in a few minutes,* thought Wren.

Chapter Thirty-One

"As I was saying," continued Wren. "Ambrose and Fiona began an affair. I would like to think it was a grand love affair. I would like that…" her voice broke for a moment, but she took a deep breath. "But we don't know that. We never will. Ambrose may have just seen her as yet another pretty girl to conquer. And Fiona may have seen a chance to get some money out of it, something to relieve her expected life of drudgery." Conor started to talk, but a look from his mother silenced him again. "As might be expected, she found herself pregnant. Yes, a pathologist confirmed that the woman found in the attic had delivered a child. She was hardly the first servant this happened to, and it might've ended there, with Greenleaf money smoothing over any difficulties, but there were two additional factors here. One was Susan Greenleaf. We have anecdotal evidence that although she was married to Benjamin she preferred Ambrose—it came down through her niece, Myrtle. Was the relationship consummated? Again, I don't think we'll ever know. But either way, it must've rankled Susan to see her beloved with a mere maid. And then the maid was pregnant—while she remained barren."

She looked around the room. Conor still looked annoyed. His mother looked sad. Everyone else was glued to her account.

"If I may," said Sergeant Ortiz, with a little hesitation. *He doesn't want to be slapped down either,* Wren realized, with some amusement. "Why wasn't I told that the body in the attic—Fiona—had had a child? I'm the detective in charge of the case."

"Which case? You made it clear Fiona Murphy was not your case—off by a century."

"Fair enough. But then, why am I here? I have to solve the murders of Karen Lavendell and Andrew Heppenstall."

"I'll get to that," said Wren. "Three murders, 120 years apart. But just one crime." He raised an eyebrow but said nothing more.

"Ambrose lived a wild life. And virtually all his money was courtesy of his brother, as head of the family. I'm willing to bet that the family had had to clean up Ambrose's messes in the past, and Fiona was just the latest. The irony was that Benjamin was a far more patient man than his brother. It wasn't the last straw for him. But it was for Ambrose. If he didn't want to spend the rest of his life under Benjamin's control, he'd have to make a big gamble. This magnificent house did not belong to Benjamin and Susan alone. It was part of a family trust and had to go to the nearest heir. Susan hadn't had any children. She might never. But Ambrose had a child. And his child could inherit Greenleaf House. His child could sit where I am now."

"He was a bastard!" said Conor. "Bastards couldn't inherit."

Before Wren could react, Mrs. Ryan slapped her son twice. "Once for foul language. Once for interrupting Miss Fontaine." He looked a little stunned—but said nothing more.

Wren hid a smile and continued: "Conor has a point—Ambrose knew that well. Now, I'd like to introduce Professor Lavinia Suisse of the Columbia University history department. You found something, professor?"

Lavinia smiled and opened her bag. "This is a photocopy of a marriage license, from the city hall in Yonkers, between Ambrose Greenleaf and Fiona Murphy. I have contacts there from my many years of research in the greater New York area, so they obliged me. It seems the couple wisely decided to marry outside of the city proper, away from family knowledge and influence. The records have been sitting there for over a century. I doubt if Benjamin thought to look there, outside of the city."

The news surprised everyone. Conor looked confused, even disappointed, as his story fell apart. Stephen had been amused, but now he was intent.

"Thank you, Lavinia. Eventually, Ambrose's child became moot when Susan had children, but that was later. For now, Fiona had a child, and she had Ambrose. Susan had neither. The marriage itself was no doubt a secret, even though her relationship with Ambrose and their child was not. A marriage like that would've been a major scandal. An illegitimate child—business as usual at that time. So anyway, I am trying to imagine Susan's rage, humiliation, and disappointment, with Fiona flaunting the fact of her child, and no doubt retaliating by showing her contempt for the servant every chance she got."

"Why didn't Ambrose just take his wife and child and leave?" asked Stephen.

"He should've. But remember, he had limited funds. He was dependent for most of his income on a family directorship, and I don't see Benjamin and the rest of the Greenleafs keeping him around if he had shamed the family by marrying a maid. I think Ambrose had another plan: essentially, blackmail his brother. Remember—at that point, Ambrose and Fiona's child was heir to the house. People died easily back then—pneumonia or an infection, and that was it. So maybe Ambrose was trying to work that angle. He would eventually reveal his marriage and promise to remain quiet about his son—a legitimate Greenleaf—in exchange for cash. Maybe they were already quietly negotiating the plan: Benjamin gives Ambrose and Fiona enough money to live in reasonable comfort far away and basically take their child out of the house's inheritance, assuming Susan never gets pregnant. But while this is going on, Ambrose didn't count on just how much Fiona and Susan hated each other. I can see Susan calling Fiona a whore once too often. And Fiona finally losing her temper and telling Susan she was a wife, not a mistress. She probably had a marriage license at hand. The thought that Fiona might someday preside over this very table as the mother of the heir to Greenleaf House was too much for Susan. She took her husband's gun and came to Fiona's room in the empty nursery wing. Susan berated Fiona. Fiona responded by turning her back on the mistress of Greenleaf House. That's when Susan shot her to death."

That stopped everyone. Conor and Stephen looked like they had been hit. Her father was raising an elegant eyebrow. Lavinia looked proud. Hadley winked at her, unconcerned that her great-great-great-aunt was a cold-blooded murderer.

"Then Benjamin covered it up. Put Fiona's body in the attic trunk. Packed his wife off for a few months rest in the country and brought in workmen to seal the attic."

"Did you find this in the diaries?" asked Conor. "I wouldn't trust a Greenleaf."

"Thank you," said Stephen drily, but Conor ignored him.

"I am not asking you to," said Wren. "There's a lot there—but I think we can find more. Sergeant Ortiz, do you think your crime scene team is done? Could you ask one of them to step in?"

"My team isn't here to help you with your historical puzzle," he said.

"I told you there's just one crime here, and it's been going on for more than a century."

"Wasting police time is a crime," he said. But Wren figured he had no other avenues, and humoring her was his only option right now. He sighed, pulled out his phone, and spoke briefly into it. Then the room was silent. Wren caught her father's eye—*Very clever, my girl, but God help you if you're wrong.*"

The crime scene detective came in.

"Did you find anything?" asked Ortiz.

"Blood on the floor, sergeant, not very old and carelessly cleaned up." He paused. "And something else. The floor in that room was probably covered by a rug or carpet at some point—we found fibers. And it would explain why the floor is in such good shape. And we found an old blood stain. Much older."

"How old?" asked Ortiz.

"Very old," said the detective. He shrugged. "That's just the preliminary info. We're still working." He gave a quick salute and left.

"Fiona Greenleaf, nee Murphy, and Karen Lavendell, killed in the same room, with the same gun, for the same reason. To control who sits where I sit now."

"Karen Lavendell was found downtown," said Ortiz. "If she was killed in that room, it had to be by someone with access to this house and the ability to move a body." He looked at Stephen. "I hope that alibi is airtight,

Mr. Greenleaf, because all the influence in the world isn't going to help you now."

Stephen looked wildly back and forth between Ortiz and Wren. "I didn't even have that damn gun—my aunt had it all along."

"You shouldn't have left it where she could get it," said Ortiz. He stood and took out his cuffs. "Mr. Greenleaf—"

"No," said Wren. "No. Mr. Greenleaf has secrets, but he isn't the murderer. Agnes Greenleaf had the gun all along. She killed Karen Lavendell."

"That's ridiculous," said Ortiz. "A ninety-year-old woman in her condition couldn't have moved a body."

"Unless she had help," said Wren. Ortiz looked at Mrs. Ryan—the loyal servant. She was so lost in the two tragedies it didn't even register that she was being accused. But Conor jumped on it.

"I knew it! At the end of the day, you blame a Murphy for this. I won't stand—"

"Just stop," said Wren. "It wasn't your mother. However, the Greenleafs have always had those who would follow them. That name still retains some of its old magic, which can work on some—like Andrew Heppenstall. I can see Lavendell naively reaching out to Miss Greenleaf to gain her as an ally in taking over this house. Maybe she promised an elegant suite here—or fame, as a figurehead to preside over this house. But she fatally misjudged Agnes Greenleaf. Horrified at what might happen to this house, fearful of who would steal those diaries, and unsure of what Stephen could, or would, do to prevent it, she invited Karen Lavendell to come here late. She had sleeping pills—and had drugged Mrs. Ryan so she wouldn't interfere. Then she brought her to Fiona's old room, the same room where another woman, a century before, had tried to take over the house and died trying. The room where Ambrose's portrait now hangs. Miss Greenleaf had been holding her grandfather's gun since he had died, probably hidden neatly in the bottom of a jewelry box."

"Are you suggesting she conspired with Heppenstall?" asked Ortiz.

"Correct me if I'm wrong, but I think the phrase is 'accessory after the fact.' She and Heppenstall had been in touch and were on the same side. She saw him as useful as they shared a hatred of PH Hospitality. She knew he'd be a likely suspect. So I think she arranged to kill Lavendell when she knew he'd have an alibi—he was delivering a lecture up in the Bronx. She didn't need him for the killing, just for the disposal. She had arranged in advance, no doubt, for him to come here and get rid of the body. He must've been horrified to come here and find out Miss Greenleaf had killed someone, and he was expected to deal with it. He was a nervous man. I think he panicked. Maybe he thought the communications he had had with Miss Greenleaf would implicate him, if not as a murderer, then as a conspirator. And Agnes Greenleaf had long experience imposing her will on others—to the point of manipulation, even blackmail. They might've had communications that would put him in a bad light. We'll probably never know. A normal man might've gone to the police, but he may have felt he'd be suspected—and he was wound a little tight. I'm guessing he carried the body away in the trunk of his car."

"A trunk is impossible to clean perfectly—his car is still parked in his garage. We didn't do this before, because he wasn't a suspect, but we can search it now," said Ortiz.

"Good. Of course, he was a loose end, and Miss Greenleaf was afraid he'd crack. She invited him back to discuss the case, get their stories straight, and then drugged him, hoping he'd die after he left. When I met with Heppenstall, he was a nervous wreck, kept denying his involvement despite an ironclad alibi. No wonder—he had covered up a murder."

Ortiz nodded. "But one more thing. We searched Heppenstall's and Lavendell's email and phone. No communication from Agnes Greenleaf—and those messages never disappear anyway, no matter how hard you erase them. She didn't have a smartphone or Internet. How did she set this up?"

Wren smiled. "Miss Greenleaf was old school. I saw it the first time I was in her room. She had stationery and stamps. Everything was conducted through the mail. I imagine in her dealings with Lavendell and Heppenstall. She told them how terrible it would be if their communications became public. She was afraid of her nephew, she said, and they humored her by destroying letters and keeping appointments secret. And Miss Greenleaf told both of them they were involved in a conspiracy against her nephew, which was shady, if not illegal, so they had their own reasons for discretion. She took a risk that almost worked."

"What almost worked?" asked Ortiz, looking confused. "I'll accept, for now, that she was a double-murderer, but what was the motive? What was she saving this house from?"

Wren smiled and looked at Stephen, and then her father. "Mr. Greenleaf can answer that. And my partner, Mr. Fontaine, knows as well, don't you? You know, Stephen, if you had been honest with me, honest with your aunt, we might have avoided all of this. Your Aunt Agnes didn't trust you with the family secret. She didn't trust you, period. She was terrified of PH Hospitality taking over her lovely home, chopping it up, those diaries made public. She had concluded that if she could hold them off, you'd move back into the house, and the Greenleafs would take their rightful place. She was cunning, but ignorant, a dangerous mixture."

Neither her father nor Stephen looked happy. Wren just waited, and Stephen spoke first, but not to her.

"Ezra, can't you do something?"

Wren watched her father closely, felt her hands grip the chair.

"Stephen. This was a mistake, yours and mine. Anyway, I can't restrain my daughter. And I'm unwilling to restrain my partner. In either role, she has grounds for complaint."

That made Stephen exasperated, but her father gave her a look: *Backing your play for now, but this better work.*

"I was wondering about the fate of this house, and why Stephen Greenleaf was so cagey. I also wondered why my obsessive partner didn't seem to care. I found out by accident, although I didn't realize it at the time. It was Heppenstall who knew. He had plenty of supporters in the architectural community, especially at Columbia, where Stephen graduated from and where the Greenleafs have long been donors. Heppenstall had found out secretly that this house was going to be donated to Columbia University, a living monument to city architecture, for seminars, meetings, residence for students and visiting scholars. Right? He let it slip. He mentioned a 'Colombia' connection, and I thought it was a reference to Ambrose's South American adventures. But Heppenstall wasn't interested in family histories—he was interested in the building. He was talking about 'Columbia' the university, which he had heard was taking over this house. That was the final piece of the puzzle—right, Stephen?"

Stephen just bounced his Mont Blanc pen with a steady beat on the table and gave her a sour look.

"Nice going, *detective* Wren," he said. "Except now it may not happen. I told you this had to be a secret. Who do you think is paying for all this, your exorbitant fees, the army of workmen, the miles of copper pipes you seem to feel are necessary? Do you think I have that much cash lying around? Do you know the people I had to rope in to make this happen? So Columbia could own it, preserved as my family's legacy to this city? And now these murders have happened, committed by my own aunt. How are we going to keep it a secret now? The police know all about this—it'll be public. Oren Perry—I was counting on him and the group he put together to finance this. Those supporters will run for the hills rather than be mixed up in this—a double murder over control of this house. The Columbia trustees will back out too. I don't have the money to keep this place. I'll have no choice but to sell to PH Hospitality if I can't keep my deal on track. Dear God. Couldn't you have kept this quiet a little longer?"

"You're wrong," said Wren. By this point, she felt she had stepped away from her own body, watching herself. She hated having to do this, having all these people watching her, arguing. She had to end it.

"I beg your pardon," said Stephen.

"Wren—" started her father.

"Oh, for God's sake, just try to look at this house for one minute! You and Conor grew up here, so you take it for granted. Did you ever step back, really step back, and realize how magnificent it is? Its utter perfection? Sergeant—Agnes Greenleaf killed Karen Lavendell and then Andrew Heppenstall just to make sure PH Partners didn't take over this house."

"Just to squash a business deal?" he asked.

"Not a deal. Her entire life. She'd kill for that. She had spent years waiting for Stephen to take his place at the head of this table. Yes, Stephen, your Aunt Agnes may have been insane, but she knew, she never forgot over 90 years, never married, never did anything, just for the privilege of living here. Unlike you and Conor, she never took it for granted. She never stopped realizing how incredible this house was. Has Perry or any members of his syndicate or Columbia trustees ever entered this place?"

"No. I couldn't bring a dozen supporters through the door or even just Perry. The press is always following him—I couldn't take that risk. Word would get out, and we couldn't show our hand to PH Hospitality. That might've sent them scrambling to outflank us with a new round of funds. I needed them complacent." He sighed. "This is New York. PH Hospitality has few friends here, but Perry and I do. The Greenleaf name still means something. I could stop PH Hospitality in the short term—they'd find banks in this town dragging their feet as a favor to me. But not forever." He looked at Ortiz. "I didn't want you poking around. Perry and his associates are very wealthy with complex business lives. They might feel that if police are investigating murders regarding control of this house, they might want to investigate them."

"I wonder why," said Ortiz drily.

"Be careful about your accusations," said Stephen. "We haven't committed any crimes. My family is connected to the death of a property developer—this will be settled in time, but I don't have a lot of time. Friends and backers will disappear if there's a scandal. If PH Hospitality regroups—"

"Everyone is missing the big picture," said Wren. "You have your murderer, sergeant, as I promised. Now, I want to talk about the house and its future. Stephen—stop focusing on any potential scandal. What you need to do is bring every donor and supporter here—Perry especially—and show it to them—show them this isn't just an item on a tax form, and they'll be begging to be a part of this, begging to see their names inscribed on a brass plaque in the foyer, never mind how many scandals, just to go down in history with their name attached to this…this…living artwork."

Stephen looked a little stunned at that. Wren kept rolling.

"I've been wrong about you, Stephen. At first, I thought you just saw this house as an asset on a balance sheet. But when I learned what you were doing to keep it, and why, I changed my mind. Don't make me change it back. You must understand the power of this house. You must be able to see it through fresh eyes, to know that just as you want to keep it, everyone else who sees it will want to be part of it as well. And if not, if I'm wrong..." she took a breath—"I guess you're just a *pompous bourgeois vulgarian.*"

That was it. She felt completely spent, leaned back in her chair to catch her breath, and waited for the blowback, wondering if she saved the day or threw her professional career into the trash. Hadley was hiding giggles in a tissue, and Lavinia was quietly fighting a smile. Her father was unreadable, and that made her more fearful than if he had been furious. But he had something to answer for too...

Stephen sighed. "A brass plaque, huh? I guess you're going to charge me a mint for that, too. We'll see, Ms. Fontaine. We'll see. But your outburst aside, you make some good points. I'm inclined to agree with you."

She saw her father quietly nod.

Conor cleared his throat. "If I may change the subject and go back in time? You still haven't told us what happened to the child that Ambrose and Fiona had. Do you know?"

Of course. This was probably the best part of all. The crimes had been dealt with. And this was going to be...interesting.

"Your mother knows. Don't you, Mrs. Ryan?" Mrs. Ryan squeezed her eyes shut, as if willing away the question. "I know." She felt bad and softened her voice. "You kept a secret. But the time for secrets is over. It's been more than a century." Yes, Mrs. Ryan knew the secret. And by knowing that, she was aware of what was happening, even if Miss Greenleaf didn't take her into her confidence. She knew how this was going to end. When Hadley had woken her up this morning, there was no surprise.

Mrs. Ryan just shook her head and looked at her lap. "I'm so sorry. I kept the secret, I never told anyone." Wren couldn't tell who she was talking to—probably to the late Miss Greenleaf.

"It was an accident," said Wren. "You said when Brian *joined* the family. It was an odd word to use. Why not just say when Brian was *born*. Because he wasn't born—not to Kevin Murphy, anyway. He was the son of Fiona and Ambrose, farmed out to her brother, Kevin. Fiona was dead—Benjamin stuffed her in the attic. He exiled Ambrose. Sent his murderous wife to the country to recover, and made sure Brian was installed as a permanent part of the Murphy household. Brian—Ambrose's son. And Conor's great-grandfather."

"Brian Murphy was a Greenleaf?" asked Stephen.

"Yes. Kevin had to be told the story, of course. I doubt if he was told his sister had been stuffed in a trunk. God knows what story they gave him for that. But he was given money and his nephew, whom he loved dearly in memory of his beloved sister. And he didn't tolerate criticism of Ambrose, whom he knew as Brian's true father. As for Ambrose, I don't know what kind of paternal feelings he had. But later in life, he must've confided in his niece, Laura, and left her any money he had for his son—a late-in-life attempt at an apology for what the family did. I can't say why you weren't told the full story, Stephen, but there it is." *The story was clear in Aunt Agnes' reactions: fiercely protective, if disgusted with Ambrose, who was a Greenleaf, although a disgraced one. Joy in Conor, who was also technically a Greenleaf. And indifference to Fiona, a servant who got above herself and paid a price.*

"You'll have to go through the diaries for more details," continued Wren. "Diaries that were behind lock and key, tormenting your Aunt Agnes, who couldn't bring herself to destroy or hide them when she had the chance. And had to live right next to them, unreachable, for the better part of the century. Just imagine that, furious at Ambrose, for marrying beneath him, but much less so at Susan, who committed murder." *It was horrifying—but as Stephen had told her, Agnes lived at another time.*

"I'm technically a Greenleaf?" asked Conor. Wren enjoyed how stunned he looked. *Serves you right for following your obsession instead of the facts.*

"You can check through a DNA test. But I'm sure it will show that you and Stephen are third cousins, once removed."

Stephen threw his head back and laughed. "A perfect end to a perfect day! This is really wonderful. I spent all these years wondering what horrible thing Uncle Ambrose did, and it turns out all he did was marry 'beneath' him." He used air quotes around *beneath*. "The killer? It was my great-grandmother Susan all along. And if there was insanity in the family, I guess Aunt Agnes inherited it." He turned to Hadley. "The story was that the Vanderwerfs were always a little off. This proves it. No offense."

"None taken," said Hadley, smiling right back.

"I'm glad this amuses you," said Conor coldly.

"For God's sake, it was more than a century ago," said Stephen. "You've spent your entire life thinking your great-great-grandfather was a rapist, and now he's been vindicated. You see, this is why I wanted to get rid of this damn place, the insane family behavior of another generation. Dear God, enough already. Conor—you didn't need to solve a century-old murder to leave your mark in the history of this house where Murphys and Greenleafs lived together. I told you you'd be part of this house's future, before I even knew we were related. This house will be owned by Columbia and supervised by a board of advisors. I am going to be the chair. There's a seat for you on the board as well. That can be the Murphy legacy—not raking up some old scandal no one cares about. Look forward, not backward."

Conor didn't say anything for a few moments. "Thank you. I would be pleased to join."

Then Stephen stood up and walked over to Mrs. Ryan and surprised her—surprised everyone—by kissing her on the cheek. "Cousin Eileen, if I may. It's still some months away, but we do a big Thanksgiving at our place. Please come with Conor, and your daughters. Arrive at 3:00, we eat at 4:00."

"Thank you, sir," she said quietly.

"Stephen," he said. "My name is Stephen." He shook Conor's hand. "Welcome to the family. We may be well-populated with murderers, I'm sorry to say, but you're stuck with us. You and I will talk about giving Fiona a proper Catholic funeral."

Conor was not quite giving in. "She's my family. I can take care of her, thank you."

"But she's my family too—Wren, isn't she? You seem to have a grasp of the genealogy."

"Fiona was your great-great aunt by marriage. Not blood, but family nonetheless."

"There you go," said Stephen. He slapped Conor on the back, chuckled, and went back to his seat.

Chapter Thirty-Two

Conor spoke quietly with his mother. She dabbed away his tears, and then Conor looked up. He nodded slowly. "Thank you, Stephen, for the welcome." Then he grinned. "How appropriate, in the end, that we're cousins. After all, we're the last two children who lived in this house."

"Yes, this house," said Ortiz. "Lots of threads, but just one story. It's always been about who will sit at the head of this table. For over a century, that's the situation?"

"Yes, exactly," said Wren.

"Okay, then," said Ortiz. "This all makes a certain amount of sense. But I'll be bringing in some other detectives, and we'll have some questions to ask."

"I'm sure," said Stephen, pulling himself together. "But no reason to make this unpleasant. Can I send out for sandwiches and coffee?"

"Sounds good, sir. This may take a while."

That seemed to be a signal for everyone to start talking. Conor talked to his mother, Ezra with Lavinia, Stephen with Hadley, and Ortiz stepped away to call for more detectives.

Stephen pulled out his cell phone. "Say, Hadley, can you imagine that, sending out for food? When this place was new, Benjamin didn't send out for sandwiches. The butler would tell the cook, and the maids would bring them up, all perfect with the crusts trimmed off."

"Oh, those days are gone, as Wren said," said Hadley. "Right?" She looked up at Wren.

But Wren was gone.

* * *

Hadley gave her some time to be by herself, before opening the door to the ballroom. Wren was lying down on the floor, in the middle of the room, staring at the ceiling. She looked up briefly when Hadley entered but said nothing. Hadley lay down next to her.

"I can't figure out what techniques they used in the 19th century to create that ceiling. It's a marvel. This room is so large—on the edge of vulgarity without quite going over. But overwhelming nonetheless."

"You were wonderful," said Hadley. "Everyone—Stephen, Conor, Sergeant Ortiz. You left them dumbfounded."

"I'm exhausted. I don't ever want to do something like that again. I don't ever want to be with people again."

"I wanted to see if you were okay. But I'll leave."

"No, I'm sorry. I said that badly. I'd like *you* to stay. I just don't want *people* right now." She reached out for Hadley's hand, and they looked at the ceiling in silence.

"I wonder about Benjamin and Ambrose and Susan and Fiona. Did any of them love each other?" asked Wren.

"It's my family, but still, I don't know. Did you wonder why Susan and Benjamin waited so long before she had children? Yes, maybe miscarriages. Or maybe it's a lot simpler—they weren't having sex. She was pining for Ambrose. And maybe Benjamin had someone on the side, too. But he was more discreet than his brother."

"One of the other maids?"

"Think out of the box, Wren. It might've been a footman. That would explain a lot."

"You're right. I wonder if it was just because it was nothing but a business deal, and they just didn't care for each other. There were plenty of Greenleafs who could inherit this when they were gone, and meanwhile, it was theirs."

"Okay. So even if they never had a grand, passionate affair, Susan really did want Ambrose. And Benjamin…" she shrugged.

"Maybe, like his favorite granddaughter, the house was enough for him.

But with that tragedy, they realized they had a duty to someone other than themselves and to produce heirs, to make sure Ambrose and Fiona's child wouldn't get control of the house. The murderess and her accomplice. "

"It's all awful. I was hoping that at the end of the day, there would be some love here. I'm not like you. The house isn't enough for me. I wanted some love here as well. And there wasn't any."

"I can only tell you the history of this house, not the emotions of the people who lived here," said Wren. Hadley pouted, and although it wasn't her fault, Wren felt she had let her down. *I spoke too harshly. I'm really bad at this.* "We could…I mean, we're here, in this house, and if you think the house needs love…."

Hadley grinned. "Are you saying what I think you're saying? I mean, really try to make it as a couple?" She lowered her eyes, in a mock bashfulness. "Are you asking that we go steady?"

The tension melted away, and Wren laughed, and Hadley laughed back and kissed her.

"Again, you were brilliant, Little Bird."

Wren shook her head. "I was naïve. Stephen wanted what every Greenleaf has always wanted, a chance to sit at the head of that table. And he will, as chair of the board of advisors. The economics have changed, but this house will be important again. And a Greenleaf will run it again. Stephen wouldn't admit it, but he really did love this house, and the real reason he just didn't sell it to PH Hospitality and walk away was that he wanted to sit at the head of that table. Susan killed for that a century ago. And Agnes killed for it today."

Hadley nodded—but then she grinned. "Okay. The Greenleafs are back in control. But don't forget a Vanderwerf oversaw the servants. So it would be appropriate if I got the catering gig here."

They had a few more minutes alone, before the door opened again, and Ezra walked in. No one spoke, and the only sound was his footsteps on the wooden floor. When he reached them, the two women sat up, and Ezra, seeing no chairs in the room, reluctantly sat on the floor next to them.

"Father, this is Hadley Vanderwerf, my girlfriend, and our client's third cousin once removed. Hadley, my father, and senior partner of my firm, Ezra Fontaine."

"A pleasure," said Ezra. "It was interesting seeing Wren come out of her shell at the meeting. I wonder if that's your doing. If so, thank you." Hadley laughed. "If both of you are free this evening, I would like to take you out to dinner."

"Super," said Hadley. She gave Wren a quick kiss and stood. "I'll leave you to it and tell the detectives you'll meet them in your good time." She skipped out of the room and closed the door behind her, leaving father and daughter in silence. "Those columns are too fussy," he finally said.

"You're wrong. Stop comparing everything to Bauhaus. This room is too big, that's true, but it would look cavernous without that design theme bringing it all together."

Ezra considered that. "Perhaps. Anyway, I just want to say again, I'm sorry. I know I wasn't honest about a number of aspects of this job. I was sworn to secrecy about Columbia's plans. Columbia and Stephen were fanatical about secrecy. But I should've included my daughter. I should've included my partner. Again, I'm sorry."

"That brings us to Perry. I was wondering what's in it for him. I'm betting there's more to it than a brass plaque in this building." Her father let her think. "He never went to college. He can't just buy a diploma. But he bought this building for Columbia, and they're giving him something he wants very much. A title, right?" She raised an eyebrow, and her father smiled back.

"Nicely reasoned. In fact, soon you'll see an announcement of his appointment as Professor of Urban Infrastructure at Columbia. An academic title for a man without a degree—indirect payment for bringing this house to the university." "Again, I'm sorry. I told you to do a partner's work, and should've trusted you to handle all this, as a partner. I've misled you twice. I was wrong twice."

"I've decided to forgive you," said Wren. "As Hadley told me, it wasn't your secret, and you were stuck with a nervous client. But no more secrets from your partner."

"I promise."

CHAPTER THIRTY-TWO

"And you are going to have to pay a penalty."

"I'm buying the two of you a nice dinner tonight—same level as our top clients."

"This is going to cost you more than a dinner. I can make deals too, Mr. Fontaine. The board of advisors that's going to oversee the use of this house, with Stephen as its chair. I assume they offered you a seat?"

"I'm a Columbia professor and alum, and the senior partner of the firm that renovated it."

"I want it. I know this house much better than you, and by the time I'm done, I'll know it better than anyone. Tell Stephen you're too busy, and I'll be a better choice."

"Wren. You'd hate it. Fussing with details of budgets and nitpicking discussions of who will provide the sound system for the seminars."

"You're probably right. But I assume the other board members will be well-connected, and now that I'm a partner, I have to pull my weight in networking. And best of all, I'll get to sit in that splendid room."

"Oh, very well. I owe you that much, if you really want it." He smiled. "This house has led to three murders. That doesn't put you off it?"

"It's not the house's fault, father! Yes, as a symbol for the powerful people who owned it—it's hard to separate it from the very imperfect people who owned it. But as a work of art, this house is perfect and understandable and eternal—unlike people." She saw her father's raised eyebrow—and smiled right back at him. "But don't worry. I'm not going to become a crazy old lady like Agnes Greenleaf. If I learned anything from this, it's about the dangers of obsession. People are messy and difficult, but gradually, I'm learning to cope with them and even like them. " She stood. "I could stare at this house all day, but it's time to go. We have a client to take care of."

Chapter Thirty-Three

There was no one alive who remembered such a party at Greenleaf House. Wren looked around—it had taken many months, but she had delivered. The house looked like it had at its peak, when the Greenleafs had ruled New York. A string quartet played in the ballroom, bartenders mixed drinks in the library, and a dessert chef served pastries in the once-again blooming conservatory.

This evening, the house opened its doors to a far more diverse group of guests than it had seen when it was first built. But one thing hadn't changed—when the Greenleafs threw a party, everyone came: Distinguished professors from Columbia, politicians, celebrities, and the wealthy donors who had made it all possible. *Oh yes*, reflected Wren. By the time she had finished giving Perry and his associates a tour, and a review of her plans, everyone was completely committed to adding their name—and their funds—to the house, and PH Hospitality quickly backed off. If anything, there was a new glamour added to the "house people would kill for." Who could pass on a chance to tie themselves to this work of art?

"Yes, you were right, and Stephen was wrong," her father had said. "But please don't make insulting our clients a habit."

Of course, the event was black tie. Wren wore a simple long black dress, and Hadley strode through the halls in a long skirt and white blouse as she supervised the hired waiters with efficiency. Why not give the catering job to family, she had said, and Stephen had agreed.

Wren watched her father look over the house with a professional eye.

"As good as it was the day it opened?" she asked him. He shook his head.

"I wouldn't say that," he said.

"Oh, what would you have done differently?" she asked.

"Nothing. I need to add it's not as good as the day it opened because it's better. Bobby is a better contractor. And we're better architects."

"Nicely said, father. A compliment wrapped in a boast. But you're right." Lavinia and Angela joined them.

"A pleasure as always," said Ezra.

"I hope that you've been complimenting your brilliant daughter," said Lavinia.

"She was always such a bright student," said Angela. "But even we didn't expect she'd reach such heights, so early in her career."

"Quite a change from when she was your flower girl," said Ezra.

"She was actually our bridesmaid," said Lavinia, with a wry smile.

"Yes, very proud," continued her father. "An excellent addition to the firm—and a wonderful daughter."

Erik Leopold sidled up to them. "So pleased to be here—thanks for wrangling the invitation for all us group members, Wren. Living in history, aren't we?"

"Oh yes," said Wren. "But although I'm still going to be an active member of the Gilded Age Society, I'm trying to focus more on the present and future."

Lavinia nodded approvingly. "You're too young to spend so much time in the past. You don't need to. You can do just fine in the present." She gave her a kiss on her cheek. "Everyone wants to congratulate you. Go mingle."

Over the course of the evening, Wren took her compliments with grace. ("Don't blush," she could hear her father saying. "Nothing is more ridiculous than false modesty.")

Eventually, Conor intercepted her in a hallway. "I wanted to thank you again for coming to Fiona's funeral. It meant a lot, you and Hadley attending. To my mother, too."

"It was a learning experience for me, seeing this house not so much as a historical curiosity than as a home for people. They were flawed. But they were people."

He smiled wryly. "It's been a learning experience for me too. My childhood resentments driving me—it wasn't me at my best. You probably suspected me at one point?" He raised an eyebrow.

"It was a close contest between you and Aunt Agnes. But she had decades more to obsess than you did."

Conor laughed. "I like that. Anyway, I convinced my mother to come tonight. She was anxious—not really her scene. But Stephen said the Archbishop of New York was coming, and I saw them a little while ago sitting in a corner, discussing their favorite hymns. You know, even after everything, she didn't want to leave this house. It's been her home too long. Stephen is having her stay on in that nicely refurbished suite as 'director of custodial services.' She'll supervise the cleaning and housekeeping staff, and it suits her nicely, and although she won't admit it, she's pleased I'm on the board." He laughed again. "It's the least Stephen can do for family!"

As the evening wore down, she found Hadley overseeing the packing up of the food and drink and conversing with Lavinia and Angela.

"...and I have never had salmon croquettes like that. Can I ask what you put into them?" asked Angela.

"It's my own recipe," said Hadley. "I don't usually share—but for you, I'll make an exception."

"Thank you. After all, we're all practically family." Hadley giggled at that.

"A triumph," said Lavinia. "We must be off to our beds, but we'll talk soon."

"She's right," said Hadley. "A triumph, Little Bird. I haven't eaten all evening because I was busy, and I bet you haven't because you forgot. What say we kick off our shoes at my place. I'll put up some tea, and we'll have some leftovers."

"That's ideal. But first, I have a present for you, and for me, and for this house. I've been planning this. Come to the ballroom."

"Everyone has been ushered out. They're shutting it down."

"Not yet," said Wren.

"Ooh...Wren being whimsical. Wow."

Wren took her hand, and they walked to the ballroom. The bartenders were putting away the bottles, and the cleaning crew was folding up the chairs.

"The quartet you found is fantastic. How did you wring that money out of Stephen?"

"I didn't. They're members of a heavy metal band, clients of mine, and they came cheap. They owed me—I've had to bail them out in the past—don't ask. Just be grateful I got them to cover up their tattoos."

The first violinist nodded at Wren, and they reached for the sheet music she had given them earlier.

"I assume you can waltz?" asked Wren.

"What? I'm Episcopalian, so yes, if I have a good lead. But—"

"This house used to have waltzes. And I decided that one final time, it will have another one." She nodded at the quartet. "May I have this dance, Miss Vanderwerf?"

"My dance card is open, Miss Fontaine."

The quartet started playing, and Wren began leading Hadley around the room.

"This house deserves music and dance," said Wren. "And love. It deserves that, too."

The Greenleafs

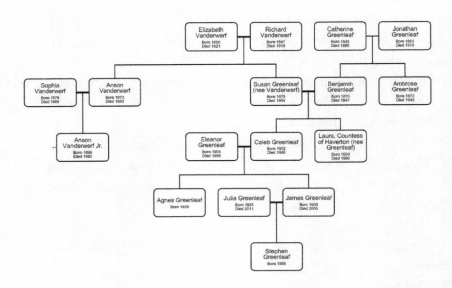

CHAPTER THIRTY-THREE

The Vanderwerfs

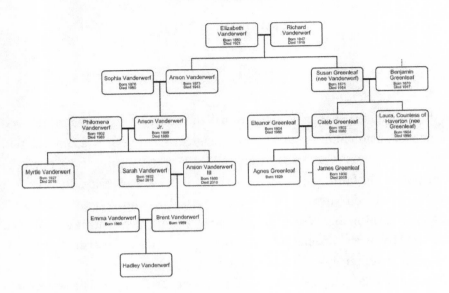

Author's Note

Although all the characters are fictional, the house is largely real. It is based on the mansion built in 1906 by steel magnate Charles Schwab (no relation to the brokerage Charles Schwab). With 75 rooms, it may have been the largest single-family residence ever built in New York City. But Schwab couldn't afford to live in it very long, and as it was located on New York's then-unfashionable West Side, it became a white elephant. It was offered to the city as the official home of the mayor, but La Guardia thought it was too ostentatious and turned it down. Developers tore it down in the 1940s and put up an apartment complex that is still there. The Greenleafs, Vanderwerfs, and Murphys are in no way based on the Schwabs, however.

I have many people to thank for this book. Noted authors Lisa Black, L.A. Chandlar, Brendan DuBois, Cate Holahan, Catriona McPherson, Art Taylor, and Victoria Thompson all read an earlier version of this manuscript. It continually startles me that while mystery writers may plan the most diabolical crimes, they are actually some of the kindest and most generous people in the world.

Special thanks to Dutch Doscher for his photo shoot. He's as generous as he is talented.

Steve Rush, author of *Kill Your Characters: Crime Scene Tips for Writers*, gave me valuable advice on bloodstains. However, any errors in the book are entirely mine.

Once again, I owe more than I can say to my agent Cynthia Zigmund, for her unflagging enthusiasm and her unerring instincts.

Deepest gratitude for my wife, Elizabeth, for her continual love, support and advice. Thanks also to my daughters, Katie and Sophie, for serving as my special advisors on Millennial behavior and understanding their father's need to write historical romantic mysteries instead of taking up a normal activity, like golf.

And last—but in no way least—thanks to Verena Rose, Shawn Reilly Simmons and the whole team at Level Best Books for their hard work and wise counsel.

About the Author

R.J. Koreto is the author of five historical mystery novels, and his short stories have appeared in multiple anthologies, *Ellery Queen Mystery Magazine*, and *Alfred Hitchcock Mystery Magazine*. He has been a book reviewer, Edgar® Award judge, and frequent panelist at mystery conferences. Koreto is also a veteran business journalist who wrote a book on practice management for financial professionals. He is a past president of the New York Financial Writers' Association and won the Gold Award from the American Society of Business Publication Editors. He has a degree in English and Latin from Vassar College. He and his wife have two grown daughters and divide their time between Suffern, N.Y., and Martha's Vineyard, Mass.

SOCIAL MEDIA HANDLES:
https://www.facebook.com/richard.koreto
https://www.facebook.com/RJKoreto
twitter: @RJKoreto

AUTHOR WEBSITE:
www.rjkoreto.com

(with newsletter signup)

Also by R. J. Koreto

Novels

Death on the Sapphire (Crooked Lane Books, 2016)

Death Among Rubies (Crooked Lane Books, 2016)

Alice and the Assassin (Crooked Lane Books, 2017)

Death at the Emerald (Crooked Lane Books, 2017)

The Body in the Ballroom (Crooked Lane Books, 2018)

Short Stories

"The Missing Motive" (*Ellery Queen Mystery Magazine*, Dec. 2015)

"Winter's Journey" (*Alfred Hitchcock Mystery Magazine*, Jan./Feb. 2017)

"The Girl on the Roof" (*Ellery Queen Mystery Magazine*, March/April 2019)

"The Hollywood Gangster" (Bouchercon *California Schemin',* anthology, 2020)

"Micaela, Whose Apartment Never Changes" (*New York: Give Me Your Best or Your Worst*, anthology, 2021)

"April, Come She Will" (*Paranoia Blues: Crime Fiction Inspired by the Songs of Paul Simon*, anthology, 2022)

"Czech Mate" (*A Question of Loyalty*, anthology, 2022)

CPSIA information can be obtained
at www.ICGtesting.com
Printed in the USA
BVHW042205031222
653396BV00007B/512

9 781685 122089